THE ROCK 'N' ROLL
DIARIES

HAVING IT

JAMIE SCALLION

Book Two of The Rock 'n' Roll Diaries series

THE ROCK 'N' ROLL DIARIES
A MADNOTES MEDIA PUBLICATION

First published in Great Britain and Ireland by Madnotes Media, 2016

ISBN 978-0-9926855-2-2

A CIP catalogue record of this book is available from the British Library.

www.therocknrolldiaries.com

THE ROCK 'N' ROLL DIARIES

HAVING IT

Written: Jamie Scallion

Produced: Penny Luithlen

Mixed: Jill Sawyer Phypers

Artwork: Melinda Elek

A&R: Mark Sheehan and Danny O'Donoghue

General Manager: Rodney Alejandro

Label: Madnotes Media

This book is best enjoyed while listening
to the greatest band on earth...

Head to Amazon and search The RockAteers to
buy the music.

or

Head to Spotify and search The RockAteers
to stream the music.

Burt - 9th May

I, Jack Skill, have everything. I'm in the coolest band in the world, I have movie star looks, a mahusive house, and I can get with any girl I want. I'm also just about to be well, proper rich.

If I had my own TV show, which I don't coz I'm too busy, that would be the opening sequence. I'd have a montage depicting my proper awesome life. I think it would definitely make people watch my shanizzle.

Except the bit about me getting with any girl is a lie, because I still don't have the one thing I've wanted since I was eleven years old - Rebecca Vargas. I started my band to impress her. I changed my name to impress her. I pretty much did everything to get her attention, then she runs off with my stroppy lead guitarist! That part's def not in the TV show.

Bex is getting fitter every day - which is a big problem for Egg, because every day she gets fitter, she moves more and more out of his league. #beautyandthegeek

We go on tour with The Desert Kings this summer! Burt Windsor AKA Jack Skill is about to be the biggest rock star on the planet. The tabloids have already started putting me front page, when this album drops that shiz is gonna go daily. The Skillmeister is ready. Bring It On.

1

SONG 1 REVIEW THE REVIEWER

Egg marched up the hill towards his old school. It seemed strange to be walking right past it to meet his insanely hot girlfriend at the café next to the park. After that they would travel into the West End and spend the day shopping, before dinner out and then on to a club, on a school night. His life had changed. A lot.

"Where you going, Smeg?" he heard from behind him.

Egg froze and twisted around slowly. George Graves stood, slightly out of breath and glaring at him, only a few feet away. Egg hadn't seen the school bully for months. He looked older, dishevelled.

"Looks like things going well for you then. Judging by all that swish gear," George sneered.

Egg glanced down at his expensive new clothes. "How are you, George? Been hitting any girls recently?"

"That was an accident."

"Right, the back of my girlfriend's head fell on your fist?"

George dropped his head. "I told her I was sorry."

Egg shrugged, turning to walk on.

"Wait," George said desperately. "I've called Burt a million times. Why don't he answer?"

Egg took a step down the hill towards him and met his eyes.

"Maybe he doesn't want to hang out with a woman beater anymore."

George glared back at him. Egg started back up the hill, half expecting to be punched in the back of the head.

He reached the café unscathed.

Burt - 14th May
I checked my bank! WHAM!! 50K!!! Kerching!!!! Egg says it's recoupable. I had to google it coz I'm not an egghead. It just means I have to pay it all back! #bigdealdonkeydildo. I will pay it back when we sell seventy-five zillion records.

As soon as I got the dough, I went straight down the betting parlour and placed a few celebratory wagers. I lost 5K in half an hour, which is 10% of the total amount I got in the first place. I wasn't overly buzzing about that, but so what!

I had a wicked Skype-off with my little sis, Millie, last night. She's doing great at her posh boarding school up in Scotland. It took her a bit of time to settle in, but she loves it now. I told her if anyone picks on her she better let me know, coz I will fly up there and start kickin teeth in. She said: "Burt, I'm the sister of Jack 'Suicide' Skill. No one picks on me." That weirded me out a bit.

We named the debut record *Set the Bench High*. This was my wicked suggestion. I explained to the lads it has a double meaning. High Bench is where we hang out and setting the bench high means

shooting for the stars. It's well clever. Egg
hated it, of course. Luckily Tea and Clipper know
genius when it lands in their faces.

Crazel has got proper big now (her boobs are
mahusive). She's got very needy and I am very
busy. Not a good combo. She wants me to go into
the hospital and actually watch the birth.
I'm seventeen! Seeing a thing like that would
traumatise me for life. No, I will do what I said I
would do – pay her maintenance and go see it when
all the blood and stuff is wiped off. I've told her
what to call it. I'm good at picking names, The
RockAteers and our wicked album name being perfect
examples. I'm just glad she hasn't sold her story to
the papers. I know she would never do that to me.

Egg opened his eyes and focused on the slender, brown back
belonging to the figure lying beside him. Her jet-black curls
cascaded across the pillow. The white sheet covering her middle
accentuated her coffee-coloured skin. Feeling like the luckiest
man on the planet, Egg pulled himself up on an elbow and started
to piece together the night before. He'd seen the record advance
hit his account and taken Bex out on the town to celebrate. No
expense had been spared. It had been a fantastic night. They'd
started with drinks in Jerome's private members' club before
dinner in China Town, and then on to a little rock 'n' roll dive in
Camden. It was gone four when they made it home.

He scanned the bedroom of the plush new flat. How did this

happen? The last year and a half had been a blur of drama and romance. What if he hadn't been approached by Burt that day in the school canteen about starting a band? What if he'd said no? He certainly wouldn't be lying in bed next to the hottest girl in the world. In the film version, Burt would have got the girl. He'd wanted her badly enough, so much so he'd tried to kill himself when he'd discovered she and Egg were together. Burt was lucky to still be here. When Egg looked back over the past year, he winced at some of the things that had happened, like the time he'd ended up passing out at Burt's party, been stripped naked and had his eyebrows shaved off. Time and again, Egg could have left the band, but he stuck at it and now the girl he couldn't even look in the eye at the band's first rehearsal was waking up with him. And as if that wasn't fantastic enough, they were off on tour in a fortnight; first time on the road supporting one of the biggest bands on the planet. Life was sweeter than sweet.

Egg's reminiscing was interrupted by the shrill ringtone of his cordless landline phone. He fumbled for the handset on the floor next to the bed.

"Hello?"

"Good morning, Edward," his mother said brightly. "Your father and I wondered if we could pop round on our way back from the garden centre later?"

"Sorry, Mum. Think I'm rehearsing with the lads today."

"Oh, OK. Is Bex there?"

"Errr, yes. Why?"

"Just wondered! So we'll see you Sunday for lunch. I'm making your favourite, apple crumble."

"That's great, Mum. I'll see you then. Love to Dad."

"Have a lovely day, then. Goodbye."

Egg hung up. His mum had phoned him daily since he had moved out. It was kind of OK. Egg smiled as he gazed at the wondrous form lying on his white percale sheets. Moving out of his parents' house was the best decision he'd made in his life.

He was thinking about getting up when there was a loud bang on the front door. Bex stirred and mumbled something incoherent before snuggling back into the pillow.

"I love you," Egg whispered, as he swung his legs out of his brand-new IKEA king size.

"Me too," Bex murmured.

Egg pulled on a pair of jeans, grabbed a grey Led Zeppelin T-shirt and padded quietly out of the room and down the hall. He opened the door, squinting as the warm sunlight flooded in. Clipper stood beaming on the step. He looked cool in new designer skinnys and a jean jerkin. The distressed, brown leather boots looked particularly expensive, as did the new, sleeker, cut and style of his sandy hair. He'd obviously been out spending his advance money too.

"All right, mate? Thought we could go down the shop and get *Sound City* together."

Egg nodded and waved him inside.

Clipper let out a long whistle as he looked around.

"Oooo, this is swish. I'm liking the white walls with the tiled flooring. Proper modern," he said, trailing his hand down the wall as he followed Egg into the kitchen.

"Bit of a change from Mum and Dad's," Egg replied.

Clipper started playing with the space-aged coffee machine sitting on the shiny, black granite surface.

"How did you get your mum to let you live on your own aged sixteen?"

Egg grinned.

"Dad persuaded her. He came and looked at places with me, sorted it all, signed my lease."

"That's wicked."

Egg nodded and sat down on one of three breakfast stools. Rubbing his temples, he pointed to the brand-new Gaggia.

"Want a coffee?"

Clipper took the stool opposite.

"No thanks, mate. I won't put you through it. Looks like you need a degree to work the thing. Where d'you go out last night?"

"Took Bex all over town. Ended up having a drink with Dave Grohl."

"Piss off!"

Egg laughed.

"No lie! He likes our sounds. Such a cool guy."

"Amazing. Did you see what Burt said in *The Sun* yesterday?" Clipper suddenly looked pensive.

Egg pulled a face.

"No. I'm not sure I want to know."

"He told Gordon Smart he wants to crack America by pulling a Hollywood A-lister like Jennifer Lawrence and making a sex tape."

Egg put his head in his hands and groaned. Suddenly there was another loud bang on the door.

"I'll get it," Clipper said, bolting out of the kitchen.

A few seconds later he returned, followed by Burt and Tea. Burt's golden hair had turned a few shades lighter in the sun, falling to his lightly tanned cheekbones and enhancing his dazzling blue eyes. Tea's glossy, black hair framed strong features and kind, dark brown eyes. Egg could see immediately that both had new outfits on and he had to admit they looked cool. He mustered a tired smile.

"What are you two doing here?"

"Clipper invited us," Burt said, gazing around at the stylish kitchen.

Egg turned to his drummer for an explanation.

"It's our first review in a big music magazine. I thought it would be cool to all go get it together," Clipper said cheerfully. "You moved into this place two weeks ago and none of us ever even got an invite, so we had to guerrilla it."

"Even I'm here," Tea grinned, "and I hate hanging out with you nobheads. It's bad enough we spend nearly every day together, without seeing you on my day off."

"OK, let's get going then," Egg said, heading for the hall.

"Where's Bex?" Burt asked.

"In bed," Egg replied.

Burt raised his eyebrows and gestured over his shoulder.

"Just gonna go say hello."

He headed off towards the bedroom. Before Egg could say anything, Tea grabbed Burt's shoulder. "Don't be a dick all your life," he said, spinning Burt around and pulling him back towards the front door. "What? Just being polite," Burt replied over his shoulder, with a mischievous grin.

Egg eyed his lead singer with weary resignation. He pulled on a pair of new suede desert boots, opened the front door and led The RockAteers out into the morning sunshine.

Egg peeled back the crisp front cover of *Sound City* magazine as if he were defusing a bomb. The band's first ever single review was contained within the pages. The lead guitarist had no idea how the music would be received; the weekly publication was notorious for giving scathing reviews. Suddenly, the nerves overwhelmed him, he shut the magazine and held his breath.

"What you doin', you plank?" Burt said.

"Building the tension," Egg replied, unconvincingly.

He reopened the magazine and began to leaf through it, flicking through the pages until he reached the reviews page. There it was, page forty. Egg's stomach lurched. It was the first time his band's name and a photograph had been printed in the infamous weekly; a magazine he had read religiously from the age of nine. The photo was from the shoot Bex had done near the recording studios: Burt in the middle looking pensive, the sun illuminating his jaw line, standing tall with his head cocked arrogantly to one side; Tea to the right, cool and moodily handsome; Clipper beside him, his friendly, wide face smiling broadly. Then Egg, hunching his lanky frame awkwardly, his shock of ginger hair stark against his milk-pale skin. Egg took a deep breath and began to read out loud.

The RockAteers

"Golden" (Single)

When the single arrived on my desk I had high hopes.
All the hype that's surrounded this band, the endless
tabloid squawking about "Jack Skill" the teenage
tearaway, the suicidal rock 'n' roller, has made it hard
not to care.

"What!? Hard not to care? Everyone cares!" Burt interjected.

"Shhhh, let Egg read it," Clipper hissed.

Egg continued.

"Golden" starts well enough, the song careers into an
anthemic chorus, announcing the new kids with firm
intention. It settles into a funky guitar and vocal verse and
progresses very much like a well written song should. It's
catchy, it's well produced, it's well played, but something
struck me as dishonest. The guys in the band are all
seventeen/eighteen. Can they really have a full grasp of
sincerity and sorrow?

"I told you it was a moody song, Egg. Why did we release it
first?" Tea demanded.

Egg stared at his bass player, unable to find the right words to
reply.

"Keep going, Egg. May as well hear the rest," Clipper said.

Egg read on gravely.

Shouldn't they be singing about sex, drugs and rock 'n'
roll? Did they read one too many "how to" books?

By the time the song finished I felt cheated. Misguided
lyrics "Get up and stand up, you're golden emboldened

by youth" are preachy and self-indulgent; the stench of
experiences faked not learned.

Burt sat back.

"You know what, she has a fair point there. What does all that
bollocks even mean?"

Clipper was shaking his head.

"Give him a break, Jack. The song is about getting bullied,
so how is Egg faking it?" He gave Egg's shoulder a reassuring
squeeze. "We need to stick together, not agree with this shit.
Read on, mate."

Egg took a deep breath.

In summary, "Golden" is sentimental tripe, all mouth
and no trousers. There is no substance to back up the
propaganda. Alas, this vacuous rubbish will probably sell by
the bucketload.

Drusilla Prior.

Egg sat back in his chair and let the magazine slide off the table
and on to the floor. He looked at his band mates, put out an
unsteady hand with splayed fingers, and watched as it shook.

Burt stormed into the newsagents. He scanned the middle shelf
of music magazines and quickly located a healthy batch of *Sound
City*. He grabbed the lot, marched over to the counter and dumped
them in front of the slightly apprehensive shopkeeper.

"You want all of them?"

"I do!"

The newsagent nodded slowly and began to count them. He looked up. "All seventeen copies?"

Burt nodded.

"As you wish," the shopkeeper said, side-stepping over to the till and ringing it up.

"That will be £76.50 please."

Burt produced a card, paid contactless, picked up the wedge of glossy paper and walked out of the shop.

Once outside he stopped, scanned the area, spotted what he was looking for and set off towards it. He reached the black council-branded trash can, stuffed all the magazines inside it and stood back in admiration of his work.

Egg, who had been buying a sandwich from the café opposite the newsagent, spotted Burt and approached.

"What you doing?"

Burt grinned triumphantly. "I just binned a shed load of *Sound City*."

Egg looked puzzled. "Did you buy them?"

"Yep."

Egg ran a hand over his face in despair. "Have you heard the expression counterproductive?"

"Have you heard the expression get to the bloody point?"

"You just gave *Sound City* money!"

Burt shook his head. "Sometimes I despair with you Egg, I really do. You can't put a price on satisfaction. Besides, if any dicksplash hipster tries to buy it now, they won't be able to. Will they?"

Egg whistled. "Your logic astounds me. Shall we get back to rehearsals?"

Burt – 20th May

Who does that idiot think she is? Dishonest? No
trousers? I'm all fucking trousers! The thing
about people like that is they're all failed
musicians. I'm a winner. That's what I do, I win.
It's all about tall poppy syndrome. They build
you up then they chop you down. But then again,
we haven't even got tall yet, so what is she
banging on about? You wait till we do get tall.
I'm gonna write a book about how stupid she is.

There's this website called ripfork. Egg told me
about it. It's when people review the reviewers.
Within twelve hours there was a review of her
review. It was so awesome I copied and pasted it
below. Right, I'm off down the bookies.

Review the review – The RockAteers' single "Golden"

I've developed a skill for telling how good a music reviewer
is by the style of the opening sentence. The most obvious
thing about Drusilla Prior's opening line, other than her
obvious lack of brain cells, is her lack of imagination. My
guess, therefore, is that she is more haircut than journalist,
all the effort put into the attitude with nothing left to spare
for any kind of constructive critique, the important stuff.

"The review" itself is the most vacuous bull I've read in
a long time, combining sloppy rhetoric with ill-conceived

suggestion. The only slightly positive thing I can say is that Drusilla has spelt vacuous correctly.

I can't believe she is allowed to write reviews for such a well known and respected magazine.

Tea - 20th May

The past few days have been all over the shop. One minute I'm chuffed because we got the money from Jerome. The next some dickhead is calling my band fake in the biggest music mag in the country. I actually feel sorry for Egg. He keeps being told he's the new Chris Martin and then – BOOM! – he gets accused of being a manufactured pop star. Probably good for him, but still, being told you're fake is well tough.

I gave Mum twenty-five grand. Didn't tell her, just transferred it. She was angry at first but I told her I don't need it all because it's a mental sum of money and I owe her big time for doing the well hard job of bringing me up on her own.

She told me not to be daft and gave me a massive hug. Next day she went out and bought new clothes, a new sofa and a new TV. Ha ha, she ain't been able to buy anything for years. Right now she's in her new dress, on her new sofa watching her new TV. I bloody love my mum. I think she's gonna miss me when we go on tour. I hope the radio stations like our single better than the tool who gave us the review in *Sound City*.

Clipper - 20th May

The lads were well pissed off about the review. I'm a bit more chilled out about it. I figure

we're gonna get bad reviews because people are
jealous of how massive we're gonna get. I'm more
worried about getting the single playlisted on
Radio One and Capital Radio. Jerome reckons it's
proper important. He thinks it's pretty likely
they will support us. But then he said that *Sound
City* would like us. We're seeing Jerome tomorrow
about the tour and to meet crew members.

✪

The conference room at Fictitious Records was minimalist. The
walls were plain. A long oak conference table, primary-coloured
designer chairs and a state-of-the-art sound system were its only
features. Burt planted himself on a red chair at the head of the
table and immediately began to speak.

"You told us we'd be supported by *Sound City* and we weren't!
I reckon it was exactly the opposite of support. I'm not sure what
that particular word is, but it's that!"

Jerome studied the unhappy faces of the band one by one. The
record company boss had already heard just how upset they were
about the scathing review from their manager, Harry Branch.

"Have you seen me carrying around a magic wand?" Jerome
said, brushing his dark hair out of his eyes. "Did I tell you I could
predict the future? Do I have the power to hypnotise people into
liking your band?" Jerome looked into each confused young
face. All were silent. "No!"

Burt was first to reply.

"Oh, I get it. Now you've eventually got round to paying us

16

and we're locked into the contract you're getting all sarcastic and showing your true colours."

Jerome waited a moment before responding.

"That's right; now I've got you in my clutches you're gonna see the real me, the evil me." He paused and his expression softened. "But you know what? That is partly true."

"What do you mean?" Clipper asked.

Jerome smiled. "I'm going to explain without sugar-coating it. Right now, you're a joke. You're the band that came out of nowhere because of an irresponsible stunt pulled by your lead singer."

Burt slammed his hand on the table.

"Hang on, mate. I wasn't pulling no stunt. I meant to do it!"

"That may be so, but a large section of the press don't see your suicide attempt like that."

"Yeah, well I'd like to see them say that to my face!"

"Don't be a doughnut, Burt. Let's hear Jerome out," Tea said.

Jerome watched as Burt flipped Tea the finger.

"OK, so we need to change people's perceptions. Perception is ninety per cent of the struggle. We want people to see the graceful swan on top of the lake, not the ugly, webbed feet paddling furiously under the water."

"I'm not following. You sayin' I'm a graceful swan or I've got ugly feet?" Burt asked.

Egg sighed.

"Let him finish."

"OK, let me put it simply. We need to turn you into a band where the music is the centrepiece. The huge media hype you guys have traded off so far is a double-edged sword. Right now all the public is concentrating on is what stupid shit Jack is going to pull next."

Burt shook his head and stared at Jerome.

"I tell you what, mate. I'm inches away from walking out of this cock-banging meeting."

"Chill out, Jack," Egg said quietly. "Why can't we just listen to Jerome? I think he has a good point."

"Me too, he's right," Tea said firmly. "We need to make it about the music again."

Clipper nodded.

"So how do we do that, Jerome?"

"Good question, Clipper," Jerome said, smiling. "We start by changing the playing field. We make our entire campaign about the music. We don't engage the hype machine."

"But how can that work?" Egg asked.

"It works because you've just recorded the best rock pop record in ten years and that's what we are gonna promote."

"Wow, do you really think so?" Clipper beamed.

Jerome nodded at the drummer.

"How are we gonna get people to talk about our record when all they're interested in is me?" Burt sneered.

"Aha, a good question. Firstly by putting a gagging order on you, Mr Skill. We need you to lie low. If you have to talk to the press, make it about the music. Basically refrain from saying stuff like you're going to crack America by making a sex tape with a Hollywood actress."

Tea let out a snort of laughter. Everyone watched as Burt processed the words.

"So it's all my fault again?"

Egg leaned forwards.

"That's not what Jerome is saying. But I think I can put it even more simply. Let the music do the talking." Egg turned to Clipper and Tea. "What do you two think?"

Tea gave Burt a sideways glance.

"No argument from me. I hate reading all the idiotic crap Burt goes on about in the papers."

"I must admit, I do think it would be better if we concentrated on the band's music and not our singer's sexual urges," Clipper added, giving Burt an awkward smile.

"Jack?" Jerome asked, turning to the singer.

Burt squirmed in his chair. Avoiding all eye contact, he muttered something inaudible.

"What? We didn't hear you," Jerome pressed.

"OK, Dad! I'll shut up and only talk about the bloody music. But I want everyone to remember that I was the one that put this band on the map, yeah?!"

There was a long silence.

"Great. So moving on." Jerome clapped his hands. "I wanted you to meet the guys I've sourced to form the core of your touring team. It's vital you gel with these guys as you will be spending a lot of time with them, so please do ask them anything you like."

"Sweet as a nut. Who you got for us?" Clipper asked.

"First up is Ged. I truly believe he is the best Tour Manager in the world. He's a perfect fit for you guys. Frankly, that he's prepared to take on such a young band is a real compliment. He's the most efficient and professional man I know. He doesn't do chitchat and he won't try and be your friend; he is there to do a job. He'll tell you where you need to be and when, so do what he says. OK?"

"Sounds like The Terminator!" Tea said.

"Your Front of House guy is Richie," Jerome continued. "He's young but the best there is. Don't mess with him either or he'll make you sound horrible."

Burt pulled a face. "These people sound like a right laugh."

"It's not about having a laugh, Burt. You guys behave and do what you do and I guarantee you will have fun as well. You'll have a chance to meet the crew on Thursday. Now if you don't mind I have to run to another meeting."

Egg waited patiently on High Bench for over half an hour in the searing spring heat. He could feel the skin on his forehead prickling. Burt was outrageously late. Why did he want to meet on their day off anyway? They'd spent almost every day for the past six months together. As usual, Burt had brow-beaten Egg into the meeting, and as usual, he had caved in and agreed.

Egg had to wait a further five minutes before he saw the figure of his now infamous lead singer swaggering up the hill, the backdrop of London sprawling against the blue-grey haze. As Burt came closer Egg noted the purposeful look on his face and groaned. A moment later the towering, elegantly dressed boy was nodding a curt hello. Egg returned the greeting.

"Why beg me to meet you and then be thirty-six minutes

late?" he asked. "We have a rehearsal tomorrow, couldn't we have talked then?"

"I'm not late am I?" Burt said with surprise. "I thought we said two-thirty?"

Egg shook his head.

"You said two. What do you want?"

Burt frowned.

"Look, I think we've got off on the wrong foot. Can we start again?"

"We don't need to start again, we haven't even started." Egg stood up, ready to walk away.

Burt raised his palms.

"All right, all right, keep your hair on and sit down."

Egg sat again and rested his elbows on his knees.

"OK, I wanted to talk tour!"

There was something about Burt's chatty tone that was ringing alarm bells.

"Great, go ahead."

"Well, I was thinking it would be a good idea to have a bird ban?"

Egg looked up and fixed Burt with a look of pure astonishment. "Have a what?"

"A bird ban. As in, no girlfriends come on tour with us."

"You brought me all the way up here to tell me that you don't want Bex to come on tour?"

"No!" Burt spluttered. "I don't mean just Bex, I mean girlfriends in general. I just think it would be better for overall morale."

"I'm the only one with a girlfriend and her name is Bex. So you are not talking about a bird ban, you are talking about a Bex ban."

"Now you're splitting hairs."

Egg put his face in his hands.

"OK, I know I'm going to regret this, but enlighten me? What's your reasoning?" he asked, through his fingers.

"I told you my reasons, haven't you seen *Spinal Tap*? Biatches be a distraction and…"

"Oh God, please no, you didn't just call my girlfriend a 'biatch', did you?"

"Don't be so sensitive. Look, Egg, for your information it's been a tough year for me and all I'm asking is that you give me a little support."

Egg had lost count how many times Burt had mentioned his attempted suicide. Sometimes it was incidental, like now. Often it was direct, like in radio interviews.

"I have to go. I will see you at rehearsal tomorrow," Egg said despondently, before starting off down the slope.

"But we haven't decided anything yet!" Burt called after him.

Egg – 22nd May

Bex and I had a chat after rehearsal. I told her about Burt not wanting her on tour and she just kissed me and said, "It's cool, baby. Who said I wanted to go on tour anyway?" I could tell she was lying, but I decided to leave it. I really, really wish she could come. I don't know what I'm gonna do being away from her that long.

I wrote a review of the review we got of "Golden" on Tumblr. I pretended to be someone else. It's had loads of hits and even trended on Twitter. I really hope no one finds out it was me. That would be so whack.

I'm still so angry she said all those things. I think about it, a lot.

Burt - 23rd May
Harry just called and said our single had just been B-listed on Radio 1 and Radio 2 and A-listed on Capital. In your face, Drusilla "face cock" Prior. I said that to Harry and he said I should calm down because it was only one review, and that radio and gigging were the most important things. Then he started telling me about the support tour. Him and Jerome are like our new dads. The two of them together make me laugh. Jerome looks like some sort of corduroy wearing ex male model who hasn't shaved for a year. He doesn't care but I suppose he still looks sorta cool. Harry is not cool at all. He has a well dodgy comb-over type deal going on and wears chinos. His whole wardrobe is from the 1990s.

Crazel has called me every hour for the past two days, and left millions of messages. It's got so bad I had to change my number, but somehow she got my new one. I accused Tea and it turns out he did give her my new number because she's preggers and he thinks I'm a bastard. The one message I did listen to she sounded so insane I have now made it Jack Skill policy never to listen to her voicemails again. She was ranting and raving about us needing to be together for the sake of our love child! I was thinking about going to the police, but they would've just said that she is a week over her due date and that's what girls up the duff get like. Besides, if that story leaked

in the press, Jerome and the lads would go buck
mental. I promised to keep a low profile.

They're going to do an epileptic on Crazel if the
baby doesn't come in the next week. Basically
they put a big needle in her spine so the baby
comes quicker and it don't hurt.

Clipper - 24th May
The first time I heard our song on the radio I
actually cried. Yes!!!! We got on all the big
radio stations! I hope now we can all get past
the doom and gloom hanging in the air since that
bad review. We're moving on!

Burt stood on the gravel drive and stared at his family home.
He'd only seen Millie twice since last September. It was still
painful recalling how she was dragged, kicking and screaming
from the house by some meat-head new boyfriend of his mum's
to be sent to boarding school. Could it really be nine months
since that awful night? So much had happened since. Anyone
would have thought he'd be too busy to miss his sister, but Burt
missed Millie every single day.

The urge to give her a giant hug was overwhelming. Burt ran up
the stairs into the house and headed straight for the kitchen. There
she was, grinning from ear to ear. She bounced across the room,
crazy wavy hair flying everywhere, into his arms. The relief hit
him in a wave.

"That was quick!" she said, her face buried between his neck and shoulder.

"Well, it's not every day your favourite sister comes home."

Millie beamed. "I'm your only sister, doughnut brain."

"All right, mate?"

Burt looked over Millie's shoulder. There, sat at the large, round kitchen table in the bay window, was George Graves.

"What you doing here?"

Millie sighed.

"Ugh! I told him you weren't here, but he said he'd wait," she said crossly.

Burt eyed the opened laptop on the table.

"He fired up your laptop when he thought I was upstairs. I was just telling him off when you walked in."

George stood up. "Piss off. It was already on!" he said, his guilty expression betraying his words.

"No. It wasn't."

"Shut up, you specky little squirt," George sneered, before turning to Burt. "I was just checking my emails, mate."

Burt frowned and stepped in front of his sister. "First off, don't ever speak to my sister like that again. Second, don't ever, ever speak to my sister like that again."

Millie folded her arms and frowned. "You were reading Burt's emails."

George's expression changed, coldness in his deep-set blue eyes.

"No I wasn't, you little witch!" he hissed.

Burt moved towards him, but Millie held him back. She took four long strides towards the bully, until she was standing right in front of him. She crossed her arms and glared.

"Don't you dare use that tone with me you … you … arse crack! Aggression is not something I respond to, George Graves. Now get out of my house and never come back." Millie frowned. "Hang on a minute, how did you get in?"

"Door was open."

"No it wasn't," Millie replied firmly.

Suddenly Burt was by his sister's side.

"Get out, George, before I tear your throat out," he hissed, eyeballing his old best friend.

George's face fell, his defiance replaced by hurt. After a long, awkward moment George dropped his head and traipsed out of the room as if he'd just received a death sentence. Burt and Millie looked at each other in silence until they heard the front door shut.

Millie looked worriedly up at Burt, her brown eyes magnified through the blue-framed glasses.

"Sorry," she said.

Burt put his arm on her shoulder. "Don't be sorry. He just showed his true colours is all."

He grinned.

"Tell me about Hogwarts."

"It's good. When I got there a carriage picked me up!"

"You're shitting me?!"

"Yes, I'm totally lying, but I like it there and I have OK friends. You're going to be off all over the place soon. It's best I'm there."

"I suppose so. I'm glad you're enjoying it. You do sound well posh though." He frowned. "Has Mum phoned you yet?"

Millie looked down.

Burt wanted to scream, but he knew it wouldn't help. "Cuppa?" He smiled adopting a posh accent. "Or should I say, would you like a cup of Earl Grey?"

✪

Burt – 25th May
What a snake George is. I've not talked to him for months and then I come back to see Millie and there he is, looking all innocent, on my laptop, more than likely reading my private shizzle. And then he gets all aggressive with Millie. So I kicked the bell-end out. I might have known him since I was five but I've had enough. Since I started being in the papers he's been acting all weird, like he's jealous or something. Ringing me all the time. Gotta cut him out for good. #greeneyedshitbags

✪

SONG 2 ON THE NOSE

A smile crept across Sir Wilson Cloom's thin lips. Reading The RockAteers' single review in *Sound City* had just made his year. After losing the battle to sign the band, he wished them only failure. He hadn't slept easily since Billy Visconti and Jack Skill had recorded him revealing the depths of his deceit. His obsession with their downfall drove him to check their website and social networking sites daily. He'd gone further and bribed a contact in the band's law firm to divulge the details of the deal with Fictitious Records. Cloom was shocked at how much the advance was; a huge sum in today's market. It seemed Jerome was confident they were destined for massive success.

Two days after the album was mastered, Cloom managed to get a digital copy. As he listened his heart sank. It was fantastic; every track a stone cold winner and he knew it. When Jerome flew to the USA to showcase The RockAteers stateside, Cloom knew about it. The word on the industry grapevine was the American bigwigs loved the band and would back Jerome in an effort to break them in the US. Cloom was powerless to stop any of it. If he used his influence to turn people against the band, Jerome would surely produce the incriminating tape recordings and destroy his reputation forever.

Cloom was shaken from his vengeful thoughts by his office buzzer.

He hit the talk button.

"Yes?"

"Just wondering what you thought of the article, sir?" his secretary, Sophia, asked.

She had dropped the magazine off that morning, a Post-it Note attached: "A treat for you on page 40, sir."

"Get in here!"

Moments later his very pretty young secretary slash junior A&R girl appeared at the glass door.

Cloom ushered her inside with the magazine. "Sit down."

Sophia took a seat opposite her boss.

"I think it might be the start of the backlash," she said.

"I'm not so sure but it's certainly something we can exploit."

Cloom fixed Sophia with one of his hard, cold stares. "How far are you prepared to take it?"

"Take what?"

"How far will you go to destroy The RockAteers' reputation?"

Sophia cast her eyes down at the floor. "As far as it takes, sir."

Cloom made a steeple with his fingers, leaned forward and nodded his praise.

"That's good, because I have an idea and I'm pretty sure it's going to ruin your ex-boyfriend's year."

"Where do I sign?" Sophia said, with a confident smile.

"First we plant the seed. That's all for now." He waved her away.

Once alone, Cloom turned his chair to face the fantastic view of central London and began to deliberate. He gazed out of the window for twenty minutes before turning back to his desk and hitting the intercom.

"Get me the chief editor of *The Daily Blog* on the phone right now," he barked.

Burt – 29th May
Behold biatches! Today I bring you a day in the life of Jack Skill – future teenage rock 'n' roll superstar. I won't get too detailed coz I can't be arsed.

I wake up and smoke a massive bifter. Then I go downstairs and get some black coffee. When I say black, I mean, like tar. It's got to give me a massive hit or it isn't worth drinking. I don't eat breakfast, because breakfast is for male lesbians.

The next bit of my day depends on if I got rehearsals or not. Let's say I haven't: at about midday I head down the bookies and spend a couple of hours in there chatting with Lenny (my bookie) and placing bets. The next bit depends on if I win or not. Let's say I win: at about 2 pm I head into town. People have started to recognise me all the time and bug me for photos, so I always take a cab. I either go to Soho and hang in a couple of members' bars or I go down Old Bond Street and hit some of the posh shops. Louis Vuitton didn't let me in once because I was a bit drunk. That got in the papers and I looked like a tool. What usually ends up happening if I have a few in a members' bar is some fitty starts chatting me up and then that's me for the night.

Drinking, frolicking and trying my hardest to keep out of the way of the paps.

Some mentalist accosted me up on Oxford Street yesterday and started giving me agg. He told me we were a novelty act and that I was an attention-seeking media whore. What??! I just stood there and took it. I wish I'd said loads of shiz back to him. I swear next time I get accosted like that I'll be prepared. Anyway, that's definitely a downside of being in the paper every week. I just don't get why he was having a go?

Isn't it bad enough that autograph hunters knock on my door at all hours without getting abuse from random strangers? I never answer the door anymore.

On the up side, on the way home I walked past a travel agents and saw this girl sitting at the desk through the window. She was so well fit I went in there and ended up booking a holiday, just because I could.

#sevenstarrocknroller

"Can you put £3K on Pink Apalachi for me, Len?"

"Each way or on the nose?" the gruff voice asked.

"On the nose."

"That takes you up to 13.2 grand," Burt's bookie replied. "At 15 to 1 you're gonna make it all back in one hit."

"Mate, I'm a superstar, course I will."

"Atta boy!" the bookie replied. "By the way, I saw you in the paper this morning, good work. I bet the slag deserved it."

"Yeah," Burt replied absently. "Listen, I gotta go. Things to do, people to see."

Burt hit the red button on his phone and started the intricacies of rolling a joint. Having his own personal bookie thrilled him, but he didn't want to get too chummy with the man. Burt first met Lenny in his local betting shop, in his native Blackheath Village. Burt felt alive around ordinary people, but things had become tricky since becoming famous and he had started placing his bets through Lenny over the phone. When he did go into the shop, Lenny kept everyone away. Burt had noticed people seemed very respectful of Lenny.

Burt's celebrity both annoyed and pleased him. At first the press agent had taken every opportunity to exploit Burt's rising star. Now there was a total shift in strategy. Burt had loved the attention, giving interviews and courting reporters. And there were perks: everything was suddenly free – clubs, bars, he was even admitted into the cinema without paying. But the fact he could no longer be anonymous was starting to bother him.

Burt stubbed the joint out on an expensive china plate and was suddenly consumed by the need for chocolate. He shut the sturdy back door and made his way down the patio steps. He hadn't seen his parents in two months and the huge garden was looking neglected. They had returned separately a day after his attempted suicide, but once they'd established he was alive and recovering, they'd returned to their lives elsewhere. His dad was in Italy now, working on some big-money project. His mum had traded the meat-head who had dragged Millie off for a Swiss banker called Sebastian. She had brought him to the hospital after Burt's suicide attempt. He stood in the door in a stiff blazer, looking like he had a bad smell under his nose.

Burt snuck over his neighbour's wall and crossed their garden. He repeated the process twice until he reached the street adjacent to his own and then doubled back along it. As he passed the house from a safe distance, he saw to his surprise that the usual bunch of four or five photographers was more like twenty.

"More famous every day, Mr Skill," he told himself, as he quickened his pace and headed towards the little corner shop. Burt loved the walk across Blackheath towards the village. The expanse of lush green grass was a pocket of paradise, with the little church and the quaint shops. As he neared the church he started to think of Bex, again.

It still distressed him every time he saw her with Egg. The worst thing about it all was that Burt could finally see what she saw in him; now he had lost the specs and spots, he actually looked half decent. It didn't occur to Burt the guitarist's looks were not what Bex was interested in. Burt would still give anything to be with her. Was he obsessed with her, like Crazel was with him? He decided not. After all, he could have any girl in the city, he was Jack Skill, and he didn't obsess about girls; *they* obsessed about *him*.

He felt a tap on his shoulder and turned to see a good-looking boy of about his age. He was styled in a very similar way to Burt.

"Hi, Jack, my name is Zander," he said, extending a hand. "So sorry to bother you, I just wanted to say I'm a huge fan and that I'm in a band, and we just got signed."

Burt ignored the hand and shrugged. "And?" he said, before turning his back and walking on.

The boy stood crestfallen in the street, staring at the disappearing rock star.

Burt arrived at the shop and headed straight for the chocolate counter next to the till. Below the sweets were piles of newspapers. He fished up a copy of *The Bugle*, *The Sun*, the *Star*, the *Mirror* and *Heat* magazine and slung them all on the counter. He then picked out a Twix, Twirl, Mars, Bounty and Snickers and added them to the pile.

By the time he made it home, he had already chewed through four bars of chocolate. The crowd of paparazzi had grown even larger. He nonchalantly trespassed back over his neighbours' lawns and re-entered his house. Once inside he made a cup of tea, rolled another joint, put the horse racing on the radio and settled back to enjoy the remaining chocolate. He demolished a finger of Twirl and started leafing through one of the red tops. He stopped in horror, dropping the remaining chocolate finger on the couch. There, in the centre pages, was a huge picture of Hazel, her face forlorn, holding her huge pregnant belly. He read the headline out loud.

"Pregnant with Suicide Singer's Love Child."

Burt continued to stare at the paper, unable to bring himself to read the blurb. He shifted his gaze to an inset picture of him with his band. Studying the tiny picture of himself, he suddenly felt completely and utterly out of place, as if he were living someone else's life. Burt tried to catch his breath. He felt dizzy. Suddenly he retched. He retched again, puking up all the chocolate on to the expensive coffee table.

Burt - 30th May
Now I know the pattern I can be prepared.
More paparazzi outside the gaff means I'm in
the papers. I wish I could stick my head in
the ground like one of them giraffe-looking
animals. How could Crazel do that to me? I rang
her and she just said it was for my own good
and that something needed to jolt me into doing
right by her. What does that even mean? Is she
talking about marriage? She better freaking not
be! Anyway, I can't think about it. It drives
me mental.

We have all these people coming on tour with us.
Jerome introduced us to them the other day. The
Tour Manager is called Ged. He's about 40, looks
proper hard and has a shiny, bald head he must
Bic shave every day. He has a well deep Scouse
accent that is impossible to understand. There's
a front-of-house fella called Richie, another
Northerner, and these three roadies dressed in
combat shorts, black T-shirts and big black
boots. Weirdos. They're from Ireland I think but
they could be Scottish. Why couldn't Jerome and
Harry sort normal London people? Ged called the
roadies "Hairies" and asked Jerome if we were
taking any "Vidiots", "Lampys" or "Swag Men" with
us. Jerome explained that a vidiot runs all the
video stuff on a tour. A swag man deals with all

the merchandise and a lampy does the lights. What
a load of total bollocks.

"I warned you, Jerome," said Harry. "I said that bloody overeager
PR person of yours could turn The RockAteers into an episode
of *EastEnders*." Harry had kind eyes, a plain, honest face and
dressed immaculately. Jerome noted time and again how people
misjudged his old friend's demeanour, all too often concluding
he was a pushover. They couldn't be more wrong.

"Give me a break, Harry. None of us could predict Jack would
be such a media whore. Our PR person lit the match, but Jack
was the one who built the bonfire. Anyway, I had a meeting only
last week telling him to stop."

Jerome and Harry had called the crisis meeting after receiving a flurry of phone calls from worried co-workers. They sat
in Jerome's spacious kitchen, each feeling the peculiarity of
seeing one another so early on a Sunday morning. Harry wasn't
used to seeing Jerome's slightly shabby alpha-male persona
in this homely setting. He studied his handsome friend. The
roughly cut salt and pepper beard, shoulder-length straggly
black hair and weather-beaten face hid high cheekbones and
fine features. If he tidied himself up and had a shave he would
definitely make a better first impression, Harry decided. But
then again, his scruffy friend had no problems gaining respect
despite his appearance.

"It's turning into a circus and we haven't even released the first album yet," Harry moaned.

"OK, let's think about damage control. How can we contain this situation?" Jerome was keeping one eye on his two small children playing outside in the sunny garden. His youngest, a boy, was eating what looked to be soil and Jerome wondered if he should intervene.

"I've been rolling that one round my head since the shit hit the fan yesterday."

Jerome put his hand up. "Hang on a sec, Harry." He got up and opened the patio door. "Jack, can you not eat the mud, please, it's not clean."

"Bloody hell, Jerome, I always forget your son is called Jack, what a waking nightmare."

Jerome shook his head and retook his seat. "Where were we?"

"I've considered various solutions," Harry said. "Paying this Hazel off, for example?"

"If we give her money and the press find out, it'll get even worse. Teenage pregnancy, bad boy rockers and unrequited love? It's a tabloid's wet dream."

"Agreed, so how do we minimise the damage?"

Jerome stared into the garden. "We both know this story will sell The RockAteers at least another hundred thousand records. Maybe we don't do anything."

Harry shook his head.

"Egg hates all this attention; he finds Jack impossible. He wants to be in Radiohead, not some kind of novelty act. His words not mine. He sees himself as a serious songwriter."

"But don't you see? That's exactly why they're going to be the biggest band in the world, Harry," Jerome countered. "That conflict, the clash of characters."

"So we ride it out?" Harry bowed his head, unconvinced. "To hell with Egg and his integrity, is that it?"

"Egg will come round eventually. Look, don't worry, everything's great. The chart rundown is tonight; I predict a top five. We have the sold-out Desert Kings tour. I know it seems like this story might derail the juggernaut, but it's probably only going to ramp it up a gear."

"This is a total reversal of the strategy we implemented last week!" Harry said.

"It is. But we have to roll with the punches."

"OK, let's do it. Is that all?"

"One last thing I want to discuss."

"You want to talk about *The Vox*?" Harry groaned.

"It's the biggest TV show in the country, Harry, and TV sells records. We can't ignore the offer."

"You know Egg won't go for it, right?"

"I do. But there are strategies to persuade integrity fixated musicians to relent."

"There are? You should write a book about it. We could be rich."

Harry left Jerome's house feeling just as uneasy as when he arrived.

Tea – 8th June

Number 1!!!! Just came home after listening
to the chart show round Egg's flat. Chuffed!!!
Only nine months since we left school and we've
smashed up the charts! Me, Bex, Egg and Clipper
all jumped around the room. Bex gave me a hug. I
think I might have clung on a bit too long.

Burk wasn't there. No one could get hold of
him. I kind of felt sorry for him. But then, if
you impregnate someone you've nicknamed Crazel,
there's a fair chance it's going to come back and
bite you on the arse.

I'm off to town now with my mum to treat her to a
posh lunch. #bestmumintheworld

Clipper – 9th June

I just spent nearly the whole day in town with
Bex, going in and out of shops. I spent a fortune
and I can't even wear any of it on stage. I don't
care. I love it. I bought a really lovely pair of
red velvet shoes from Gucci, a studded belt from
Prada and a silver jacket from Vivienne Westwood.
I didn't even know these type of clothing stores
existed before Bex showed me them. It was one of
the best days of my life. I love Bex. We chat
like I've never talked to anyone before. It was
so cool walking down Bond Street arm in arm with
her, she's properly my best friend.

I still can't believe the single went to #1. We
have over two million followers on Twitter and
all the other reviews have been so awesome.
I didn't know what the expression "pinch
yourself" meant before now.

Egg - 12th June
"Having a great intellect is no path to being happy." Stephen Fry.

I've been over the reviews. All positive. I think I may be a little obsessed. Thing is, it's all going great but I'm still stressed. I feel a sort of weight on me.

I've not been able to bring myself to write anything for a few days. After the playback of the album, Alex Bear, the producer, turned to me and said. "It won't ever sound as good as it does right now in this moment, it won't ever be purer than this, savour the moment. Soon people are going to pull it apart, judge it and want things you never expected anyone would want from you."

Now I know what he meant. Harry said that I shouldn't worry about one bad review. He was one of about thirty people to tell me that very same thing. When I reread it I actually start to believe I'm a fake, that I really do just write a bunch of over-sentimental, meaningless rubbish.

It doesn't help that I keep telling Bex I love her and that she always replies, "Me too." I hadn't really noticed properly until me and her watched this old film called *Ghost*. Demi Moore tells Patrick Swayze she loves him and he always replies, "Ditto." That's when it suddenly dawned on me that Bex has never actually said the words "I love you" and that I'm Demi Moore. What made matters worse was that right after the film finished, to test my theory, I told her I loved her and she just said, "Me too."

It's left me feeling very insecure and we go on tour with The Desert Kings soon. Burt's girlfriend ban means I'm going to be in limbo for months. I already can't sleep. I need to sort myself out.

Burt seems to have gone AWOL. He was supposed to meet for rehearsals this morning but didn't turn up.

It's times like these I could do with seeing Mum and Dad a bit more. Life might feel closer to normal.

Tea – 13th June
We've lost Burt. He ain't at home and his phone's off. No one's seen him for five days. He's not gone to see Millie either, because Bex managed to find out without telling her he was missing. I even called Hazel and now she's ringing me every five minutes. If that bastard doesn't show up by the weekend, we are one hundred per cent fully shafted.

Harry Branch sat at his desk staring up at the platinum discs on his ego wall. No doubt there would be a RockAteers disc up there soon. It would be the hardest earned, no question.

He rubbed his eyes but the worry would not subside. The RockAteers were going on a UK arena tour in two days, the album was coming out in a week and Jack Skill had vanished from the face of the earth. He picked up the landline and dialled Jerome's mobile.

"Jack's disappeared," Harry said flatly.

"What do you mean?" Harry could tell Jerome was on the move. The street noise was making it hard to hear him.

"I mean the tour starts in two days and our lead singer has gone missing."

"How long?"

"Five days. I asked Ged to search for him but we can't find any trace. He's checked airlines, pubs, all his usual hang-outs. No one has a clue."

There was a long pause before Jerome spoke. "How am I just hearing about this now?"

"I didn't want to worry you," Harry replied. "I should have listened to my gut about these kids. As soon as I met Mr Skill I knew he would be trouble. A suicidal seventeen-year-old megalomaniac! What was I thinking?"

"Calm down. We'll find him and don't start complaining about signing potentially the biggest band on the planet. Let's just figure out how we find him."

Suddenly the buzzer on Harry's desk flashed.

"What is it, Tammy? I expressly told you no interruptions."

"I know, Mr Branch, but Jack's here to see you."

"You are joking?"

"No, Mr Branch, he's here." She giggled. "All 'andsome and tanned he is."

"You're not so bad yourself, Tam!" Harry heard the unmistakable voice over the speaker.

"Send him in." Harry paused and then hit the call button again. "And, Tammy, what have I told you about flirting with clients?"

"I weren't flirtin', Mr Harry, sir, it's Jack!"

"Jerome, Jack's here. Call you back," Harry said, cutting the call.

Jack glided into the office. He looked like a man who had been on holiday for six months: beautifully tanned and festooned with a vast array of love beads. Harry stared at Jack's lower half slack-jawed.

"Why are you wearing a dress?"

"All right, Harry?" Burt said, plonking himself down in the chair opposite with a casual flounce.

Harry had intended to use calm managerial tones, the cool interpersonal skills he'd honed over years of dealing with conceited clients. There had been plenty of time to plan this moment, when he would confront his wayward artist and explain who wore the trousers.

"Where the hell have you been?" he barked.

"India. I needed a rest," Burt replied, distracted by something through the window.

Harry stared at him. Burt put his feet up on the desk, his floaty skirt slipped to reveal his hairy, brown legs, an act that almost sent his furious manager diving across the desk and at his throat.

"India? You're on tour in forty-eight hours. You've missed interviews with *Q*, *Sound City*, and a cover shoot with *Clash Magazine*! What the HELL were you doing in India?"

"I told you, taking a break. I deserve a bloody break, Harry. You work us like dogs."

"A break!? You haven't even started your debut tour, how can you need a break?" Harry had worked with some of the biggest divas on earth, yet he had never, in his long, distinguished career, raised his voice to one of his artists. "Look, Burt—" he said, lowering his tone.

"Jack, call me Jack. It is my working title after all, and we do work together, don't we, Harry?"

"Look, Jack," Harry began again through gritted teeth. "I can't have you disappear whenever you feel like it. It's just not on. The rest of the band aren't pleased with you either."

"I was with Brad and his wife."

"What?"

"Pitt!"

"You're telling me you've been in India with Brad Pitt and Angelina Jolie?"

"I am!" Jack said. "Well, they were staying at the same spot and we got to know each other." He grinned. "I'm pretty sure she fancied me."

Harry put his elbows on the table and stared, despondently, down at his clenched hands.

"When you became our manager you told us we should try and network and socialise. It was how you got up the ladder, you said."

Harry rolled his eyes, the urge to wring the boy's neck almost too much to control.

"And it's not a dress. It's a lungi. It's what men wear in India."

Harry shook his head slowly and stared at Jack for a long moment.

"What am I going to do with you?" he said eventually.

Burt smiled.

"You're going to take twenty per cent of everything I earn, Harry, that's what you're going to do with me."

"You're too smart for your own good, Jack Skill," Harry said, sitting back in the chair.

"Thank you," Burt said, standing up. "Right, I'm off to see a man about a horse."

"There is something else, Jack," Harry said, raising his arm. "*The Vox* want you to play live on the show next Sunday."

Burt sat back down. "Really? But that's *wicked*, right?" He declared loudly. "We would sell loads more records going on that show, yeah?"

Harry nodded. "You would indeed, but there's a problem."

Burt looked concerned. "What? Don't they have a dressing room big enough for my gigantic horse penis?"

"I don't think Egg will go for it," Harry told him.

Burt looked away and narrowed his eyes. After a moment he turned back to Harry.

"Let me call him," he said, pulling out his phone.

Harry looked at the singer in confusion. Before he could say anything, Burt had reached his guitarist.

"Egg, it's Jack. I'm good thanks, mate. Look, I'm with Harry. He wants us to play *The Vox* next week. They want to do it all tasteful and shit. Make sure it's cool and serious rock 'n' roll, etc., etc." Burt paused, looked up at Harry and winked.

Burt put his hand over the receiver. "Egg asked how much?"

"Not much. They're doing us a favour, exposing us to millions of potential new fans. Remember, television is king."

"How much, Harry?" Burt pressed.

"Around 10K."

Jack got back on the phone. "Harry says about ten. It's good promo, he reckons. You cool with that?"

Harry strained to hear Egg's answer but couldn't catch anything. "Sweet." Burt nodded and hung up.

"He'll do it. No probs," Burt said, with a smug grin.

Harry shook his head slowly, feeling fatigued but relieved. He allowed himself a smile. The sooner Jack Skill was on tour and out of his hair the better.

Burt – 16th June
I could live in India. I could have Brad as me bezzie mate and we could both be married to Angelina Jolie. Like those lads from The Killers. Marmites or whatever they're called. She might be old but in the flesh she is a work of art. In truth they only loved me coz their kids knew me from the Internet. They gave me loads of wicked advice about keeping out of the public glare.

I had to pretend to ring Egg about doin' *The Vox* show. #iamgenius! I knew as soon as Harry said it that he wouldn't do it. I think it's called forcing his hand. #eggisgonnagoyokemental

Met Jerome's new digital girl, Tyra, this morning. She just come up to me in the street and said she works for me. Weird. To think there are people who work for me that I have never even met. I must admit there is a proper right fitty in there somewhere. Quality legs. As it is now though she looks like a ginger punk with geeky glasses.

Clipper had transformed the rehearsal space into a cosy hang-out. The large, soundproofed, windowless space on an industrial estate next to the river had been soulless until he'd worked his magic on it. He had chosen neutral colours and soothing artwork, to calm the environment. He knew the other boys liked it, even if some of them didn't say so.

The RockAteers had progressed from the school hall, but remnants of familiarity remained. Clipper had acquired the same school chairs they had always used. There was a large cream corner sofa surrounding a teak table, coffee- and tea-making facilities, and a fridge.

The advance money had been put to good use. Egg had chosen the gear, a state-of-the-art PA system for Burt and two amplification units for himself, one electric, one acoustic. The giant Marshall stack he'd purchased took up nearly half of one wall. Tea had an equally giant Ampeg bass rig on the opposite wall. When it was turned up loud it made a man vibrate, Tea joked.

Clipper's drum kit was positioned in the middle of the room. His three band mates stood around him like satellites circling the earth. Or at least that's how Clipper thought about it. The new DW kit sparkled.

"Let's take a break, shall we?" Burt said into the microphone.

Egg turned off his guitar and placed it on the rack.

"Cuppa, anyone?" Clipper asked, placing his sticks on the snare drum.

Tea went over to the tiny kitchenette.

"My turn."

"So, we all set for *The Vox* tomorrow then?" Burt said, glancing at Egg.

Egg stared at his singer.

"What are you talking about?"

Clipper looked sheepish. "Egg, mate, we thought you'd prefer not to know until the last minute. You know, because of your worrying and everything."

Egg eyed the other three in turn.

"And I suppose this was Burt's brilliant idea?" he said angrily.

"It *was* my idea as it goes," Burt said, unapologetically. "You're such an integrity-obsessed freakoid and I knew you'd be nervous about the gig. I saved you a load of sleepless nights, mate."

Egg shook his head furiously.

"You don't even know the meaning of the word integrity, which isn't ironic, because you have none. Why didn't our manager consult me on this? It's not your job to manipulate my band mates into keeping something as big as this a secret."

"I know what integrity means, piss bag. It means being an arrogant tit, and anyway, don't blame Harry. I told him I talked to you because I knew you would have a ginger freak out if we asked you," the singer sneered.

"You're right, Burt, we would have had a conversation about it, because I don't think we should do a reality TV talent contest right now. It's not bloody cool. Especially before we've even released our album."

"What you chattin' about? *The Vox* is an amazing show. We'll sell loads of records off the back of it," Burt shouted, as Tea arrived quietly and set the tray down on the coffee table.

Egg returned the glare and replied slowly, "Read my lips. I … AM … NOT … DOING … IT."

SONG 3 GET UP, STAND UP

Egg - 21st June
Didn't sleep a wink last night, I really mean
that, not a wink. Bex stayed over again and she
eventually got really annoyed with me fidgeting
about. I told her it was because I had more or
less left the band and she sat up in bed, with no
top on and said *The Vox* was a great show and that
I was being stubborn and biting off my nose to
spite my face. So I texted the boys at 3 am and
said I would be there. Only Clipper replied to
say he was glad. God knows what he was doing up
at that time. Probably playing FIFA.

I'm worried about forgetting my guitar parts now.
I'm worried that Burt might say or do something
insane on national television. He's way past
loose cannon status now. He's a primed, nuclear
missile. Bex said that Burt would never toe the
line and whether I liked it or not, he was a rock
'n' roll superstar waiting to happen. I told her
that he was a car crash waiting to happen and she
laughed. That's when I told her that I loved her
again and she said, "Me too."

#Heartbreaker.

✪

Egg chose to sit right at the back of the Addison Lee seven-seater taxi. The rest of the band and Harry left him to it, chatting excitedly about the upcoming tour and promo campaign. After an hour's journey, they pulled into the world-famous Pinewood Studios, a sprawling city of hangars, connected by a web of single-lane streets.

"Look! 007!" Clipper shrieked, pointing at a sign way up on the top of a huge warehouse.

Burt pulled a face.

"I thought it would look a bit more swish than this." He shrugged.

The taxi drew up outside a small office block. A man and woman, both in their twenties, with cool hair and clothes, greeted them with wide, perfect smiles. The man was pointing a small hand-held camera at them.

"Hi, guys, I'm Kendal, we are soooooo excited to have you on *The Vox*," the girl said, with rehearsed delivery.

"Proper zinged to be here," Clipper gushed back. "I watch the show all the time. It's so well zing to be invited…"

Burt stepped up behind the drummer, grabbed his collar and hissed into his ear. "Shut up, Clip; stop saying zing every five seconds. You sound mental."

Clipper looked as though he'd been slapped. "I mean … yes. You should be excited coz we are gonna rock this party … hard," he trailed off weakly.

Burt dragged a hand across his face in despair.

"OK, great! Let me show you to your dressing room," Kendal said, smiling broadly. The group followed on behind her. "This is Stan, he'll get you anything you need whilst you're here. You don't mind him filming, it probably won't be used," she added, nodding towards her equally smiley companion walking backwards as his camera rolled.

They reached a small but smart-looking dressing room with a sofa, two chairs and a TV.

"We have you scheduled for a sound check at 11 am. Yusef will come and say hi just before then."

"Who?" Tea asked.

"Yusef, he's the contestant you'll be singing a duet with."

The band members looked from Kendal to Harry and back again in confusion.

"We didn't agree to a duet with anyone," Harry said.

Kendal frowned.

"It's in the contract you signed, Mr Branch."

"We only received the contract three days ago and it was thicker than a five-year record deal. We didn't even sign it."

"I see. Shall I call our producer?"

"I think you'd better," Harry said, sternly.

"Okey dokey, before I go grab him, just so you know, Yusuf is a huge fan. He has all your records and knows all your songs by heart. He will be heartbroken if he's the only one that doesn't get to sing with a star."

"Wait, is Yusuf the wheelchair refugee? From Iraq?" Clipper asked.

"Iran. He escaped because homosexuality is banned in his country," Kendal replied.

Stan nodded in sombre accordance. "As he was escaping

he was in a car accident and suffered spinal damage," he told them gravely.

Clipper looked imploringly at his band mates. "We gotta do it, lads. He's been through so much already."

Egg studied his shoes. Tea frowned in thought. Burt exploded.

"Listen here, sugar tits. We haven't released a record yet so how can this Yusuf have it and anyway, if you think I'm doing a duet with a disabled, cock-munching Arab, you got another thing coming."

Kendal and Stan stared at Burt slack jawed. Egg clapped both hands to his face, covering his eyes. Tea looked out of the window, shaking his head. Clipper glared at the singer. Harry stepped towards Kendal, shooting Burt a look of disdain.

"I think what Jack is *trying* to say, is that we haven't prepared for this. There is no time for us to even rehearse, which is madness. How about you go get your producer and we get this sorted out."

Kendal nodded gravely and left the room with Stan in tow.

"Right, close that door, Tea, and all of you sit down," Harry ordered.

Once seated Harry stood and stared down at Burt. "Jack, you cannot say those things. My God, it's not the nineteen hundreds!"

"You really are a vicious wanker," Clipper hissed. "I suppose you think I'm a cock-muncher?"

"I do," Burt said flatly. "You are."

"You realise we have to do the duet now? Because of what you just said," Egg said.

"Piss off, Smeg," Burt sneered.

"I'm afraid he's right, Jack," Harry said. "In about five minutes an equally annoying but slightly older man will come into this room and he will introduce himself as the producer."

"So what? I'll bite his nuts off," Burt said.

"He will have concern smeared across his smug TV industry face and will say something like: 'How are we going to sort this mess out then?'"

"By calling us a cab and him pissing off back to his studio," Burt blasted.

"Ah yes, but then he will point out that the things you said about one of the show's contestants were racist, homophobic and anti-disabled people. And that he would hate for the press to get hold of a story like that, because he can just see the headline: SUICIDE SINGER QUITS SHOW BECAUSE HE WOULDN'T PLAY WITH A WHEELCHAIR BOUND GAY MUSLIM."

Burt looked confused. "How was I disablist?"

Harry locked eyes with the singer.

"The thing is, Burt, we could and should have quit the show. We haven't signed the contract and we could have walked free, but they have you on camera saying those dreadful things."

There was a loud knock on the door. Harry got up and answered it. He was greeted by a man in his late thirties, with a stylish haircut and sleek, dark clothes.

"I'm Ed, the producer of the show. This is Yusuf."

Harry stared down at Yusuf, a handsome lad in his late teens. He looked back to the producer and nodded with quiet respect.

"I thought I would come down, so I could introduce him to your group," Ed said, already pushing past the band's manager and into the room.

Yusuf wheeled through the door in his slipstream.

"Which one you bastards call me bad things?" Yusuf said, in a husky, heavily accented voice.

The band stared back at him, except Burt, who avoided everyone's gaze.

"Hi, I'm Clipper. I play drums. I hear you're a wicked singer." Clipper offered a hand to Yusuf.

"I love to sing. It is my life. That and cock-munching," he replied with a smirk.

Tea was the first to crack. Soon they were all in hysterics. Apart from Burt. His eyes darted as his face reddened. It was the first time any of them had ever witnessed Burt Windsor humiliated.

Burt stared out at the audience. They were all on their feet, clearly loving it. He looked over at Yusuf, just as he began to sing, and winked. The Iranian beamed back at him as he jived, side to side, in his chair. Burt gazed at Tea. Why was he pulling a face like that on live TV? Why did he look so upset? Or did he look ill? Maybe he was nervous. They hadn't even reached the first chorus yet.

Suddenly it hit him like a brick in the face. The chorus! Oh my God – the words in the chorus. THE CHORUS!! Burt spun on his heel and stared at Clipper. The drummer grinned back at him as he bashed away, totally unaware of what was about to happen on live television. Burt turned, still singing and looked at Egg. The guitarist raised an eyebrow and turned his back. Burt stared at the mic in his hand as he sang into it. He couldn't just stop, could he?! NO. This would all be on him. He couldn't focus, he forgot a lyric but managed to replace it with something similar. The chorus was in four bars. There was only one thing for it. He had to go for it. What the hell, he thought. He took a deep breath, turned to Yusef, and belted out the Chorus to "Golden".

"Get up, stand up…"

Egg – 23rd June
It was only a few seconds before we started
singing the chorus that I realised. The crowd
reacted first. They started turning to each other
nervously. Some looked confused, some offended,
some hadn't cottoned on. How the hell did someone
not flag it before performing that song live on TV
in front of millions of people? Everyone from the
TV people, to our label had heard the song. Why
didn't someone say something!?

I've watched it back and we all look mortified. Of
course, Burt didn't let it show. He was singing
his lungs out, playing to the crowd, ignoring the
uncomfortable-looking judges. I stared at Yusuf.
He knew exactly what was going on and he was
milking it for all it was worth, grinning from
ear to ear at the irony as he sung the harmony on
the chorus. Thank God he's got an awesome sense
of humour. It all hinged on him. When the second
chorus rolled around I think Yusuf had somehow
convinced the crowd that it had been planned,
and that we were all in on the joke. So he sung
the words even louder. "Get up, stand up." Burt
started grinning too. For the third and last
chorus I watched, horrified as Burt picked Yusuf

out of his chair and held him up. With their arms
round each other's necks. When we finished everyone
went crazy and got to their feet, shouting and
screaming, including the four judges.

It's taken me a few days to get my head around
all that happened that night. If I'm going to be
in a band with Burt Windsor, AKA Jack Skill, then
I'm either going to lose my mind or accept the
manipulation, deception and circus that seems to
follow him around everywhere he goes.

A few said it was in bad taste but mainly
everyone loved it. The newspapers said that it
was TV gold. We made the nine o'clock news.
Twitter and Facebook lit up. #getupstandup,
#yusufwalks and #thevoxmiracle all trended
worldwide.

Truth is, even without the blunder we were
brilliant. I mean musically, we were bang on. It was
well zing to have that experience under my belt.

Damn, I swore I wouldn't use zing!

Burt – 23rd June
Yusuf is a proper legend! After we did *The Vox*
we hung out. We had a bottle of wine and then he
let me have a go on his wheelchair. I got on the
back and we went zooming about the studios. The
funniest bit was when I leant over, took hold
of the joystick and zoomed us towards a set of
stairs. Yusuf just shouted, "Go for it!", so I
bloody did. We ended up in a heap at the bottom,
laughing our heads off.

Once I'd got Yusuf back in the chair we found
this little back alley. He took out a ready
rolled spliff and we blazed it up. I asked him
all about his childhood and he didn't moan, he
just told me it plain and simple. It sounded
proper hardcore, but he said he's happy even
though he can't use his legs no more and doesn't
know if his parents are alive or dead. I decided
to apologise for calling him a cock-muncher. He
told me that he appreciated the apology and that
I should try and be a bit more respectful in
future. No one ever tells me stuff like that and
it kinda made me respect him even more. He said
just stuff like me getting on the back of his
chair and having a laugh felt like a normal thing
for a young person to do, but people are always
so serious around him. He told me he hates pity.
He had escaped with his life and he was going to
enjoy it. That got me to thinking that I should
appreciate my life more. I am well lucky.

I think Yusuf fancies Clipper. He asked me a few
questions about him. When it was time to go, just
as I was about to get in the cab I whispered to
Yusuf, "You can't have him. He's mine," and gave
Clipper a big smacker on the lips. Last thing I
saw as I was leaving Pinewood was Yusuf cracking
up. Clipper looked like I'd slapped him in the
face with my pork salami.

Clipper – 23rd June
Oh yeah baby! Absolutely magic! We slammed *The
Vox* yesterday. We played "Golden" with Yusuf.
It was quite a fitting song really coz the lyrics
are all about being yourself. Which is a bit
ironical, because it turns out Burt is a racist,
homophobic, disablist pig.

Yusuf can really sing. And he's such a good laugh. He had us all in stitches before the show. He's proper handsome too. Just before we left the studio, he said:

"In case you're wondering. It's all in working order."

I nearly died of embarrassment. How the hell did he know? He must have a great gay-dar or something. I wouldn't have guessed he was gay. He is pretty masculine, apart from his perfect eyebrows.

Just before we left the studios Burt kissed me on the lips. He put his hands on my cheeks as well. It wasn't really how I'd imagined it to be.

Tea − 23rd June
My uncle Frank rang to say he and Mum watched me on *The Vox*. He sounded different, like he was impressed he'd seen me on TV.

Harry and Jerome reckon this is just the beginning. Famous people say that it don't change them, but I'm not havin' any of that bull. I already don't go on buses no more because I don't want to be recognised.

When I was moving from my mum's into my flat the other day I had to pack up all my old clothes. I realised I've totally changed my image. All my branded trainers, sweats and hoodies I wouldn't be seen dead in now. All my long stylie Abandon Ship T's I am probably never gonna wear again. Mental.

I used to hate rich people, now I'm going to be one of them.

I need to stay connected. I reckon my mum and Frank will make well sure I do.

★

"I want a proper big mountain of chocolate buttons," Clipper blurted, before anyone else could say a word.

The band were in their rehearsal studio, making a list of what they wanted on their rider for the upcoming tour.

"Clip, you're supposed to choose booze, not chocolate bloody buttons," Burt scowled.

"Well that's what I want. Harry said we can choose whatever we want and that's what I want."

"Jelly Babies. But only Bighearts," Tea said.

"What are you going on about?" Burt said, rubbing his eyes.

"Bighearts are the purple ones," Tea explained. "They've all got names."

Burt stared at the bass player for a long moment.

"Why do you even know the different Jelly Baby names? Why aren't you lot demanding shitloads of whisky?"

"I'd like some fruit. I think Vitamin C would be good," Egg said. Burt turned and faked the motion of smashing his head against the wall.

"At least try and *pretend* to be in a rock 'n' roll band?" he implored.

Clipper stared down at the list.

"Twenty-four Coronas, a bottle of Grey Goose, Talisker single malt, big bowl of ice…"

"That's more like it," Burt said.

"… and a bowl of fruit, giant bag of purple Jelly Babies and shitloads of chocolate buttons," Clipper finished, as Burt grimaced.

Burt – 25th June
I'm a dad! I'm a dad! I'm a dad! I thought I wouldn't give a toss but I do. I have a son. Baby Burt, Double B. I'm over the moon, I shit you not! Crazel, I mean Hazel (I need to show the mother of my child more respect), was in labour for twelve hours. Millie said I should go over the hospital and support her.

I was proper freaked out when I went into the birthing room. There was Hazel, grunting in a big, blue paddling pool. It was all smoky and hot. She had this air canister that she was sucking the life out of. #WTF? I found out it was gas and air. I think Hazel must have gone through ten canisters. I had a massive toke on it when no one was looking and it was a decent hit. When I went in, she grabbed hold of my arm and squeezed so tight my hand started going blue. She yelled a lot about me being selfish, but then the next minute she said I was amazing. I think she was off her head.

What I realise now is just how boring giving birth is. It takes sooo long. I actually fell asleep on the chair for about four hours, which was a miracle the amount of noise she was making.

Luckily I woke up just in time to see Baby Burt popping out. His puny little purple body looked so weird, kind of like an alien, but as soon as I clapped eyes on him I loved him.

We go on tour in ten days. I think I might miss the midget.

⭐

"Jimmy, it's Wilson."

Cloom smiled when he heard the groan on the other end of the line.

"Jesus, Wilson, I haven't heard from you in ten years," Jim Lake replied. "No one calls me Jimmy anymore."

"What do they call you?"

"Just plain Jim."

There was a pause on the other end of the line.

"You know, Wilson, I reminisce about our buccaneering days from time to time. You used to go up to girls and say: 'Hi, I'm Wilson and I'm going to be the biggest music mogul in the world.'"

"Did I?" Cloom replied. "I don't remember. Although I was right."

Jim snorted with laughter. "You certainly were."

"Looks like we both did OK," Cloom said. "I heard they made you Editor in Chief. Congrats."

"Why thank you. Anyway, what can I do for you?" Jim asked.

Wilson cut directly to the chase:

"You know all that rubbish you've been writing about Jack Skill and his band The RockAteers?"

"Still a charmer I see," Jim grunted.

"I want you to stop heaping praise on them," Wilson said flatly. "Aside from it being wholly irresponsible to glorify teenage suicide and pregnancy, I know for a fact they are complete and utter fakes."

Wilson could almost hear the newspaper man's interest sparking. "Tell me more."

"Have you read the *Sound City* single review? Read the subtext. It questions the band's authenticity. Could it be suggesting that someone else wrote the songs?"

"Do you know for a fact that someone else wrote the songs, Wilson?" Jim asked.

"Of course I don't. It's your job to unravel that jumper. I'm just pointing out the loose thread. Bye for now, Jim."

Wilson put the phone down and leant back on his chair.

Egg – 2nd July

```
I went round to Mum and Dad's yesterday evening
and it was really nice. When I lived there it was
so difficult between Mum and me, but now it's more
chilled. I spent the entire time moaning about
Burt. Dad was his usual placid self and Mum told
me it was my penance for giving up on becoming
a proper musician. So, actually, not everything
changes. I kind of miss them, even though Mum's
still on my case.
```

We've done a few warm-up shows in London in preparation for the tour. Burt has this knack of getting the audience to do exactly what he says. "Put your hands up and clap with me." And, "Let's jump," etc., etc. I have to hand it to him, he does create an electrifying atmosphere and the crowds love it. Everyone jumps about on the spot like mental fleas. It baffles me how much influence one man can have over a crowd. The more powerful Burt becomes, the worse he's going to get.

We got a few good live reviews from the warm-ups. Of course it's all gone to Burt's head. He keeps coming into rehearsals with the magazines and squashing them into our faces and saying, "Eat that, *Sound City*!"

I can't believe we go on tour with The Desert Kings tomorrow.

Tea – 3rd July
We're meeting outside Burt's gaff at 9 pm today. I don't see why it has to be his house, but I can't be arsed to argue. We will load our gear on to the bus and then go all the way up to Glasgow and sleep on the way.

I had no clue what to pack for this tour so I went with a tonne of boxers and socks, new T's and jeans, leather jacket, gigging shoes, Adidas trainers, MacBook and one ounce of proper wicked hydroponic ganga weed.

Clipper – 4th July
WE'RE HERE!!!! It's HAPPENING!!!!

We tweeted that we were on the bus with a pic of

us in the lounge and the tweet went buck mental. We got 2,897 RTs and 2,787 Faves. Thing is, I wanted to tweet about everything. It's all so well proper zing!

Like, how the bus travels all night while you sleep in your little bunks and there are two lounges, one at the front and one at the back. There are massive flat-screen TVs that you can play FIFA on all night and you can have a beer from the fridge, whenever you want.

I don't think anyone is going to mess with Ged, our Tour Manager. He's like a shiny-headed machine with a big grey beard. He just gives you commands, and I get the idea he thinks we are all little dickheads. He is kinda awesome.

Ged went to bed very early but we all stayed up and got well drunk. Even Egg got a bit pissed. It was like the old days, when we first started, with all of us ready to take on the world. Even Burt was being cool and having a laugh.

When we eventually went to bed the bus had already arrived at the arena in Glasgow. Then I slept like a baby in the bunk. There is this little curtain you draw across and it's all cosy.

Ged woke us all up at 11 am and took us into the venue. That's the first time I shat myself. It was mahusive. Ged took us to catering where we got some breakfast. The Desert Kings are so massive they have their own catering on the tour, so we can eat decent food three times a day. I think I might get fat. After some well nice grub we went to do a few interviews in our dressing room.

Our rider was exactly how we'd written it. Even though I had just eaten brekkie, I got stuck into the chocolate buttons.

After that we all went on our computers and answered loads of tweets and Facebook messages. This was our new digital girl, Tyra's, idea. It's important to interact with the fans.

Then before we knew it, it was time to sound-check. Our sound man, Richie, is cool. He's younger than I thought he would be. He told us not to worry about the sound when there was no one in the venue. He said once there were bodies inside it would be just right.

I'm absolutely terrified and excited about the gig tonight.

★

SONG 4 CALIFORNIA GUNS

Cab Jones entered the dressing room without knocking and introduced himself. The leather waistcoat the Desert Kings singer wore revealed sleek, tanned arms. His square jaw was covered in salty blond stubble. He was shorter than expected but he had an unmistakable air about him and the kind of looks that sent his female fans wild. Egg, Tea and Clipper greeted the famous rocker warmly. Burt glanced over his newspaper and nodded lazily.

"Holy shit, man, that song, 'Satellites', that's one hell of a song, dude," Cab told Egg. "I caught some of your set last night in Glasgow. Jeeze, it's a huge song. And that tune 'Love and War' is awesome too. Hey and 'Golden'. You have some great songs, guys."

Clipper responded eagerly.

"Wow, really? We love all your stuff. We're all so chuffed to be on tour with such an incredible bunch of guys. I just wanted to say a massive thanks," he gushed.

"The pleasure is all mine, dude. You're the drummer, right? I can tell by the guns," Cab said, pointing at Clipper's well-muscled arms.

Clipper blushed. "Wow, not as toned as yours, mate."

Burt groaned from behind his newspaper.

Cab nodded awkwardly. "You guys lookin' forward to the gig tonight?"

"Yeah, man. Looks like a full house again," Tea said.

"A lot of them are here to see you guys and I ain't surprised. Jerome played me your stuff over a year ago now and I was really impressed. Been a fan ever since. Now I've seen you live, I'm an über fan."

"You got any advice for us, Cab?" Clipper blurted.

"Not really, man, just enjoy the ride, stay clean and keep away from the pen pushers."

"Cool, that's great advice." Clipper paused and looked confused for a moment. "Who are the pen pushers?"

"The newspaper men. The guys that shove their cameras up your ass every day," Cab replied, glancing at Burt, who was still buried deep in the pages of *The Sun*. "OK guys, anyway, nice to nearly meet you all. Have a great show."

Cab lifted an arm in farewell. As soon as he was gone, Clipper turned on Burt.

"What the hell was that?"

Burt looked up slowly.

"What the hell was what?"

"Why didn't you talk to Cab? You were proper rude!"

"Because I'm preparing."

"Preparing what, exactly?!"

"I'm preparing myself to rock the shit out of ten thousand people. I don't give a monkey's who interrupts us."

"That's the stupidest thing I've ever heard," Clipper replied.

"It's not stupid. I need an hour to centre myself, run through lyrics, things I might say on stage. If I mess up, we all look like dickheads. I am the focal point, you know!"

Clipper turned to Egg for help, but the guitarist was looking thoughtful.

"I agree with him," Egg said. "I think we should tell Ged not to let anyone near us for an hour before we go on stage."

"It's not a bad shout. I like warming my fingers up," Tea agreed.

Clipper glanced from one to the other as if they were all mad. "Well I don't need a bloody hour, and anyway, even if I did, I'd make an exception for the man that invited us on this massive tour!" Clipper paused and raised his voice. "In fact, even if he came on stage for a chat while we're playing, I'd be bloody polite to him."

Ged came in. "Five minutes till show time," he said. "Let's have you side of stage, guys."

Tea - 6th July
Clipper puked three times and had five dumps before the gig in Glasgow. I reckon it was a combination of nerves, eating too many chocolate buttons and meeting his pin-up, Cab Jones. We all took the piss out of him after the gig for being such a bum-licker.

First night we walked on stage the noise was deafening. The second night wasn't any different, except I knew what to expect. I have never ever seen that many people all squashed into one place,

with so many faces looking at me. They were
shouting so loud, it was as if they were there
for us, not The Desert Kings. I could see the
lads were as blown away as I was. Except Burt,
who looked as though he was born for it. The first
thing he said, before we had played a note was,
"We are The Desert Kings," and then he sang an a
cappella chorus of their biggest hit "California
Guns". I must admit it was proper funny. He sung
it perfect too. The crowd went mental. Burt just
smiled, then looked over at Clipper. Clip raised
his sticks over his head and clicked them four
times. I felt my guts lurch and – boom! – we
were playing.

Egg – 6th July
Before I left London, Bex told me I should ignore
the media circus and get on with the job of
"rocking people". That made me smile. She told
me I should carry on writing songs because I was
going to need them. The support and faith just
made me love her more. She still hasn't told me
she loves me back though.

Right now we are on the tour bus in the vast car
park at Aberdeen Arena where we played the night
before. The amount of people waiting outside the
gig both nights has been insane. Everyone wants
pictures with us. Jack got the most attention
of course. The way the girls stared at him, and
all of us really, was a bit intense. I couldn't
really deal with all the eye contact. Burt stayed
in the car park for a good hour and a half. He
craves the attention, but I have to admit, he is
a grafter.

I was gobsmacked when we played "Golden" and people
started singing the words back at us – words I'd

written in my bedroom years ago. I knew the crowd
were there to see The Desert Kings, but by the
end of our gig it felt like they were there to
see us. The noise they made was so intense my
ears are still ringing now.

After the Aberdeen gig we watched The Desert
Kings' set and that's when I actually realised
the crowd were there to see them. They blew me
away with their stage craft and professionalism.
It was a whole different level and so was the
noise from the crowd. Incredible.

Burt – 7th July
I am thirty G in the hole with that prick
Lenny and he wants his money back. I can't
ask my parents. My dad would laugh and my mum
hasn't spoken to me since she kidnapped Millie.
Anyway, I wouldn't ask my dad if he was the
last man on earth.

Lenny said if I didn't pay up by next week, he
was gonna come down to the 02, get up on stage
and slap me about like a bitch in front of all my
fans. When I told him he wouldn't get past the
security, he said that they don't call him Lenny
the Butcher for nothing and that I should ask
around about him.

I told him I didn't have any money and he said
I couldn't be in the papers as much as I was
without having any money. I tried to explain that
it didn't work like that, but he hung up.

I asked Jerome and Harry to lend me it, but the
nosey gits asked what it was for.

At least the tour is going wicked though.
Everyone proper loves us. I like being on tour,
but there's loads to do and it's also a bit
boring sometimes. Talk to music interviewers on
the phone in the morning, do a sound check, do
the gig and then get pissed. That's what the
last few days have been like, and I can't see it
changing much over the next month. #groundhogday

Hazel texts me pics of Double B all the time. I
love it.

I've decided I'm gonna ask Tea if his Uncle Frank
knows who Lenny is.

I wrote a song called "Pictures of Me" the other
day and it's much better than anything Egg ever
wrote. It's about this seventeen-year-old girl
who's in love with me, and starts stalking me. I
played it to Clipper on acoustic guitar and he
told me I was a genius. I told him I wrote it so
the first word of each stanza made up the words.
I FOUND YOU OUT. He said he thought it was a
smash hit and asked if it was about Bex and
Crazel all rolled into one. I told him he was an
idiot, but after I thought about it for a while I
reckon he might be right. Here are the words.

Pictures of Me
I, got something to say
I didn't mean to do it and I didn't mean to make your
day
Found, you hold too tight
Behind your double mirrors lies a burn it all
blinding light
You, You're turning off style
A triple whisky chaser and a know-it-all secret smile

Out, I found you out
You're barely bloody legal now your mother is set
to shout
You're sweet seventeen you're the queen of the
scene
Could have a million other lovers but you carry
round pictures of me.

Clipper – 10th July

I've been having proper levels of fun previously
unreached by someone from Charlton. I am now best
mates with The Desert Kings (they love me) and
we have a beer after every gig. They have this
game called corn-holing, where you have to throw
a hacky sack into a hole cut into sloping planks
of wood. I am beating Cab and Nate Jones 89-79-82
respectively.

I saw the live review in the paper from the
Birmingham gig and it said: "This band is as
happy in front of thirteen thousand people as
three hundred, they give you everything they
have and the audience lap it up with a fervour
I have seldom seen." This is the best bit: "The
drummer is a powerhouse." Yes! I am a powerhouse!
Now everyone on the tour calls me Powerhouse. I
absolutely love it.

I walked in on some kind of secret meeting Tea
and Burt were having the other day. I asked them
both separately about it, but neither of them
would tell me anything. Burt looked a bit shaken
up. In fact, he hasn't been himself for a couple
of days.

Tea – 10th July

Just when I'm starting to think that Burt is not that bad, he does something even more stupid than all the other stupid shit he's constantly doing.

He owes Lenny "The Butcher" Brown thirty K. I explained he has that nickname because he chops people's fingers and toes off when they mess with him. Then I asked him if he had asked Lenny to do him any favours?

When I saw the look on Burt's face at that moment, I knew he was finished. Before I could find out, Clipper walked in and Burt legged it.

Uncle Frank always dressed the same: leather suit jacket, black jeans and suede loafers with a brass buckle. The porkpie hat that perched on his relaxed afro was his trademark. Tea thought the look was pure class.

The pair sat in Frank's local – a run-down pub that looked as though it hadn't had a refit in decades. The curtains were shredded and streaked with grime. The wallpaper was grey and peeling. They sat in a secluded corner, the red velvet upholstery pock-marked with a thousand cigarette burns. There was no smoking ban at the The Highwayman.

"You shouldn't have told me is all I'm sayin'," Frank said, with a disappointed shake of his head.

"I'm only tellin' you because my band is in double trouble,

Unc. If it all goes tits up because Burt owes some dickhead money, I don't know what I'll do," Tea pleaded.

"Not a dickhead, boy, a lunatic!" Frank paused and looked thoughtful. "Lenny bent a fella's head in with a breeze block just coz he was the dad of someone who broke his nephew's skateboard. Do you understand? He's utterly nutterly and he has his fingers in some big billy shit – drugs, weapons, whores. Things you don't even wanna know about."

Tea nodded solemnly, suddenly wishing he was back at the 02 in the plush dressing room, with his hands around Burt's neck.

Frank sucked hard on a cigarette. "So, you don't have a clue what Lenny has done for this Burt fella?"

Tea shook his head.

"So, what is it exactly you want me to do about all this?"

"Would you have a word with him, like for Burt? Try and smooth things over?"

Frank gave his nephew a hard stare, slowly stubbed his cigarette out on the underside of the table and spoke very precisely.

"I'd do it in a heartbeat if it was for you, Tea," he said. "But what you're asking me is proper risky. I don't want to go down certain roads unless I absolutely have to, you get me?"

The hope in Tea's face fell away and worry began to take a hold in his gut. He registered the adamant look on his uncle's face and his heart sank.

"I'd never ask unless it was important. If he gets this wrong then my band might not survive. I don't know who else to turn to, Unc."

Frank studied his nephew for a long moment across the worn

pub table. Then he stood, put his hand on his nephew's shoulder and shook his head.

"I'm sorry, boy. I can't do it," he said, before turning and leaving the pub.

✪

"I missed you loads."

Egg kissed her on the lips and sat back with a happy smile.

"Me too, I've missed you like crazy."

He shook his head.

"Every day when I wake up on the tour bus, I have to pinch myself. Same when I come off stage. But I'm pinching myself more than ever now. It's so amazing to be back with you."

Bex smiled back and nodded happily.

It was a perfect hot, sunny day. They sat on High Bench bunched close, Egg with his arm around Bex, her head resting on his shoulder. It had only been ten days since they'd seen one another, but it felt like an eternity. Bex was relieved Egg seemed cheerful. He'd been so worried before he left. She imagined for a moment they were skiving final lesson and it was like it used to be: just her and him. He seemed more self-assured somehow, more grown up. The boy she had watched come out of his shell had a new intensity to him now, a new coolness.

Bex grabbed his arm.

"Hey, did I tell you my dad watched you on *The Vox*? He bloody loved it! He reckons I should enter the show next year. He's heard me singing around the house and says I've got an amazing voice. He's my dad so he would say that, wouldn't he? I've never really thought about it."

"Wow, did he!? He loved us? That's great." Egg paused and looked at her. "Am I ever going to meet him?"

Bex felt her smile begin to fade. Egg and her dad were like chalk and cheese. She didn't want them to meet. She would feel awkward, worried they wouldn't get on.

"One day, maybe, when we get serious."

Egg sat back and stared at her. "What do you mean, 'serious'? We are serious, aren't we? I love you."

Bex felt caught out.

"You're in the hottest new band in the world, Egg!"

"What is that supposed to mean?"

"It means that we're going to be spending loads of time miles apart and we need to manage our expectations." She smiled again. "Anyway, look, let's not talk about this now. Let's enjoy seeing each other." Bex nudged him playfully, but her heart was sinking and she didn't know why. Something had happened in that moment, and it scared her.

Egg stood up and turned to face her.

"No, I want to talk about it now." He scowled. "Are you saying you want an open relationship?"

"Of course not, stop stressing. It's OK. I'm just sayin' we need to be realistic."

Egg sat back down on the end of the bench, as far from Bex as he could. He turned and looked at her like a small, spoilt child.

"Why haven't you ever told me you love me?" he asked flatly, staring at his shoes.

"Jesus, Egg, I don't know!" She sighed, the question rattling around inside her head. "I don't know what all these feelings are. I just know I want to be with you. Isn't that enough?"

She put her hand out and smiled sadly. Egg looked up. He waited a moment, then nodded and moved back up the bench towards her.

He held her hand tightly and they stayed on High Bench in silence until the sun disappeared behind the London skyline.

Burt – 23rd July
The looming disaster of Lenny the Butcher coming on to the 02 stage and bitch-slapping me to death is really bumming me out. Tea told me his uncle can't help me. So, I'll just have to come up with the dough myself. I will just have to sell my story to *The Daily Blog* or something.

The 02 gigs start tomorrow and I had the day off, so I invited Crazel and Baby Burt round my gaff. Wow, what a little spud Double B is! He's so teeny weeny but he knows exactly what's occurring. He's like his old man. Crazel said he sleeps OK. He didn't cry when I held him. Just to have his little squirmy body against my chest was the best feeling I ever had. Crazel reckons I'm a natural dad. It was kind of pretty cool to see her as well. She's a great mum.

So, it's OUR hometown gig tomorrow night. I told Ged I wanted him to go get a bunch of fit birds from the audience and bring them back to our dressing room after the show. The Tour Manager

for The Desert Kings does the same for them every
night. Ged told me that when I headline *my* own
tour he will elect someone to do that job. I
didn't kick off. I just rang Harry and told him
that someone better get that shit done or I'm not
doing the show. Why should The Denim Kings get
all the perks in our manor, stealing our women?

#imworkingmyballssoffhere

Egg - 24th July
I really just can't figure Bex out. At all. I've
decided to stop trying for a bit. She really
sounded like she missed me, but then she turned
it all to nothing.

At the aftershow parties girls come up to me and
start conversations. It's difficult to get used
to, given I've been ignored for the majority of
my life. The fact that I lap it up with a spoon
makes me feel somehow cheap. Jerome and Harry
keep telling us to keep our feet on the ground
but it's hard. For the past week all I do is
get up, have breakfast, play computer, watch TV,
have lunch, read my book, do sound check, have
dinner, do the gig and go to the aftershow. For
the hour we are on stage and afterwards I'm being
saturated in adoration. In realistic terms, how
can that not rub off on a person?

I go back to my bunk, pull the little bunk
curtain across and try to sleep over the rumbling
of the road. Sometimes I wonder if it's not the
noise of the road that keeps me awake, but the
ticking of my mind.

I've decided not to introduce Bex to Cab Jones. He and I have become mates, of sorts. He isn't at all what I expected. Burt says he's like a good-looking geography teacher who won the lottery. I disagree. He's thoughtful, witty and sensitive, but after watching how girls act around him I'm a bit dubious about introducing him to Bex. It is universally believed that she is the most attractive woman on earth and with Cab being her male equivalent, introducing them might cause a tornado of pure jealousy. Or worse, they could run off together. Added to this, I remember very well that before we got together she said she fancied him.

I have four more weeks on the road and I really would like Bex with me some of the time. I've decided to bring the "girlfriends on tour" issue up in the meeting with the label and management after the 02 shows.

I'm worried she wouldn't come, even if I asked her.

Egg scanned the spacious VIP backstage area. He'd already called Bex's mobile five times and it had gone straight to answer machine. He asked people if they'd seen her. All of them said they hadn't. Egg suddenly started to question whether she had been at the gig at all. He marched over to Jerome, who was at the bar discussing something with a smartly dressed man who looked like he was in his early fifties.

"Did Bex come to the show? Have you seen her?" Egg blurted, interrupting the older man in mid-flow.

Jerome turned with a frown. "Egg, this is Hans Molander. He's the promoter that put this tour together."

"Hi," Egg said shortly, glancing at Hans before turning back to Jerome. "Have you seen her?"

"I thought you were wonderful tonight," Hans said, in a heavy Swedish accent, extending a hand in greeting.

Egg, forced to converse, turned to him, nodded and shook his hand. "Thanks."

"I haven't seen her since before the gig," Jerome told him. "She did see the show. I sat two rows back from her."

"OK, cheers," Egg said, moving off.

"Hey, hold on a minute," Jerome said, lightly taking the guitarist's arm. "Hans and I were just talking. We think a head-line theatre tour is next on the agenda. A short 'A' city run in October – Manchester, Leeds, Glasgow, Birmingham, etc. Isn't that great?" he said, beaming.

"Shepherd's Bush Empire, that sort of size show," Hans added. "To be honest you could probably go bigger, but I think let's grow you in an organic way."

"You make us sound like a vegetable," Egg replied with a frown. "Sorry, I have to go," he said, as politely as he could manage.

Jerome and Hans watched him leave. "Love is too young to know what conscience is," Hans shrugged.

"Russell Brand?" Jerome asked.

"Shakespeare!" Hans winked. "You should know this. You are British."

The music professionals watched as Egg tore around the room, stopping to ask people where his girlfriend was, checking his phone every few seconds.

"I heard rumours Wilson Cloom was gunning for you again," Hans said gravely, turning back to his friend.

Jerome studied Hans carefully. "Really? Does he not know when he's been beaten?"

"I have known the man thirty years and I say honestly that he does not know when he is beaten and it is this fact that makes him so dangerous, and also so successful," Hans said.

"So what is he scheming now?"

"I only heard that he was asking about the songs and who exactly wrote them."

Jerome nodded thoughtfully and looked back out across the busy room, just in time to spot Egg marching out, his phone pressed hard to his ear.

"But I don't understand. You said you were coming to the after-show?" Egg said, as he made his way through the winding corridors of the 02 and back towards his dressing room.

"I just don't feel sociable tonight," Bex replied. "I think I might be coming down with something. Look, I will see you tomorrow. Don't fret. You guys were awesome!"

"OK, well how about I head home now? You could meet me there."

"I'm already in bed, sweetheart."

Egg tried to keep the desperation out of his voice, but failed.

"OK, but I will see you tomorrow, right?"

"Course you will! Goodnight, darlin'."

Before Egg could reply, the phone went dead. Head down, he walked into The RockAteers' spacious dressing room. What had he done wrong? Why hadn't she wanted to see him after the gig? Was she jealous of the attention? Worried he wouldn't be around anymore? Or was she just bored of him?

"Hi, Egg, sorry, Jerome said it'd be cool to come in here for the Wi-Fi, so I can answer all the fan tweets after the show."

The pretty redhead sat on the black leather two-seat sofa, a MacBook on her lap.

Egg frowned. He had thought he would be alone.

"Cool," he managed. "Want a drink?"

"Yes, please. You got any vodka?" she replied, in a sturdy city-of-Dublin accent.

"We do. Grey Goose any good for you? Mixer?"

"Cranberry or orange or both if you have it."

Egg mixed the drinks and brought them over to the sofa.

"Mind if I sit down?" he gestured to the other half of the sofa. "I'd like to see what people are saying about the gig. I need cheering up."

Egg sat down next to her, noticing for the first time her slim, long and lightly tanned legs.

"I'm Tyra, by the way," she said brightly. "I'm the head of your in-house digital team." She turned awkwardly, holding out her hand in the confined sofa space.

Egg shook it.

"I'm Egg, I massage the strings in the band."

Tyra smirked. "Jaysas, that's a corny thing to say."

Egg frowned, taken aback. A smile started to creep into his lips. "I could have you fired for impudence!"

Tyra smirked.

"It's my impudence that makes me the big bucks."

"How so?" Egg said, leaning in and staring at the screen in front of her.

"You really want to know?" Tyra turned towards him, narrowing her eyes.

Egg nodded.

"OK, see this Twitter feed? These are people commenting on the awesome show you just played right?"

"Hang on, did you really think it was awesome?" Egg interrupted.

Tyra nodded casually and continued to tap away.

"Yep."

"OK, cool, so what are they saying?" Egg asked.

"They're saying you massaged that guitar to sleep," she winked.

"Ha ha. I asked for that."

"You did. Nothing attractive about an ego fisherman," she said, returning his gaze.

"Is that some sort of an Irish idiom?"

"No, that's one of me own." She laughed. "Right, so they're saying all the usual – that you're great, asking when the album is out and can they meet you all in person. They're also talking about which member they love the most. That's where I come in. If I reply to one person and ask what they like about 'Egg' it engages hundreds more. They jump on the question and it spreads. The key is remembering people are behind these screens, they're not just a thumbnail inside a box. They want to be tested, amused and engaged. And that's where cheekiness comes in handy. If a person wonders if Jack Skill is a good kisser I might reply, 'I heard he tastes of strawberries. What do you think he tastes of?'"

"Get them hot under the collar, you mean. For the record, Jack tastes of whisky and cigarettes."

"Really, you have personal experience?"

Egg smiled, drained his triple vodka and moved off the sofa. He was finding the gentle and slightly flirtatious chat calming. He hadn't thought of Bex for over five minutes now. "Another?"

"OK, but not quite so much vodka this time, please."

Tyra placed her laptop on the table in front of her and watched Egg as he fixed the drinks.

"So, why do you need cheering up?" she asked.

"Oh, nothing really, it's just my girlfriend is going cold on me."

"Wow, that's unusual."

"How so?" Egg drained a large shot of vodka, before refilling it.

"Well, usually girls get hotter for guys in bands, not colder. Especially ones that are getting as big as you guys are."

"Is that what's happening?"

"Oh, yes. I don't want to geek you out, but the social interaction you're getting is growing by around five hundred thousand a day."

"Wow, I don't think I can handle the pressure."

Egg plonked himself back down on the sofa and handed her the drink. He felt the alcohol beginning to take effect and the stress start to dissipate. He turned and smiled.

"And don't worry about geeking me out, there is no one on this planet that can out-geek me."

"Oh really? You think…" she replied, her eyes twinkling behind the black frames.

Egg stared back at her. Her eyes really were quite stunning, her make-up classic, full red lips and a flick of black eyeliner adorning long brown lashes. She looked really, really sexy.

All of a sudden Egg lunged across the space between them with an awkward determination, his lips puckered and eyes closed. Tyra took the kiss full on the chin, before pulling away.

"Whoa there, tiger! What are ya playin' at?" she said, pushing him away. She pulled herself up on to a sofa arm, putting a good distance between them.

Egg sat staring at her as he began to colour.

Before he could think of how to reply there was a loud crack as the door was flung back on its hinges against the breeze-block wall. Tea barged into the dressing room, clutching a bottle of rum and accompanied by a pretty black girl with bright pink hair. The bassist stopped dead in his tracks and studied the awkward scene before him. Egg and Tyra stared back at him in alarm.

"What be goin' on here then? A ginger convention?" Tea said, narrowing his eyes suspiciously.

Egg scrambled up from the sofa and fled the room.

SONG 5 SHARK TANK

It was a rain-soaked August morning when Sophia Clark made the long journey by Tube and train from her pretty north London suburb to south-east London.

It took her nearly two hours to reach the Frog and Radiator pub. She dropped her phone back into her Fendi handbag and pushed her way through the heavy doors. The inside of the pub was bleak. Stained walls adorned with pictures of animals playing cards and cheap mismatched furniture combined to give it a depressed and unsavoury look. She had never set foot in such a dump in her entire life.

George Graves sat in the furthest corner of the bar. It was with surprise she noted how attractive the boy was. She approached steadily, her Manolo Blahnik heels clip-clopping across the hard wooden floor. Only when she was standing over the table did he look up. She considered buying a drink, but one look at the tattooed barman was enough to make her abstain.

"You said on the phone that this was to do with The RockAteers?" George said.

"That's right, I wanted to ask a few questions, get your take on your friends' success."

George's eyes narrowed.

"They ain't no friends of mine," he began. "More like back-stabbing wankers with god complexes."

Sophia listened quietly as George ranted for over ten minutes, occasionally nodding to make sure he knew she understood, or empathised with what he was saying. She established very quickly that the level of betrayal, humiliation and vengefulness George felt far exceeded her and Wilson Cloom's estimates.

"… it's got to the point where I don't turn on the TV or radio because I think I might see or hear them on it. Everywhere I go I see The RockAteers. What's so special about them anyway? They're not even any good." He jabbed a finger at his own chest bitterly. "I know I have greatness in me, I'm just not sure what it is yet."

Sophia reached out and placed an understanding hand on his.

"How would you like to earn one hundred thousand pounds and wreak revenge on those bastard RockAteers?"

George's eyes widened. He picked up his glass and tipped back the remainder of his drink. "How?"

Sophia reached into her handbag, pulled out two identical notebooks and slid them across the table.

George picked one up and studied the faded tan cover.

"'Secrets of the Fearless by George Graves'? Why has it got my name on the front?"

"It's the exact same one Egg uses to write his songs in. He let it slip in an interview with *Q* magazine."

"Why are there two?"

"One is for you to copy word for word." Sophia picked up the book George wasn't holding. "See, look this one doesn't have your name on the front. It's empty. Take a look inside yours."

George flicked the pages. "Lyrics! Why all the doodles and scrubbed-out words? I don't get it?"

"We need the lyric book to be authentic. The doodles are there to add to the authenticity. Songs evolve; we need to see that in the book, there needs to be words crossed out, doodles and such. You need to add the dates at the top of each song. It needs to be written in different pens. The detail is what will make this stick."

Sophia pulled out a pencil case and unzipped it.

"On each page I have marked what pen you use, see," she said, pointing to the top right-hand corner of a random page. "In this pencil case I have labelled the pens that correspond."

"Jesus, it's proper James Bond stuff. But I still don't get it. How can this work?"

"A backdated lyric book, with every word from The RockAteers' album documented in your handwriting will start a rumour. If that rumour is substantiated by a real-life ex-school friend and all that is allowed to ferment on the web and that juicy gossip matures then newspapers will pick up on it. Once it hits the press it will stick like glue. It will be the start of them being discredited."

Sophia sat back.

"So what do you think?"

George's deep-set eyes narrowed as he thought for a short moment.

"I'm in," he said. "I'll get the drinks." George nodded towards the bar. "Let's celebrate!"

"Make mine a vodka, lime and soda. I'm guessing they don't do much in the way of wine."

The pair didn't talk about The RockAteers again that day. Sophia had executed Wilson Cloom's task to perfection. It had almost been too easy, and now she would allow herself to get drunk with this surprisingly hot young man.

At exactly five o'clock, feeling very merry, they made their way out of the pub into bright evening sunshine.

"Why hang out in this dump, George?" Sophia swung around a lamppost. George caught her and pulled her close. She giggled.

"Mum and Dad's is only five minutes down the road, they're at bingo tonight, you wanna come round for a coffee?" he said, leaning in, so his face was close to hers.

"Bingo, how delightful!" Sophia pushed him away and hooked her arm in his. "Lead the way, sir, a nightcap would be most welcome."

Tea – 5th August
If someone told me when we started this band that I'd be playing in front of 15,000 people at the 02 in Greenwich, a half-mile from my gaff, then I would have laughed right in their eye socket. Mum came to both shows and said seeing me on stage was the happiest day of her life. Uncle Frank couldn't make it. He sent me a text saying sorry. I was well gutted, but Mum's pure joy made up for it.

I caught Egg getting off with our nerdy-fit digital girl the other day. I told Clipper and he's proper angry. Next day Egg couldn't look me in the face and Clipper didn't say one word

to him. I don't reckon Egg noticed, but he will
soon, because Clip's on the warpath.

We've had a little break and we're in Cardiff
now. Europe leg of the tour is gonna be
interesting.

✪

Burt's arranged Skype chat wasn't going quite as he envisaged.
Four girls crowded the screen, firing questions at him: Alix,
Georgina, Jasmine and Lilly, though Burt had no idea who was
who. It had started off with quite a formal and polite tone, the
girls giggly and shy, but as they grew in confidence, the questions had become more risqué. Burt was wondering how he could
bring proceedings to a close.

"Tea's well sexy," a blonde girl told Burt. She looked a lot
older than the other three and was wearing a tonne of make-up.
"I like his tight black jeans. Yours are tighter though."

"Really. You think?" Burt replied awkwardly.

"Are you very rich now?" asked another girl – with brown
bobbed hair.

"I've always been rich, darlin'."

"What kind of girls does Clipper like?"

Burt grimaced. "Erm, boyish ones."

"What kind of pants do you wear?" another blurted.

"Right! Girls, it's been great, but can I have Millie back
now, please?"

"Have you got a big one?" the older, blonde girl blurted as the others shrieked with laughter.

Burt shook his head, but chuckled as he heard Millie ushering them out. The laughter continued until the door banged shut.

"Jeez, Mills. Where did you get that lot from? I'll get arrested!"

"Yeah, sorry, but it *was* kinda funny?"

"How old was the blonde one?"

"Er, fifteen. She paid me to be in the room when you called."

Burt gasped. "That is not good, Millie. I can't condone shit like that!"

"What?! I can get a Minecraft foam pixel sword from Amazon now."

"I'll get you ten Mineshaft pixel swords. You'll get expelled. That's the kind of thing I would do!"

Millie laughed loudly. "The others are all eleven and are my friends."

"They're bloody cheeky for eleven-year-olds."

"Mum would be thrilled with my choice of mates, wouldn't she?"

"Not sure thrilled is the word! So what's not to love about Hogwarts then?"

"PE. They make us run around in the freezing cold."

Millie paused, leaned towards the screen, and peered at her brother.

"Burt, are you looking at your own thumbnail!?"

"No! I'm looking at you."

"What did I say then?"

"You said you hate PE. Maybe I could get you out of it.

What's your headmaster like?"

"He's a she and she would kick your arse."

Burt laughed and shook his head so his long hair fell over his eyes. "Hey, you think I should cut my fringe?"

"No, I think your hair looks great," Millie replied, rolling her eyes.

"Cool, I thought it was looking good but I just thought maybe a trim might be cool." He paused and gave his sister a huge smile. "So everything's cool?"

"Yeah, it's all cool. Got a couple of weird calls on my mobile though. I always answer, because I think it's you. Both times it's silent, but in the background I can hear The RockAteers song 'Shop Till You Drop'."

Burt sat up and stared at his sister, his eyes widening.

"Really?"

He regained his composure and smiled awkwardly.

"I'm sure it's nothing. Don't worry about it, OK?"

"Don't call them days off if you still have us working," Burt spat. "If I'm in bed smoking ganja all day, or getting pissed in Soho, then it's a day off. If I spend the day talking to nobheads, then it's a work day." He paused to wave a hand at the room. "I include this meeting as work."

"And do you include us as nobheads?" Harry asked, with a long sigh.

The RockAteers were at the label headquarters. Ged, Tyra and Harry were also present. Jerome sat at one end of the long conference table regarding the young faces. Clipper was smiley and eager, Tea low-key and relaxed. Egg was looking intense. As usual, Burt had positioned himself at the head of the table. Jerome wondered why on earth he had brought a guitar with him. Last time he checked, Burt couldn't really play one. There was a belligerent air about Burt today, even more so than usual. Jerome took a deep breath.

"Right, guys!" he began brightly. "I wanted to have this meeting before you guys set off on the European leg of the tour. So that we can air any problems and reflect on how it's all been going." He beamed. "Well done, guys, the UK leg of the tour has been a triumph, it's a dream start. Tyra ran our social numbers and our engagement is up eighty per cent since it kicked off. The album pre-release is selling by the bucketload." He stopped to scan the room. "So, anybody want to kick us off?"

"I will," Burt jumped in. "We reckon Ged should go get a load of girls to come see us after the shows."

Ged glanced at Burt, his expression unchanged.

Jerome frowned. "I'm sure we can sort something out."

Burt looked surprised, then grinned at Ged. The Tour Manager raised an eyebrow.

"Let's move on! The pre-order sales of the debut album are standing at two hundred thousand. It's immense. You guys are on fire. But of course, we strive for more."

"No offence, Jerome, but you insisted we come here to talk about things? We get enough praise from the fans," Egg said, looking down at the table.

Jerome looked blankly at the guitarist for a moment before shooting Harry a look.

"OK, Egg. So sorry to be a bore."

"I need some money. That's something else I would like to air!" Burt said. "I've been living on nothing and it's not good enough. If we are doing as well as you say, why haven't I got any money? Two hundred thousand times £12.99 is a lot of dough..."

Everyone watched as Burt fished out his phone and started to tap away.

"Oh my God!" he screamed, as he stared at the screen. "Two and a half million!"

Burt passed Clipper his phone. "Is that right?"

Clipper studied it, looked confused, shrugged and passed the phone to Tea.

"Yes, it's two and a half mill," Tea confirmed, unable to suppress a smile.

"What happened to the fifty thousand you got from the label advance?" Jerome asked.

"Spent it," Burt said, taking back his phone. "So, when we getting some of that money then?"

"Harry will deal with you on that score but I will remind you that we have giant PR bills and tour expenses – basically lots to pay back. You won't see any of that money for a good while, besides, it has to be paid to us first."

Burt looked disgusted.

"I've written a song and it's a hit and I want to play it right now because I reckon some people in my own band are trying to stifle my genius."

Clipper glanced at Tea. The bassist mouthed the word "dick".

"Can't it wait until the end of the meeting, Jack?" Harry asked, looking at Jerome.

"No, it can't."

Burt put the guitar on his lap and struck up a rough, fast-paced rhythm. For three minutes he sang at the top of his lungs. His voice was honed from gigging: husky and perfectly pitched. His tone seemed different, frustrated and angry. He finished and the room was silent. After a few moments Clipper began to clap, looking around the room, trying to encourage others to join in. Reluctantly Jerome and Harry obliged.

"What's it called?" Jerome asked.

"It's called 'Pictures of Me' and it's a hit," Burt replied, with a pout.

"It's good. I'd like to hear what the band do with it," Harry said, awkwardly.

"It's for my solo record," Burt replied.

"Come on, Jack, you've only been in the band five minutes," Jerome said nervously. "Are you leaving already?"

"How am I gonna earn a living? I need a poxy thirty grand and I can't raise it. I work my nut sack off every night. Singing his songs." Burt jabbed a finger at Egg. "There's massive talent right here in this chair, know what I'm sayin'?"

Tea pulled a face. "No. There's a massive dick right there in that chair."

Egg clapped a hand over his mouth to stop the laughter escaping.

"Look, guys, I know it's a stressful time for you all, but..." Jerome started.

"It's not stressful!" Clipper shouted. "It's a dream come true.

I don't understand you, Burt. Why are you being like this?" he implored, his eyes welling up. "I've still got loads of my advance left, what happened to yours? And why are you talking about a solo project? We've only just started doing well! None of it makes any sense."

"Bollocks, Clipper, you got no idea," Burt said, without looking at him. "And how many times do I have to tell you? Don't call me Burt! I'M JACK PISSING SKILL," he screamed.

"I WANT THE GIRLFRIEND BAN LIFTED!" Egg exploded.

Burt gave Egg a withering look, stood up and took a step towards the door.

"What are you doing now?" Clipper asked. "Why are you mucking all this up!? It don't make any sense."

Just as Burt was about to reach for the handle, he turned and stuck his middle finger up before slamming the door behind him.

"That went well. What do you think, Jerome?" Harry said, with a shake of his head.

"A triumph," Jerome replied, with a weary smile.

"I'm glad you find all this bloody amusing," Clipper said, horrified.

Tea put his hand up.

"I need to tell you all something," the bassist said. "Burt's mental but I know the reason why he's acting even more mental than usual."

"Go on," Jerome encouraged.

"He owes thirty grand to a proper nasty geezer."

Everyone stared at Tea.

"Who?" Harry asked.

"Doesn't matter, all you need to know is he's nasty. Proper nasty. I went to see my Uncle Frank, who is the hardest bloke I know, and even he wouldn't go anywhere near him," Tea said grimly. "Burt is in serious trouble."

"I see," Harry said.

"We'll just have to pay him off then!" Jerome nodded. "I will sort out the money in the morning."

Tea shook his head.

"Burt did something else. Something that means he's in Lenny's debt somehow."

"What debt for God's sake, Tea? Why you being so mysterious?" Clipper shouted. "What did he do?"

"He won't tell me," Tea said finally. "But it's obviously proper bad."

"OK, so he's in deep, surely the first thing to do is to pay this guy his money?" Jerome suggested.

Tea looked thoughtful for a long moment.

"Give me the money then," he said eventually. "But if he knows I've told you, he will, knowing him, fake his own death and leave on the next plane to Nepal."

Burt – 15th August

Really don't matter how much shit I cram down my neck or how hard I party, I just can't stop thinking about Lenny. I tried to figure out what this feeling I'm carrying around with me is and I gotta say I think it's fear. I'm scared. I can't wait to get to Europe and try and take my

mind off it all. I'm really gonna miss Double B
though. Can't write no more. Feel sick.

Tea − 16th August
I'm gonna go up to High Bench and take a chance
that Burt turns up. I've texted him a million times
but no reply. I watched *The Godfather* the other
day. The word dread was used. It's a good word to
describe what I feel like right now. I dread what
is going to happen to Burt. I just keep thinking
that if Burt is murdered then it's the end of the
band and my career. I feel bad for thinking of
myself, but I can't help it. I couldn't even think
about doing anything for my birthday yesterday.
My mum and I just went out for a meal. It was my
eighteenth, but I can't celebrate with this bloody
nightmare hanging over me. I will make it up to
myself if we come out the other side.

Mum has been really supportive. I told her all
about it and she just said that it would all work
itself out and I should try and chill.

Europe tomorrow. Be good to get out and see the
world. I've never been out of the UK or Ireland.
In fact I'd never been outta London until this
tour. Mad times. Mum had to remind me to go get
a passport. Took me a whole day to sort it. I've
never needed one before.

A wet and windy spell of weather had stolen the summer from
Greenwich Park. Leaves had blown from the trees and the

persistent rain had turned the rolling lawns into slick, treacherous marshland. A place that had been filled with life and colour only days before now seemed withdrawn and grey, heading for an early autumn.

High Bench was especially exposed to the elements. Its elevated position, lack of cover and the driving rain combined to make the seat almost unbearable to occupy. Despite this, Tea waited patiently for Burt, hoping the cause was his habitual lateness, rather than a no-show. Tea ran through what he wanted to say. He'd already been over it a million times.

He spotted the tall, slim figure in the distance, entering through the park gates at the bottom of the hill, hunched against the wind and rain. As Burt trudged up the hill, closer and closer, Tea ran through what he wanted to say one final time.

"What's so urgent?" Burt said, as he arrived at the bench and loomed over Tea.

"Hello back at you, mate," Tea said.

Burt was wearing a T-shirt, tracksuit bottoms and what looked like slippers. He was drenched to the skin. "You need thirty grand right, I thought *that* was urgent?"

Burt sat down on the sodden bench and stared down miserably at his mud-caked shoes.

"It is urgent, but I don't understand?" Burt said. He shook his feet, one at a time, in a lame attempt to dry the suede Gucci slip-ons.

"I've brought you the money," Tea said flatly.

Burt turned and frowned.

"How the hell did you get hold of that kind of money?"

Tea shook his head.

"Not all of us spend our money on the horses, mate! I had it saved from my advance."

Burt's blue eyes widened with a mixture of shock and confusion.

"Whoa, Tea, man. I don't know what to say!"

His tone took Tea by surprise.

"How about 'I couldn't take your hard-earned money'?"

Tea suddenly found himself wrapped in a hug.

"Thanks, thanks a million, bruv! I'm overwhelmed. I thought you hated me."

Burt was looking at Tea in a way he'd never done before. It was as though he'd noticed the person behind the quiet, tough exterior for the first time. Tea was taken aback.

"Don't get too excited. There's conditions," he said, narrowing his eyes.

"What conditions?" Burt asked, pulling a face.

"If I give you this money I need to know what you asked Lenny to do for you. You also have to swear that you will never do anything this stupid ever again."

"Are you joking?"

"No, I'm not joking. I mean it. I'm lending you thirty freaking grand," Tea said. "Look, you and me don't always see eye to eye. If it wasn't for the band we wouldn't even know each other, but you don't realise how much I love The RockAteers. I know I'm the moody one and I don't talk much or get that excited when we go to number one or shit like that. But the thing is I do care, I *really* care. I just don't show it much."

Burt stared back as if his band mate were talking another language.

"You're emotionally stunted, you mean?" he said eventually.

Tea laughed. "Well, that's one way of putting it."

"And a little bit boring?" Burt smiled.

"We can't all be attention-seeking egomaniacs like you, you tit. Look, I'm saying I have your back on this, but you have to tell me what hold Lenny Brown has over you."

"Lenny Brown?" Burt said, suddenly looking worried.

"Yes, Lenny 'The Butcher' Brown, *you know*, the guy that wants you dead!" Tea replied.

"His surname is Brown?" Burt said, beginning to pale visibly.

"What's that got to do with anything?"

Burt leaned in, looked right and left and whispered nervously.

"Hazel's second name is Brown."

Tea pulled away, puzzled.

"Mate, loads of people are called Brown," he said. "It's a proper common name."

Burt shook his head furiously and shuddered. "No, no, no. Don't you see? He followed me."

Burt began staring around wildly.

Tea scanned the area surrounding the bench but couldn't see a single soul.

"What makes you think he's following you? Start at the beginning."

Burt nodded frantically.

"OK, OK. He came up to me in the betting shop in Blackheath. He gave me this amazing tip," Burt started. "I won two hundred quid, I thanked him for the heads up and that's when we got talking. He told me he had the inside track and had an eighty per cent success rate. I believed him."

"So you started laying bets with him?"

"Yeah, he said he'd take a five per cent handling fee. The first few times I won, I scooped nearly a grand. Then I started to bet bigger and bigger."

Burt stopped and put his head in his hands.

"Go on," Tea encouraged.

"He was always really chatty on the phone, always asking me about the band and about the newspaper stories about me. All that stuff."

"Hold on, before you jump ahead. How did you run up a tab of thirty K?"

"I said a number; he fronted the money and told me we would sort it later." Burt paused and his eyes grew wider. "Oh shit, it all makes sense now!" he exclaimed.

Tea put a hand on his shoulder.

"Slow down, you're all over the shop. What makes sense?"

"Don't you see, I was winning money, I'd seen his formula work. When I started losing he just kept saying it would come good next time. I don't think he was even putting the money on."

Tea shook his head. "How could you be so thick?"

"I'm not thick, mate. I'm a sucker for the horses, there's a big difference."

"OK, let's forget about that for a second. You said he was always chatting about your personal life. What did he ask you about?"

Burt stared into space and Tea suddenly realised how totally lost he looked. The dark circles under the singer's eyes were more pronounced than he had ever seen them, his jittery demeanour more akin to a drug addict than an excessive gambler. Even his ever-present tan now seemed grey and worn-out.

"He asked me about girls a lot. When Hazel came out in the papers he asked me loads of stuff about her." Burt paused and fixed Tea a grim look. "I asked him if there was anything I could do about a mad bitch like that."

Tea turned sharply, his face was full of bewilderment. "You mean you asked him to kill her?"

"No, no, no. Jesus no! Of course I didn't. I wasn't asking that, I was thinking he might know someone who could have a word with her, you know, so she would shut up going on about me."

Tea groaned and put his head in his hands.

"You absolute mentalist. Don't you see you implied it?" he said, hissing through gritted teeth. "If Lenny is Hazel's dad then you're really up shit creek!"

Tea tried to think straight, but now everything was jumbled. Everything was destroyed. How could Burt be so stupid?

Burt sat in silence beside his bass player, staring at the ground. Eventually Tea broke the silence.

"Burt, I can't even tell you how I feel about you right now, but here are some possible facts." He held up his hand and started to count the points out on his fingers. "One, Lenny Brown never betted that money for you, two, it's too much of a coincidence that he has the same surname as Hazel and three, according to my Uncle Frank the man murders people." Tea shook his head. "I think we need to prepare for the worst-case scenario."

Burt stared ahead across the expanse of the park.

"And what's the worst-case scenario?" he whispered.

"You know what it is."

"You think he's gonna kill me?" Burt asked miserably.

"I dunno. I need to talk to my Uncle Frank again. You just lie low for now. Go and stay at Harry's, don't use the phone, all that stuff they say on TV."

"But we fly to Germany tomorrow!"

"Exactly, and you can bet that Lenny knows that, so whatever you do keep clear of your house."

"But I need to get my stuff!"

"I'll get your stuff," Tea snapped. "For once, do as I say."

"What about the thirty grand?"

"No point in giving money away if the outcome stays the same."

Burt stared hopelessly at Tea, then stood up, nodded and left Tea alone on the cold bench.

Tea watched as Burt trudged away. He remained on High Bench staring out at the bitter grey sky, shivering against the cold. Only when the dark set in did he get up and make his way down the hill.

Tea – 22nd August
I spent the whole journey to Germany with Burt's
face imprinted on the inside of my brain. He
looked so beaten when we talked in the park.
I've been going over and over it in my head.
One minute I think everything will be OK, the
next I'm half-expecting a call saying he's dead.
Either way I hope I made the right decision not
giving Burt the dough.

SONG 6 GIRAFFE STATE

Clipper - 23rd August
BERLIN, BABY!!!! I've never even stayed in
a 1 star hotel before. This is like a whole
different world. OMG!! OMG!! It's amazing!
The bed is the size of my entire bedroom
back home. The décor is well over the top
but I LOVE IT. The sheets and duvet are like
velvet or something. The view of the city is
unbelievable. I could live in this room for the
rest of my life.

When I went down for brekkie with the lads, Egg
and Tea tried to pretend they weren't impressed
but they bloody were. Even Burt thought it was
shit hot. I HEART GERMANY.

Tea - 23rd August
I didn't think places like this existed! I
keep expecting someone to put their hand on my
shoulder and kick me out. I feel sort of awkward
when I walk through the lobby, like the other
guests are thinking I've snuck in so I can rob
them blind. I wish Mum was here to see this shit.
#differentworld

Burt - 23rd August
The hotel bumped me up to a suite. I had to
hustle for it but it was worth it. The lads

don't know anything about staying in nice
hotels, but I've been in places like this
since I was a kid. Luxury five star hotels don't
expect hustlers and even if they do, they can't
argue with them. If you say the room smells of
smoke, they have to sort it. Usually with an
upgrade. BOOM!

My mum was the hustling master. From seven till
when I was about thirteen she took me everywhere
with her. I even think she loved me back then. I
was always just so glad to be away from my dad
and their constant arguing. Millie had to stay
with the nannies. Mum didn't have to take me with
her, but she did. Sometimes I think about that.
Maybe she didn't want to leave me with Dad.

I thought she was so cool when I was a kid. Her
best friends were all models. They were so sexy
and they really loved me.

Anyway, memory lane and this hotel have settled
me down a bit. Lenny feels a million miles away.
Thank God.

Egg – 23rd August
Ha ha ha! This place is mental. I rang Mum and
Dad from the room and tried to describe it. All
I could say was there was a TV in the bathroom
and electric curtains. I press a button and they
draw themselves. Every time I go out and come
back in someone has been in the room and tidied
up. Everyone who works in this hotel is so
courteous it's bordering on obsequious.

AND THE BREAKFAST BUFFET!!!! I have honestly
never eaten more great food in my life. I hate

to say it, but I could seriously get used to it. It's my birthday tomorrow and I couldn't be in a better place

Bex would love it here.

The broad quayside swarmed with people waiting to get into the venue. The queue for the gig was ten deep and stretched all the way up and round Oak Strasse and back towards the River Spree. That morning The RockAteers performed their debut single "Golden" on the biggest breakfast show in Germany, *Das Morgenmagazin*. Afterwards, the Internet lit up with love for the teenagers from South London.

Only eight thousand Berliners would be lucky enough to see them play, but it hadn't stopped hundreds more descending on the district of Alt-Treptow in the hope they might catch a glimpse of the new kids on the block.

Clipper sat in the plain, well-stocked dressing room, drumming on his practice pads. He watched his fellow band mates as they went through their individual pre-gig ritual. Tea sat hunched over his bass guitar, his fingers flying across the fretboard. Burt paced the room, performing vocal trills to warm his voice. The noise levels he reached never ceased to amaze Clipper. He had a foghorn of a voice. Egg never warmed up; instead he sat and listened quietly to music, most of which Clipper had never heard of: obscure folk or blues, hardcore, hardstep or grimy jazz. When he did recognise a song it was always a classic, like The Beatles or The Stone Roses.

Egg came into the dressing room and greeted Clipper with a nod.

"Why do you always go and stare at the crowd before we go on?" Clipper asked.

Egg appeared to contemplate this for a moment. "I guess I want to see them normal, before they get all excited."

Clipper's guts lurched. He dropped his sticks on the carpeted floor and rocketed towards the bathroom.

Tea and Egg watched him go and smiled knowingly at each other.

"How they looking, then?" Tea asked.

Egg nodded cheerfully.

"They look good, there are loads of banners out there for us."

"What do they say?" Tea asked.

"They're mostly in German, but I saw one that said 'I shed tears of rock for The RockAteers. Super toll erstaunlich'."

"What does that mean?" Burt asked, reclining on the deep leather sofa, having finished his warm-up.

"I think it means 'Super Amazing' or something like that."

"I like it. Could be the name of the new album."

"Bit long!" Tea replied.

"Just the tears of rock bit, I mean," Burt said.

Tea nodded.

"That's actually not bad,"

"The artwork could be a mountain with a crying face," Burt said eagerly.

Egg frowned, but before he could voice any negative thoughts, Ged opened the dressing room door and leant in.

"Ten minutes," he said, before disappearing again.

"It's day off's eve tonight," Clipper said. "Let's go and have a few jars for Egg's birthday, yeah? We don't have to be back on the bus till noon tomorrow."

Suddenly the door opened and Bex walked in. Egg stared at her in shocked silence. She looked stunning; her jet-black hair fell over one shoulder in glossy waves, smoky eyeliner accentuating her glittering green eyes. She wore skinny black jeans and her customary leather biker jacket. Her sexy, Burberry perfume punctured the male-only space. She smiled at Egg and then noticed the deep-set frown developing on Burt's features.

"Before you have a go, Burt, Clipper invited me, I'm here as his friend, not Egg's girlfriend. All right?" Bex told Burt.

Burt's scowl remained, as Tea put his bass guitar down and greeted her affectionately. Then Bex threw her arms around her stunned boyfriend.

"Why didn't you tell me you were coming?" Egg asked eventually, holding her around the waist.

"It was a birthday surprise." She beamed.

"I thought you were here as Clipper's friend?" Burt groaned, as Clipper returned.

"Bex!" Clipper ran over and the pair hugged.

"She didn't want a big fuss. She's only staying two nights. So, give her a break, yeah?" he told Burt, clearly over the moon to see his best friend.

Burt shrugged.

Ged was in the room again.

"Five minutes. Let's get side of stage."

The band stood up and gathered themselves.

"We'll talk after the gig," Egg told her, with a slight shake of his head.

The rest of the band followed, leaving Bex alone. Moments later a muffled roar filled the dressing room.

Clipper – 25th August
Tea keeps telling me not to worry but I feel something really bad is around the corner. I know it has something to do with this money Burt owes Lenny the Butcher, but when I ask Tea about it he just looks all sheepish and doesn't say anything.

Bex is going to stay a couple of days before taking the Eurostar home from Paris. Burt was mad for a little while, but he calmed down pretty quickly. It was as if he didn't have the energy to keep the annoyance up. That just worried me even more. Something's gotta be proper wrong when Burt can't be arsed to argue.

Germany is a lovely place. Berlin: what a town! We went out and it was like London only better. I met this really nice guy called Marco and he suggested we go out for beers in this place Nollendorfplatz that they call Nolli. I was a bit amazed at what I saw on those streets and bars. I've been up Old Compton Street in Soho before, but this was proper different. It was well swish!

Marco tried to kiss me. Basically I freaked out
and sort of slapped him. I don't really know
why, I left Nolli and went back to the hotel a
bit freaked out. On the way back I texted Bex.
Egg was asleep so she came to my room and we sat
up chatting about everything. She asked me why I
didn't just kiss him back. I told her I didn't
really know. She said there was no harm trying
a kiss, seeing as I was gay and I haven't ever
kissed a boy.

When I asked about her and Egg she just shrugged
and said he seemed different somehow.

Egg - 26th August
"I believe in everything until it's disproved. So
I believe in fairies, the myths, dragons. It all
exists, even if it's in your mind. Who's to say
that dreams and nightmares aren't as real as the
here and now?" John Lennon.

I woke up and she wasn't in the bed. I had a
few drinks to celebrate my birthday and then
felt tired. Apparently she spent the night
chatting with Clipper. That's cool. But then I
go downstairs and there she is having breakfast
with Tea. They were laughing at something when
I turned up. It kind of looked like flirting. I'm
paranoid he will tell her I tried it on
with Tyra.

Sometimes Burt's words come back to haunt me:
"Sooner or later she is going to leave you for
someone good-looking".

I saw Cab Jones from The Desert Kings checking
her out. I wanted to go up to him and shout

in his face, "SHE'S SEVENTEEN, YOU DIRTY OLD
BASTARD!!" But I didn't because she looks twenty
and she turns eighteen next week.

I had this dream where this lanky, ginger boy
giraffe and this beautiful sleek girl panther are
walking side by side through a shopping mall.
Suddenly, out of nowhere, this male lion with
massive furry balls jumps on the giraffe's lanky
neck and drags it to the ground. As the giraffe
is lying on the floor with its neck bleeding, it
watches the big cats walking away together, the
lion's massive, furry balls swinging, as they
nuzzle each other's heads like cats do. All I
could hear in the background is very loud purring.

I woke up in a pool of sweat. I'm not an idiot,
I know I'm the ginger giraffe and Bex is the
panther, but who is the big-bollocked lion? I
thought it was Burt at first, but I know Bex
would never cheat on me with him. So now I've
seen her and Tea together, I think maybe he's
the lion. Or is Clipper lying about being gay?
Or is it Cab Jones?

I'm having a nervous breakdown. Fuck my life!

Tea walked into the production office and stood waiting while
Ged finished his phone call. The bassist rarely entered the business hub of the tour. He watched as the Production Manager, Bob,
his assistant, Jane, and the Stage Manager, Tyrone, busily worked

away on their laptops. Then, to Tea's relief, they all grabbed their phones and headed out of the office together. Tea was relieved that Joey, The Desert Kings' Tour Manager, wasn't in the office. The burly New Yorker wasn't a big fan of The RockAteers. Every time he saw one of them he made a back-handed remark. Tea wasn't sure exactly where the animosity stemmed from, but he had a good idea. Tea, Clipper and Egg had all been tarred with Burt's brush.

Ged logged out of his email. The strip lighting reflected off his shiny bald head and his permanent frown was deeper than usual.

"What do you need?" he asked Tea.

"I need to use a landline if poss. I want to call London," Tea told him.

Ged stood up and gestured to his chair.

"Sure, jump in. Have to go sort a bitch-fight out between our swagman and theirs. Make your phone call," Ged said, before heading off.

Tea sat down and dialled. Frank answered on the third ring.

"Unc, it's Tea."

"'Ello, kid, I thought you were in Russia?"

"I'm in Paris. It's great."

"Paris, eh? I took a girl to a French restaurant once. Cracking body she had. Where you off to next?"

"Madrid. Then we fly home." Tea paused. "Have you listened to our CD yet?"

"I had a listen the other day."

"And?"

"I thought it was wicked, boy, reminded me of the The Beatles,

Bob Marley and The Beach Boys all rolled into one. It's right up my alley… So, what's it like being famous, kid?"

"Weird," Tea replied, suppressing the desire to laugh at how genuinely the question was put. "We've stayed in some proper wicked hotels. Five star gaffs. And I'm seeing the world."

"That's great, enjoy every day as if it's your last," Frank said.

Tea took a breath.

"I need to ask you a favour, Uncle. There's thirty thousand pounds in it for ya."

There was a long silence.

"Lenny Brown?" Frank said eventually.

"Yes."

"I told you I can't. Money isn't gonna change that."

"I know, but I got no choice, things just got even worse. The only reason I mentioned the dough was because it cushions it a bit."

"What good is cash when you got no hands to spend it with?"

"Unc, I swear this could mean the end of my band," Tea said, desperately. "There is talk of us making it big in the USA. I'm so excited about everything, but if we don't do something, Burt will ruin it all."

"How's it got worse?"

Tea relayed what Burt had told him on High Bench. He finished and waited for Frank to speak. The silence from the London end of the line was painful.

"I'll think on it, kid," Frank said eventually. "Now get back to your band and don't worry about nothing at this end. You got me?"

Tea replaced the receiver and sat staring blankly at Ged's laptop screen. He knew he should push the worry aside like his uncle had suggested, but the sinking feeling in the pit of his gut was only getting deeper.

Egg - 27th August

The amount of times Tea and Burt have said "Gay Clipper in Gay Paris" is hitting the hundreds. For some reason it makes us all laugh, Clipper included. It's another "day off's eve" and we're staying in another amazing hotel.

We play the Bercy tonight, in the heart of Paris. It's a fantastic-looking venue, covered in grass. I had a stroll to the top of the hill with Bex. It took me a day to get used to her being with us, but I've decided that having her here is amazing. I'm feeling good and writing songs again. I wrote this one called "Shelter" the other day. The hook line is "You're the roof over my head." I know there is this big thing about girlfriends causing issues within bands but Bex gets on with everyone. The band and the crew love her. She stays out of band business and actually gets on with the other three better than I do. Even her and Burt seem to be OK these days. Burt is still in love with her of course. It's obvious. Clipper is her best friend. I know this because she tells me every day. She and Tea get on really well too. Maybe too well. Tea is so chilled out. He's funny too, in a dry kind of way. On stage he's like a statue, leaning back nodding his head along to the music. I have to say, it's pretty cool. At the end of every gig the front row demand he get his top off. He never does, instead he throws his plectrum into the crowd and everyone scrabbles around after it.

I'm still not used to all the girls waiting for us outside the venues. I was worried that Bex might get jealous. There must be a million photos of girls kissing me on Twitter and Facebook but she doesn't seem bothered.

Harry phoned me yesterday and said we're on the front cover of *Sound City* back in the UK. Seriously!? One minute they trash our single and the next we're on the front cover? Harry said that he's been told the album will be favourably reviewed. BY WHO? *Sound City*? Really?! It all sounds very two-faced. Harry said the CD would go to a reviewer that likes our genre of music. So I asked him to find out what kind of music Drusilla Prior was into, he said that she was into Electro/New age/Punk. I thought about that for a long time. Surely it's a more noble aim and a greater accolade for us to change her opinions about the band than to play it safe?

I'm going to ring him tomorrow and make sure it's Drusilla Prior who reviews the album and let the chips fall where they may. Better that, than this dishonest gut feeling I can't shake.

Jerome stood next to Bex outside the George V Hotel and watched the tour bus leave. The forty or so fans that had gathered outside for a glimpse of the famous four started to disperse as soon as the bus pulled off. Jerome was brimming with pride, but years of working with over-sensitive artists had taught him to suppress it. He turned to Bex.

"The Eurostar doesn't leave for another two hours, Bee. I'm taking you for a proper lunch," Jerome said, as his mobile rang.

"Cool, can we have steak?"

"Steak it is, let me just take this."

Jerome noted the unrecognised UK number on the incoming call and put the iPhone to his ear.

"Is that Jerome Clincher?"

"It is, who's calling?"

"Jim Lake from *The Bugle*. Have you got a moment?"

"Not really, I'm just running into a meeting," Jerome said, winking at Bex.

"We're running a story about your band, The RockAteers. I wanted to give you a chance to refute the allegations."

"What allegations?!"

"We have a man on record claiming he wrote all The RockAteers songs. We're running the story in tomorrow's early edition."

Burt – 1st September

```
As we flew into Heathrow Airport, I could see the
grey spitting sky and I couldn't help thinking
what a steaming puddle of cat piss England is. I
didn't see one drop of rain when we were in Spain.
I don't know why I don't just live there? The
weather is wicked and the birds are really fit.


When we got through passport control, loads of
skanky press arseholes were there and started
shouting questions about whether we wrote our
own songs. WTF?! They were shoving The Bugle
```

in our faces. Whose picture did I see? George
Shithead Graves.

Egg went off his head and said it was my fault.
He accused my ego of creating someone so full
of hatred he would make up a story like this.
Then with actual tears in his little squinty
eyes he tells me that mud sticks and that we'll
be branded as fakes forever, even if we prove
otherwise.

The worst thing about us fighting in public was
the paps snapping us.

Then, when we got out of the airport, about a
million women came running up to us, screaming
and shouting. We are number 1 in the album and
single charts now and, of course, it's a big
bloody deal. Apparently our fans don't give a
flying bollock about who wrote our songs. I loved
it because next the paps are snapping us being
absolutely worshipped by loads of girls. We were
like conquering heroes returning from a crusade.
Egg sloped off like a moody little girl.

The girls skipped down the high street, thrilled to be allowed out
of school for a few hours in the late summer sun. The Year Nines
who had accompanied them deliberately hung back, which was
a good thing.

Jasmine peered through the window of a shop and pointed to a mannequin wearing a gold skirt. "I'd marry Tea and wear THAT to our wedding," she said determinedly, causing Millie to laugh out loud.

The RockAteers were always a hot topic amongst Millie's friends. Now they'd all met Jack Skill over Skype, a new level of mania had been reached.

"God, Jazz, it's horrible!" Lilly commented, dragging Jasmine away from the shop front. "FYI, I'm thinking about chopping my hair." She turned to Millie. "Your brother said Clipper likes tomboys, right?"

"You're both utterly mental," Georgie squawked poshly. "Jack's so hot. Sorry, Mills, I know he's your brother and everything."

"I think Egg's cool," Millie said absently. "He was nice when he came round to my house."

"Booooooringgggg," Georgie replied. "But cool that he's been, like, actually IN your house."

Suddenly Millie felt a tight grip on her arm. She was yanked roughly backwards and turned to face a scary, wide-faced man with dark eyes. He was wearing a shabby, black shell suit. He glowered down at her, tightening his grip, so she gasped in pain. Her friends stood rooted to the spot, watching in horrified silence.

"I have a message for your brother," the man hissed, with stale breath. "If he doesn't pay up, the consequences will be the worst you can think of. For him and you!"

Before Millie could reply, the man let go and disappeared up a side alley.

Millie stood staring after him as her friends rushed towards her. She tried hard not to cry, but as they all gathered around, offering soothing words and comforting hugs, she felt big, fat tears beginning to brim over.

Bex sat up on High Bench, hoping the crisp air would help clear her head. Despite the fantastic two days in Europe, the doubts could not simply be brushed away. The fact was that Egg hadn't been entirely pleased to see her in the Berlin dressing room. After all that planning of the surprise, it was Clipper and Tea who had seemed thrilled to see her. Egg appeared disoriented, almost pissed off. He remained intense, hardly managing a smile all night. The next day he seemed to lighten up and even enjoy her company. But something was up. He started asking her leading questions, like who she thought was sexier, him or Tea. Bex felt a terrible sinking feeling when she tried to picture a future with Egg. Sure, he had come out of his shell, but there was an entirely new intensity to her boyfriend now, firmly centred around himself. Having been a man who found it almost impossible to express an opinion, he now said "I" more than anyone else she spent time with. Egg had placed himself firmly at the centre of this new universe and in her heart, Bex knew it was driving her away.

She suddenly stood up and walked back down the hill. She wouldn't go to Egg's flat today. She needed time to get her thoughts together – and now there was an added complication.

Burt – 10th September
I'll kill him. I was scared before, now I'm
proper murderous. You don't threaten little kids.
Millie cried for half an hour after she told me.
Hasn't Lenny Brown read the rule book?

I'm not scared anymore. It's time to sharpen up.
Shit needs to get done.

✪

SONG 7 GOLDEN

The 53 bus crawled towards the Elephant and Castle. Tea sat on the top deck, at the back. He'd chosen to take the bus for nostalgic reasons, but so far it had been anything but. The back of the top deck was packed full of teens and school kids. It was loud, uncomfortable and hot. What was he thinking? Why hadn't he got a cab?

A pretty girl of around seventeen, with blonde hair scraped up into a doughnut, turned and grinned at him.

"You that geezer in that band, right?" she shouted above the din, chewing gum open-mouthed. Tea saw the glint of several gold teeth.

"No," Tea replied, realising that the entire bus had turned around to see what was going on. The girl's friend had also twisted in her seat. She wore a white shell suit, had a relaxed afro and bright purple lipstick on.

"Why you on a bus? Don't you get limos everywhere?" Gold teeth asked.

"No."

"You ain't as fit as your lead singer."

"I think I am," Tea replied with a smirk.

"Don't get me wrong, you is fit enough!" she shrieked, and

paused to pout at him, casting an eye from Tea's face down to his crotch. "Fancy comin' round mine for a quickie?"

"How old are you?" Tea asked the girl, with a grimace.

"Old enough, guitar boy."

"I play bass."

"Keep your knickers on!" she said with a wink. "So? Fancy it?"

The observers on the bus sniggered as Tea studied her further. She wore a gold tracksuit, had big hooped earrings and a silver stud in her nose. Tea definitely fancied her, and for the first time in months wished he wasn't in his skinny jeans.

"I'm eighteen. 'Ere, take a look."

She pulled out a card and thrust it at Tea.

Tea looked at the provisional driving licence and nodded. "You're older than me."

"Cool, so you can be me toy boy. So you coming round mine or what then?"

The bus erupted in laughter.

"Oh look, this is my stop," Tea said, getting up.

"You ain't going anywhere until you've signed my tits," the blonde girl screeched, barring his way.

Tea was caught between kissing her and pushing her over.

"Latisha, give him that marker pen out your bag!" she ordered, lifting up her tracksuit top and pulling down her bra in one fluid motion. The bus gasped, as Latisha handed Tea the pen.

"Go on then, before they get cold."

Tea stared down at the milky white breasts and suddenly laughed. "This has gotta be a set-up. I'm on *Punk'd* or some shit, right?"

The girl bared her teeth in disgust, her gum sticking out between the gold ones.

"What you on about? SIGN MY TITS!"

Tea signed his name across her left breast and heard the camera phones snap. He pushed past her and fled down the stairs. Once on the lower deck he waited, willing the bus to stop. He got off first and sprinted down the Walworth Road.

He glanced up as the bus pulled away and saw two flattened backsides pressed up against the rear window of the bus, one black and one white; Latisha and her gold-toothed friend.

Tea walked all the way up the Walworth Road to Elephant and Castle. He reached the corner of Elephant Road and spotted Uncle Frank through the window of the greasy spoon café. He put a hand up in greeting and walked in.

"I nearly got mugged on the bus up here," he said, sitting down, still breathing hard. He noticed Frank's hand was heavily bandaged. "What happened?"

"Don't matter. How was the tour?"

Tea smiled, happy to tell the story of faraway cities, tour buses and packed gigs. Before he knew it, he'd been talking for over half an hour and he hadn't even ordered a cup of tea.

"Sounds like you had the time of your life." Frank smiled.

Tea nodded.

"Also, sounds a bit like you fancy your best mate's bird," he said, with an amiable wink.

Tea shook his head vigorously. Had he talked about Bex a lot? "Nah! She's just really good company. So what happened to your hand then?" He felt the need to change the subject fast.

"OK. I'd better start at the beginning!" Frank paused. "You sure you're not eating, kid?"

Tea shook his head.

"I went to see Lenny Brown at the pub."

"What pub?"

"His pub, the Frog and Radiator, on the lower road by the petrol garage. Anyway, so we sit down over a glass of Scotch. I ask him right off the bat if he knows some kid called Jack Skill 'So what if I do?' he says. So I tell him I need a favour and explain that you're my nephew and that if we pay back the dough that's owed, will he leave Jack Skill alone. Then before I know it, wallop…"

Frank stopped mid-sentence. A boy of around fifteen was standing beside the table, holding a pen and a napkin. He thrust them at Tea.

"Can you make it out to my brother Kai, please?"

Tea nodded politely, took the pen and signed the napkin. Frank watched, beaming from ear to ear. When the autograph hunter had gone, Tea turned back to his uncle.

"So what happened?"

"Two of his lads held me down while the butcher went to work and suddenly I've got one less finger!"

"Jesus Christ, Unc!" Tea hissed, leaning over the table, his eyes wide. "I got you into this!"

"Did you bollocks, I'm a grown man," Frank said, patting his nephew on the shoulder with his good hand before continuing. "So then he sits me back down, throws me a dirty dish rag and waggles my own, cut-off, finger at me." He paused and shook his head. "Course by this time I'm delirious with the pain. I tell you, boy, you have no idea how much getting your finger hacked off hurts."

Tea was shaking his head, wide-eyed, staring at Frank's bandaged hand.

"'I've always liked you, Frankie,' Lenny tells me. 'But blood is thicker than water. Jack Skill got my Hazel up the duff, and he'll pay with more than just money.' So then I ask him what he had in mind in way of a reprimand."

Frank paused to look around himself.

Tea held his breath.

"What did he say?"

"His exact words were…" Frank leaned over the table and hissed the words, "I'm gonna eunuch the fuck."

Tea dropped his head in despair and fought the urge to scream.

"I told him I couldn't let that happen, because that would mean the end of my nephew's band."

"You threatened him?" Tea said, looking up in dismay.

"I never threatened him, I facted him!" Frank winked. "Anyway, Lenny looked at me all odd for a second and said, 'You got some brass balls threatening me with only seven fingers, Frank Sheehan.'"

Tea watched on tenterhooks as Frank lit a cigarette. "And?"

"And we cut a deal," Frank revealed, smoke billowing out as he spoke the words. "Either Jack takes the deal or he lives the rest of his days with a serious lack of knackers, you get me?"

Tea nodded and Frank explained in meticulous detail what his nephew should do next.

★

Burt - 25th September

I just passed my test. Bang off in your face!
I didn't even do one lesson either. I got back
from Spain and just booked it. I'm like a driving
superhero. I didn't even get any minor faults.
The instructor or whatever you call him said that
it was "the perfect drive". Basically I ripped
the test a new arsehole. All the other bitches
in the band can't even drive! Just another reason
why I'm the daddy.

We go into the rehearsal studio again next
week and Egg promised we would do my new song
"Pictures of Me". Maybe I should threaten to keep
all the publishing wonga from that?

Harry showed us our schedule for the next hundred
years. Radio Tours, TV shows, Interviews. Every
bleeding day he has us doing something. I told
him we should get a day off once in a while and
he got all cheeky and implied I'm lazy.

I feel surprisingly relaxed considering I have a
cockney terrorist up my ring piece. Mind you, I
did have half a bottle of Jack Daniels and about
a million spliffs before I wrote this.

Tea keeps texting saying we have to meet up
urgently.

★

Jerome glanced at the laptop screen and smiled across his desk at Harry.

"It's gone gold. By the end of the month, we could be looking at platinum."

"All of a sudden, that thirty thousand Jack owes doesn't seem so much," Harry said.

"You have to hand it to Mr Skill," Jerome said. "I know he's a pain, but he really is a one-man publicity machine. You couldn't buy this kind of exposure. Not for a billion quid." He smiled and shook his head. "OK, enough self-congratulating. Let's chat about America?"

Harry looked at Jerome, thoughtfully.

"It's a tough one, The RockAteers are uniquely British – that can be a curse, or it can be a blessing," Harry said. "I'm just not sure what the Yanks will make of Jack Skill and the shit storm that follows him. We've seen lots of huge UK bands struggle to get even a foothold in the US."

"Many of those bands had no real ambition to break America though, did they?" Jerome replied. "It takes months of touring and huge effort over there. Besides, our lads are way younger than most of the other bands that have tried, with one obvious exception. Youth and naivety gives them huge advantages."

Jerome paused and gave Harry a grin.

"So I've spoken to the US label this morning and they're thrilled about the recent sales figures. They're prepared to spend big on making it work across the pond."

Harry grimaced.

"I'm not sure they can hold it together for an American tour just now. It's tough on any band let alone this lot."

"I know they're volatile," Jerome conceded. "But we have to give them a shot at the title. Besides, we can deal with the fallout after they've become the biggest band on the planet. Look, we have the chance of a clean slate over there. The tabloids reach doesn't extend that far."

"I wouldn't be so sure." Harry put his head in his hands. "How the hell is it possible for someone to accuse a band of being fakes with no real proof?"

"It's a new age, mate. People make unsubstantiated claims all the time, the gossip takes hold and in minutes it's spread all over the web and it's suddenly hard fact."

Harry twirled his phone around in his hand and shrugged.

"All publicity is good publicity, right?" Jerome said.

"Right! Remember what Warhol said: 'Don't pay attention to what they write about you. Just measure it in inches.' The RockAteers are riding the crest of a wave. No one cares who wrote the songs.

"Do we know anything about this kid who claims to have written the songs?"

"Only that he was Jack's best friend at school. Have you seen the photo of him holding up that fake lyric book? He looks inconsolable. He's very convincing."

"There is just no way anyone else but Egg wrote 'Satellites'."

"The truth will come out, right?"

"I hope so, meanwhile, let's start opening up America, keep plugging away at the UK and Europe." Jerome tapped another key on his laptop. "Anything else we need to chat about?"

"Yes, I'm afraid there is one more thing," Harry said, with a groan. "Egg is upset the album's being reviewed by a sympathetic journalist at *Sound City*."

"There is nothing we can do. It's in the shops tomorrow. He needs to get over it and move on."

Harry winced. "I'll talk to him," he said.

Egg - 10th October
"If you are sexist, racist, judgmental or anything don't buy my CD. I don't care if you like me, I fucking hate you." Kurt Cobain.

I don't understand how an imbecile like George Bastard Graves has managed to convince the entire country he can write a song? Let alone a good song! He has taken away the one thing I hold most dear - my integrity.

Bex and I met up in the local café yesterday and had an argument about her spending loads of time with Tea on tour. She told me to stop being so paranoid and that I'd changed since the band started getting big. Suddenly, this teenage girl came over and actually asked me to sign a newspaper article with George's face all over it. Then Bex told me she had to go. I am sure she wanted to tell me something important.

We are doing Burt's song "Pictures of Me" in rehearsals at the moment. I'm not saying the song isn't good, it is, I just can't handle him bossing me around. To make matters worse, Burt had

the bright idea to video the whole song-writing
process. "To prove to everyone we do write our own
songs," he said. He went ahead and hired an entire
film crew, complete with a very loquacious director.
Are we now actually creating a reality TV show?

Bex keeps saying surely this was everything I've
ever dreamt about. Well, no, it isn't actually.

★

"Shout it loud from the ramparts of the castle of rock. The sav-
iours of music have cometh," Tea read aloud.

The band sat around the rehearsal space, newspapers and magazines strewn across the floor, a stack of papers on the table. Tea
tossed the magazine he was reading aside and picked another
from the pile.

"Listen to this one: 'I had low expectations of The RockAteers'
debut album, but this is a record that lives up to the hype. I might
even say exceeds it'," Clipper said, grinning.

"Have you seen Yusuf in *The Bugle*, talking about how we
changed his life?" Burt said.

"Our press agent is one clever bird. She said she'd concentrate
the press in one giant push, and she has. Boom! We are literally
everywhere," Tea said.

"We should hang out with Yusuf again. He was brilliant,"
Clipper said.

"He was," Burt agreed, discarding *The Bugle* and grabbing
another from the floor.

"We haven't had anything less than a 9/10 or 4/5," Tea said.

"Have any of you looked in *Kerrang*? We won't get a good one in there," Egg said, staring gloomily at *Sound City*.

"Why you always gotta put a downer on things, Egg?" Clipper said, frowning. "Don't you get it? People love our music. People love your songs. Why doesn't that make you happy?"

"Because I believed in a publication and it's as corrupt as all the others," Egg snapped back.

"Will you stop whining on about *Sound City*, Egg – just because you wanked over it when you were twelve doesn't mean it's any good," Burt said, rolling his eyes as Clipper and Tea sniggered.

Egg's phone began to ring. He stared at the screen for a moment before answering.

"Hello."

"Egg, it's Harry. Are you with the boys?"

"I am."

"Great, put me on speaker. I have some wonderful news."

Egg pulled the phone from his ear, hit the speaker button and held his arm out.

"Hi, guys, just wanted you to know the album has gone platinum in the UK," Harry gushed.

Clipper shrieked with delight, shot off his chair and hurled himself at Tea, catching him full in the chest so the pair went crashing backwards to the floor. Burt laughed loudly and sprang up from the sofa. "Bundle!!!!" he shouted, before jumping bum first on top of the grappling rhythm section. Egg stood and observed the yelping mass. Finally, he shrugged, grinned broadly and dived head first into the pile.

As the magazines and newspapers flew about the room, Harry's tinny voice could still be heard on Egg's phone.

"Guys, guys, is everything OK? Did you hear what I said?"

None of them could hear, they were having too much fun.

SONG 8 PROBLEM SOLVER

Egg – 31st October
The reviewer at *Sound City* actually said that
it was the "5th greatest British album of all
time." I rang Jerome and demanded the album be
re-reviewed by Drusilla Prior. I told him people
think I'm a fake and the only reason that we're
big is because our lead singer tried to kill
himself. Jerome seemed disappointed and said I
was focusing on the negatives. He told me I had
to try harder to enjoy what was happening, that
my songs were wonderful and that George would be
exposed soon enough.

I think I caught Burt doing coke in the rehearsal
room toilet.

I read up on the effects of cocaine and I'm not
sure his giant ego needs stoking.

Tea had been waiting for fifteen minutes, his shoulders
hunched and arms bound tight around his torso against the bitter
wind that whipped across the heights of Greenwich Park. He

felt his backside begin to numb and wished he'd worn warmer trousers. How many hours had he spent on this bench waiting for Burt Windsor?

He spotted the singer coming through the main gates and swallowed hard. Uncle Frank's parting revelation and subsequent advice had consumed Tea since they'd met in the café. He had already been with Burt for two rehearsals and a TV interview, all with the knowledge weighing heavily. He had no idea how Burt would react. All he knew was the band could not fail because of this. He had to handle the situation with care.

"All right, mate." Burt nodded, rubbing his gloved hands and sitting down. "Nippy, ain't it?"

Tea studied Burt with a sideways gaze. He looked different to the boy who had handed him the flyer on the top deck of the 53 bus. He had aged two years, of course, and his hair was shorter, but it was more than that; he seemed worn down, stretched somehow.

"Yeah, freezing," Tea agreed.

"What's up?" Burt asked with a frown. "You look like someone wanked off in your face."

Tea fidgeted on the bench for a moment, his head bowed. "I have some bad news, mate, but before I tell you I want you to promise me something."

"Piss off, just tell me."

"No, I want you to consider the consequences your decision might have on the people around you."

He put his hand on Burt's shoulder firmly.

"Whatever you decide will affect us all, including Millie."

"Just tell me," Burt said again.

"Uncle Frank went to see Lenny Brown last week."

"And?"

"And he cut my uncle's finger off."

"Bullshit!" Burt said, his eyes widening in panic. "That's bollocks."

Tea sprung from the bench, grabbed Burt by the scruff of his jacket and pulled him close.

"My uncle went to see Lenny to try and get you out of this shit," he hissed, his face centimetres from Burt's. "Everyone always runs around after you. What do you give back?"

Burt stared wildly at his band mate.

"Nothing! Nothing, is what you give back. You owe my uncle a finger."

Tea let go and sat back.

"Lenny gave my uncle an ultimatum, specially for you, mate. Here's the choices: marry Crazel or Lenny chops your balls off."

Burt's face twisted.

"I'll go to the police. Tell them what's going on," he said at last, shakily.

"Yeah! Great idea. They'll arrest Lenny, put a protection detail on you and lock him up for the rest of his life."

"Problem solved," Burt said unconvincingly.

Tea shook his head.

"Don't you get it? You knocked up his daughter. He thinks you wanted her dead. He's coming for you, Burt."

Burt hung his head. "So what do I do?"

"You marry Hazel and you keep your vegetables." Tea stood up. "You have two weeks," he said, before heading off.

Burt sat and stared across at the wintry view. The enormity of his predicament was sinking in, like the sun into the London skyline. Only when darkness had descended completely did he think about leaving, his decision made. There was only one way he could keep his promise to Millie, but make it all go away.

Clipper – 7th November
Me and Bex have been going out loads recently. I can't do without her. She told me a tonne of stuff about her and Egg. She was a bit drunk and said they haven't had sex since getting back from tour and they were arguing a lot.

She persuaded me to go to Heaven, this gay nightclub. I couldn't believe it when I saw Yusuf in there. He introduced me to this tall black guy called Trevor. He was older than me, twenty-three, and works as a radio presenter. He has the nicest smile I ever saw. He asked me back to his flat in Pimlico, but I said no. We kissed in a really private place in case we got papped. He said that people at work don't know for sure he's gay. I told him I was in a rock band and he asked me if I was the drummer from The RockAteers, when I said I was, he screamed like a girl.

Me and Trevor talked for ages and I got worried about Bex but she was on the dance floor with Yusuf and loads of other girls. The girls were all getting well close to Bex. But then she is the best-looking woman I ever saw in my life. I loved hanging out with Yusuf again. He's made it into *The Vox* final. Good on him.

Me and Bex got back to my new flat at 3 am, opened a bottle of champagne and talked about Trevor till 6 am. It was an amazing night. Little by little, I'm getting my head around it all.

Burt - 10th November
I haven't slept a wink in two days. My brain feels like mushy peas. I stink. I didn't turn up to rehearsals last night. My phone goes off every minute. People have been knocking at my door constantly. The stuff I got was very strong and I think it was meant to be taken with other people around, you know - for safety. I have a beard, but I haven't been able to bring myself to look in the mirror.

If I choose getting married to Hazel the hot celebrity girls won't want to know, and if I have no balls then it's all pointless anyway. I can't get over this thing my old maths teacher once told me: "Every puzzle has a solution." It literally goes round and round in my head until I want to smash my head against the wall.

"Every puzzle has a solution" is all I've been thinking about for two days. As a last resort, I think about going to the police, I think about running away too, but both are not really proper solutions. I could kill Lenny - but that's mental.

I counted up all the missed calls I've had: Harry 12, Tea 2, Clipper 18, Jerome 6, Bex 1 and Egg 0. I've decided that this makes Clipper my best mate. He also actually came round the house, knocking for me twice. I think he was with Bex one time and that was when she phoned

me. I nearly answered it too. She could save
me, I could easily run away with her. I would
give everything up for her. The gambling, the
music, the drugs, the girls. I would marry
Bex in a heartbeat. I can't shake wanting her.
#willieverstoplovingher

I've drunk my dad's drinks cabinet almost dry
now. When I was a kid I remember my dad always
had a drink in his hand. He never really came
out of his study. When he did, I kept out of his
way. Drinking all his booze is giving me a little
bit of satisfaction. I've been thinking about
why he was so nasty to me when I was small a lot
recently. I can't work it out.

Perhaps every puzzle doesn't have a solution.

Production rehearsals for the UK headline tour were in full swing.
The giant hangar-like sound stage in West London teemed with
life. Sound men, guitar techs, roadies, stage managers, carpen-
ters, lighting guys and video techs were all busy road-testing the
various elements that combined to make the theatre tour. A huge
screen projected imagery to complement the video backdrop to
the stage. The lights were being mapped so each song triggered
a different light show and screen visual. An ego ramp was being
built so Burt could walk into the crowd without being mobbed.

The band had rehearsed with their sound man, Richie, on a
handful of occasions at their small practice room. Now it was

time to test it in a big space. Burt's absence did not hold proceedings up. Egg could sing the lead proficiently enough for Richie to get what he needed, and the band was getting tighter with every run-through.

"Is this really what Burt likes to hear in his 'in ears'?" Egg said into the microphone, as the band paused between songs for Richie to get level.

"Yeah, mate," Richie said into the mic, as he stood behind the huge sound desk in the middle of the sound stage. "Kick drum and his voice as loud as it goes. A tiny bit of guitar to pitch to."

"Weird!" Egg replied.

He spotted Ged gesturing to him from side of stage. Egg unslung his guitar and headed stage left towards his Tour Manager.

"You have a phone interview with Heart Radio," Ged said, as Egg reached him.

Egg nodded. Much of the promo since Burt's "mystery illness" had been undertaken by the lead guitarist. Egg waited a moment before his mobile phone rang.

"Hi, I'm Trevor Hardcastle, the host of drive time here on Heart. Is that Egg?"

"Hi, Trevor, good to meet you."

"Great to meet you too, look, before we go on air I just wondered if, when you see him next, you could say hello to Clipper and tell him I loved hanging out the other night. You and I won't get a chance to talk after the interview."

"Course I will."

After the interview Egg tracked Clipper down. The drummer was smoking outside with most of the crew.

"Clip, I just did a phoner with Heart, and Trevor the DJ said to say hi and he loved hanging out the other night."

Clipper glanced around at the crew members, suddenly wearing a hard scowl. He began to redden. Finally, he threw his cigarette on the floor and stalked off. Egg followed.

"What's up?" Egg called after him, once they were back inside.

"What are you trying to do?" Clipper hissed, his face blazing with anger. "Tell everyone in the whole world?"

Egg held his hands out and pulled a face.

"I have no idea what you're going on about, Clip."

"I think you do! And by the way I know all about you trying to kiss Tyra. How could you do that to Bex?!"

Clipper turned and marched away again. Egg stared after him in shock.

Burt had spent the day drinking discreetly in the corner of The Crown public house on Blackheath Hill. He'd picked the pub because of its hidden side room. The more he tried to block it out with drink and drugs, the more the thoughts came raging back. Inevitably, when he considered marriage to Hazel, he thought of the life with Bex he had fantasised about since he was eleven years old.

When sober, which he hadn't been for well over a week, Burt thought about Double B, and what it might be like to be a real father, to wake up with him in the morning, to watch him grow, to get to know the little soul. Suddenly his thoughts were broken by an alert on his iPhone. It was from an unknown number.

WHERE ARE YOU? IM AT THE HOUSE. Millie

He couldn't face his sister in this state. He stood up, wobbled and knocked his empty pint glass on the floor. Using the walls to steady himself, he tottered to the gents. Once inside the cramped cubicle, he fumbled inside his shirt pocket, fished out the tiny rectangular envelope, unwrapped it and poured a generous amount of white powder on to the porcelain cistern. He took a fifty-pound note from his wallet and began to roll it up. His fingers were unresponsive and clumsy. The note slipped from his hands and fell into the toilet bowl. Burt cursed and bent down; the wrap fell from his breast pocket and joined the cash in the toilet. He cursed again, fished out the wrap and opened it hastily. The powder had turned to paste.

"You all right in there?" said a voice from outside the cubicle.

"Bugger off," he barked.

Rolling his eyes, he began to lick the paste greedily. After demolishing the bitter-tasting glue, he lent over the cistern, blocked his left nostril and snorted the line.

He exited the cubicle and stopped abruptly. A medium-sized man barred his way.

"You told me to bugger off," the man stated nervously, his arms crossed.

"I did, sir," Burt slurred. "I was frustrated. You would too if you'd dropped all your drugs down the toilet."

Burt gave a drunken salute and pushed past him.

As Burt zigzagged across Blackheath Common towards home, the effects of the powerful drug hit his heart like a hammer blow. He tried to light the joint he'd rolled earlier. It took him four attempts, but once it sparked he took long, deep drags, hoping it might slow his heart rate. By the time he reached the other side of the common he was struggling to focus, the downer of the weed and alcohol unable to dull the effects of the upper. He saw shapes behind him. Had he gone the back way to avoid the photographers? He wasn't sure. No, this was his driveway. Shit! Were they taking photos of him? He hurled an arm in the air and threw up his middle finger just in case they were. He thought he heard jeering but didn't want to risk turning around. He was almost home, sanctuary was almost his.

He reached his front door and checked every pocket twice before locating his keys. He tried the lock. It wasn't working. Again and again he attempted to force the key into the slot but it was no use. He banged on the door. Some distant memory told him there was someone there. Millie! he realised. Millie was in the house. He found his voice.

"Mills, Mills," he croaked loudly.

Suddenly he heard a voice shout from somewhere above him and craned his neck to see. Who was it? Who was this person in his house?

"Whatthafffu you doin in my 'ouse?" he slurred at the man, who was hanging out of the first-floor window. He looked vaguely familiar.

"What are you doing?! You're drunk! You live three doors down. Go away, before I call the police."

"How dare you!" Burt screamed. "I've lived here all my life, do you think I don't know MY OWN HOUSE!?"

The man shook his head.

"I am absolutely positive at this moment you have no idea which is your own house. Look at the number on the door, you lunatic," he shouted back.

Burt took a step backwards, steadied himself and attempted to focus on the number on the door.

"Fif-teen," he mumbled to himself with a frown. "But I live at number nine."

He looked up at the man in confusion. "This is NOT my house! This is YOUR house."

"That's right, now kindly go away."

Suddenly Burt became aware of movement behind him. He turned, bewildered, to see a cluster of figures pointing their long lenses at him.

Burt – 13th November
I got home in a bad state last night. I don't remember how I got in. My dad was here, I do know that. I remember because he slapped me around the face. I woke up in the sitting room. He's gone now, thank God.

I rang Millie and asked her where she was. She told me she was in Scotland at school. It must have been my devious dick of a dad who sent that text yesterday. He knew I would come home if Millie was here. What an arsehole.

I didn't tell her that dad had been home. I
reckon she'll be a bit worried coz she mentioned
I was all over the papers this morning.
Apparently I tried to get into my neighbour's
house and my neighbour happens to be a Member
of Parliament. #memberbeingtheoperativeword. I
told Millie not to worry. I wanted to cry when I
talked to her, but I had to hold it together.

I got a note from my dad saying he was trying to
slap some sense into me so he could ask me to
play at his business partner's daughter's sweet
sixteenth.

When you gonna get it, Dad? I WILL NEVER EVER DO
ANYTHING FOR YOU EVER.

Tea had been fending off enquiries from Harry and Jerome
about Burt all week. He was fast running out of excuses. A cold
didn't last this long. Clipper had been providing Tea with hourly
updates on his attempts to get in touch with their lead singer.
Eventually, with the feeling of impending doom too great, Tea
made the decision to go and find Burt.

It was a good fifteen-minute walk from the rehearsal studio
to Burt's house; up the hill and across Blackheath. It was a calm
morning with a soft breeze, sending the few remaining autumn
leaves floating gracefully down from their bare branches. By the
time Tea's feet crunched the gravel drive he'd almost shaken off
the bad feelings. He half-expected Burt to answer his front door

as if nothing had happened, wearing some outlandish get-up, like the bullet-hole shorts and flip-flops he'd appeared in when Tea had brought a stolen car to his house.

There was no response to Tea's sharp raps on the knocker or his incessant ringing of the doorbell.

"He hasn't come out for two days."

Tea turned to see a photographer pointing a camera at him, with seven or eight of his friends bunched around, snapping away. The sensation of impending doom started to return.

"You considered the possibility he ain't coming out because you bastards won't give him a minute's peace?"

The photographer shrugged.

"Fame isn't a tap you can turn on and off when you feel like it, you know, mate!" he sneered.

Tea shook his head and marched over to the large, high bay window that faced out on to the driveway.

He scrambled up and peered through the kitchen window. It was a disaster area: the huge round table strewn with junk, the surfaces piled high with crockery. Tea pushed himself off the sill and landed heavily on the gravel. He dusted himself off and stepped back to take another view of the house. The only option was to force his way in through one of the windows, and he wasn't about to do that with an audience.

Somehow, he needed to get in through the back door. Tea hung his head and walked out of the drive, ignoring the paparazzi as they snapped away. He turned left and left again. Once he was a good fifty metres down the side street he stopped and looked up at the high wall. He would need to go through at least three gardens. Not a feat he was particularly keen on undertaking in broad daylight, but he had to do something.

Tea took a run-up, jumped, hooked his fingertips and pulled hard, hoisting himself over the wall, landing in a beautifully landscaped garden on the other side. He crossed the lawn and scaled the next wall. Within a minute he was in the familiar surroundings of Burt's garden. He paused to catch his breath and made his way up to the house. He peered in through the back door, but could see nothing. Tea decided to see if he could get a look into the living room. He jumped and managed to scrabble his way up on to the ledge, almost losing his balance as he steadied himself against the windowpane. He peered into the sitting room and gasped. A cold shock of horror swept over him. There on the sofa lay Burt, his head lolling, dried vomit splattered across his chest and caked around his mouth. He looked dead.

SONG 9 THE OUTING

The Cloominater studied the two young faces carefully. He could see why they were drawn to one another. Both were easy on the eye, both had an IQ lower than one hundred. The public school girl and the street urchin fulfilled the adage that opposites attract. It shouldn't have surprised him, Sophia seemed to like her teen-age lads. Despite him blackmailing her into starting the affair, he knew she had enjoyed her dalliance with Jack Skill greatly.

It was the first time Wilson had set eyes on George Graves in the flesh. He had of course seen him in the papers, looking heartbroken and betrayed, forlornly holding up the stolen lyric book. Jim Lake had done a good job exposing The RockAteers as frauds. Cloom especially applauded the comparison piece Jim had run; George's council flat and Jack's mansion pictured next to one another with the headline: "The Prince and the Pauper". If Cloom had learnt anything from working on *X-Finder*, it was the public couldn't get enough of pathos and conflict. The smear campaign hadn't stopped The RockAteers going platinum, but it had undoubtedly dented their ultra-cool image. Overall, Sir Wilson Cloom was pleased with the operation.

The pair across his desk looked distinctly uncomfortable – George possibly even terrified. Or was he just starstruck?

Cloom cleared his throat loftily and started to speak slowly and deliberately.

"I have risked a lot calling you both here today. But I felt it necessary that I make something crystal clear."

Sophia and George listened intently, their eyes fixed firmly on the music mogul.

"The rumour is that you've been seeing a lot of each other." He paused and swivelled back to face them. "Is that true?"

George looked at Sophia for help. Her eyes were downcast and she was beginning to colour. The reaction told Cloom everything he needed to know.

"Sophia, I told you specifically that you were to do your job and never speak of it again. I paid you very well and now I see you have betrayed my trust."

"I don't know what happened, sir. I made a huge mistake, please forgive me," she garbled through red cheeks.

"I know what happened, we fell in love," George said, grabbing Sophia's hand.

Sophia grimaced and pulled her hand away.

"You will finish this relationship today. Do you understand? Do you realise how serious fraud is, George? You could be jailed for a very long time indeed."

George continued to stare at Sophia.

"Yes, sir," Sophia said, standing up. "Consider it ended."

George stared at her in disbelief. Cloom nodded firmly.

"You may leave now."

Cloom watched as the young man tried to gather himself. He looked pale and shaken. Could he really be in love with Sophia?

Could anyone love such an ambitious little trollop? Cloom liked his women stunning and subservient. Ambition was not tolerated. After the pair had left the office, he turned back to his beloved view. Maybe he could turn their relationship into a plus? Perhaps he could use it to destroy The RockAteers once and for all?

Tea — 15th November
I thought the dickhead was a goner. I had to
break the back door down. It took me three
goes. The room stank. Burt stank, but I could
see his chest moving up and down. He was alive.
The coffee table was a mess of smudged mirrors,
spirit bottles, overflowing ashtrays and takeaway
cartons. I yelled at him to wake up, but he
didn't move. I slapped his face and pinched him
hard on the arm, but he didn't respond. I tried
to pick him up off the sofa and take him to the
bathroom, but he was too heavy. I was gonna call
an ambulance, but I remembered the paparazzi
outside the house.

Suddenly his phone went off. I had to dig around
on the messy coffee table to find it. It was
Clipper. I answered and filled him in, doing my
best to play it down. He was really worried, but
I said I would deal with it and call him back. I
scrolled to the letter H on his phone and found
Hannah, Harry and Heidi. I thought about it for
a moment and then bashed the letter C into the
search. Chelsea, Cherrie, Constance and then I
found what I was looking for — Crazel.

"Hazel, it's Tea."

"Why are you calling me from Burt's phone?"

"Because he's in trouble, Hazel, and he could do with a real friend."

Tea glanced at the mess on the couch.

"What's wrong? I didn't want to make him mad by going to the paper, but what else could I do? He left me on my own, Tea. All I want is to look after him and for us to be a family. Baby Burt, me and him."

"I hear ya. Can you get round here? You gotta come alone, round the back way, through the neighbours' gardens."

"I've been in Burt's garden loads of times, I go there sometimes when I miss him so much I could die."

Tea grimaced. "Right."

"I'll be there in ten minutes," Hazel said, hanging up.

Tea leant against the wall, his heart hammering. He looked down at his lead singer, his mouth open, his jaw lolling on to his shoulder. "I hope I made the right call, ringing her mate, but what else can I do?" he whispered.

Tea left the living room, made his way to the kitchen and rang Clipper.

"How is he?" Clipper asked.

"He's in proper well bad shape."

"Tea, you have to tell me what's happened. Why he's behaving like this?"

"All right, all right." Tea sat down at the round table. "Lenny is Hazel's dad and he is threatening to cut Burt's balls off unless he marries her."

"But that's insane!"

"He cut my Uncle Frank's finger off. He's insane all right."

Suddenly Tea heard the back door.

"Clip, gotta go. Hazel's here."

"Crazel? What the fuck—" Clipper said, before Tea hung up.

Tea rushed back to the front room. Hazel came in like a whirl-wind, pushing straight past him to Burt. She bent over him and felt his brow.

"He's hot. Tea, help me with his clothes."

Tea stared at her "I…" Hazel was fresh-faced, her hair piled loosely on her head. Despite the frantic situation Tea saw just how pretty she was underneath all the make-up she usually wore.

"Help me, now!" she demanded.

They began to strip him. Once undressed, they dragged Burt to the downstairs shower room and propped him up. Hazel turned the shower head on him.

"Why so hot?" Tea asked, alarmed to see her turn the gauge to the maximum temperature setting.

The pair stood back and watched from a safe distance as the shower blasted the top of Burt's head, steam building quickly.

"Hot is better. Burn the devil out of him. You ever seen that scar on his back?"

Tea pulled a face and shrugged. "Nah. Where is it?"

"Don't matter now," Hazel replied. Tea looked at her, puzzled.

Suddenly Burt let out a high, squealing shriek. Hazel darted into the shower and shut it off. Burt tried to move, but only managed a defeated slump, his head still lolling as he gazed about in confusion. The scalding water had burnt red streaks into his naked flesh. Hazel squatted next to him and started to towel him down.

"Go get bedding from his room upstairs. Bring it to the lounge," she ordered, cradling Burt's head.

Tea sprinted upstairs. When he returned Hazel had dried Burt off and had somehow moved him out of the shower cubicle.

"Right, let's take him back into the lounge and settle him down," she said.

They half dragged, half lifted him back to the front room and laid him out on the clean sofa. Hazel covered him over with the duvet and kissed his forehead. Burt fell straight back to sleep.

"Right, let's get this all cleared up," she said. "I will deal with the puke-stained sofa, you deal with the crack-den coffee table."

It took the pair forty-five minutes to make the room somewhere near right again. When it was clear of drug paraphernalia, takeaway boxes and bottles, Hazel sprayed an entire can of air freshener into the room. She and Tea sneezed repeatedly. Burt didn't stir throughout the whole operation.

"I'm going to stay here with him for as long as he needs," Hazel declared, dragging a chair over to the sofa. She sat down and began to stroke his brow, staring down at him, a mixture of concern and contentment etched on her pretty face.

"OK, I will too then."

Tea slumped down against the sitting room wall and crossed his arms.

"I've been meaning to ask you something," Tea said, breaking the silence. "Are you sure the baby isn't mine?"

Hazel frowned. "Of course not. It's Burt's baby. We had sex five months before I got pregnant."

Relieved, Tea nodded and switched on the TV. While Hazel maintained her vigil he watched reruns of *Breaking Bad* on Netflix. Hours passed until, eventually, exhausted he curled up on the floor and dozed off. He was awoken by Burt's screams.

"It burns. BURNING ME!! Aaargh!" he cried.

Hazel was up in a flash.

"Hush, baby," she whispered, gently cradling his head. "Sweetheart, I'm here." Burt focused on her, a mix of fear and confusion in his eyes. "I will look after you until you're better, OK?" she said softly.

"OK," Burt croaked.

"What happened?" she asked.

"I don't know. I've been sad," he managed. "My dad was hurting me."

Hazel bit her lip.

"I'm here now, baby. Don't worry. Is there anything I can do to make it better?"

Tea saw a twinkle in Burt's bloodshot eyes.

"A blow job might help?" he said sorrowfully.

Hazel shook her head. "Jack Skill! What you like?"

She reached under the covers.

"How about we compromise?"

Tea stared in horrified fascination. As Burt moaned, Tea sprang up and darted for the door.

Tea – 16th November
Yesterday was the weirdest night of my life. Burt
has got to pull himself together.

I can't decide if Burt and Crazel are made for
each other or if their joint mentalism could
cause a tsunami. It's proper weird shit, the way
they talk to each other. I think Burt's just
gotta marry her. He hasn't got much choice anyway
and at least that way he gets to see his baby and
the band has a chance of existing past the end of
this week.

If I was seeing a girl, I would show her proper
respect. Sometimes I think I wouldn't mind having
a girlfriend. But I reckon they might just want
me because I'm in a band now. Bex isn't like
that. She doesn't care about Egg being famous.
I sorta think someone like Bex would be who I'd
choose.

Burt – 20th November
Hazel is a special person. I'm glad I said it out
loud.

She has moved in and so has Double B. I love it
and I feel so much better. I'm off the drugs
and alcohol and down to only six spliffs a day.
Having the baby here is a game changer. I don't
want to be messed up on drugs around him. He's
too awesome. I went back to rehearsals and I must
admit we are all having a laugh. I'm trying to
keep the idea of having to marry Hazel out of my
head until I get back from the tour. I'm hoping

she told her nut job of a dad that she's moved in
and I'm making an effort. I texted my mum to tell
her about Hazel and Baby Burt moving in and she
wrote back with one word. "Fine."

I had a great chat with Millie. She is well
pleased I have someone looking after me.

#notetoself I think I overheard Tea telling Clip
that Egg tried it on with Tyra. She is fit! But
why eat carrots when you got steak at home? Is
he mental?! I need to get the whole story when
we get back out on tour. Funny thing is Tyra is
actually joining us on tour for a few days. I saw
it in a scheduling email from Harry's assistant
today. I wonder if Smeg can keep his Eggs and
Bacon on the plate?

I must be feeling better coz I'm looking forward
to finding out.

"Have you seen the freaking bus?" Clipper skidded into the
rehearsal room with his wheelie suitcase sliding behind him.

"No, what's wrong with it?" Burt said in alarm.

"Nothing, it's awesome! It's a double decker and has much
bigger bunks than the last one. There's enough room to sit up in
bed." Clipper took a deep breath. "It's got three lounges and two
PlayStations. It's totally zing!"

"Sounds legit." Tea nodded.

Harry and Ged walked in.

"How you doing, chaps? I thought I'd come and see you off." Harry smiled, looking around. "Nice place. I can't believe I haven't been here before."

Clipper looked chuffed.

"Will there be catering?"

"Did you see what games they had on the bus, Clip? Or should I bring some of mine?" Tea asked.

"Yes, there's catering," Ged told them in monotonous Scouse. "Tea, there are plenty of games on the bus."

The band nodded in unison.

"Right. Let's get a move on," Ged said. "Leeds isn't a long drive but I'd like to get there in good time. It's bad enough having to pick you up from the wrong side of London."

"Oi, this isn't the wrong side. This is the heart of London," Clipper said.

"It's the heel of London more like," Ged retorted.

"I baggsy the front two beds with the lounge room attached," Clipper shouted, jogging out of the door.

Ged called after him,

"Not a good idea, Clipper. There's eight bunks and only six of you on the bus, including the driver. I suggest Burt takes the area at the back top of the bus."

Clipper turned, looking crestfallen. Tea picked up his suitcase.

"Not sure of the logic there, Ged, but let's just go with it and get out of here," Tea said.

"Why should any of us get their own area?" Egg scowled.

"I think Ged's right," Burt said, picking up his huge case.

"I need space to entertain all the girls I'll be bringing back."

Ged shook his head.

"You know what my company's name is?" he asked them. The RockAteers shook their heads. "YOU KNOW BEST," he said slowly. "So named, because my job requires me to facilitate your needs whilst at the same time making sure you know where you are, who you are and how long you're on stage for."

Clipper started to snigger. "How can someone not know who they are?"

"It's happened, Clipper, and that person was a lead singer." Ged paused. "Let Jack have the bunks and back lounge. You will thank me."

"OK," Clipper said mournfully.

Tea rolled his eyes and shrugged. Egg nodded.

"Great, so shall we go do this tour now, ladies?" Burt said, grinning from ear to ear.

Clipper - 29th November - 08:02 pm - Tour Blog
Hi, everyone. I thought the first thing I would write about is what we get to see before any of you lovely lot do. We get a tour schedule from our manager. Below is a list of gigs we are going to do. The UK leg is announced of course, so you will need to scroll down to see the ones we are doing in the US of A. When I got all the dates I was buzzing. You can leave a comment on my blog. I will try and read as many as I can. I am actually backstage with Burt, Egg and Tea as I write this. I know it sounds weird but this is like a really intimate gig after doing

arenas with The Desert Kings. And no, I won't be answering any questions on how to meet, marry or kiss Burt. LOL.

Egg swaggered off stage, sweat dripping from every pore. He collected a towel and bottle of water from Ged and headed back to the dressing room. The arena tour with The Desert Kings had been a learning curve. They had gained their touring legs, honed their stage craft and consigned their songs to muscle memory. Now they were in front of their own dedicated fans, the leash was off and the energy was intensified. Egg felt the freedom in every perfectly timed beat, every vocal swell, in every plucked, strummed or bent note he played on his guitar. It had been electrifying and soul purging. For the first time ever, he had joined Tea and Burt in the whirling, gyrating fury that had become part of every RockAteers show. The crowd had responded in kind. He had let himself go, forgotten where he was, who he was and what problems he had in his life. He had let the music take him over completely.

"Jesus, Egg, Man of the Match, bruv. You were on fire out there tonight," Clipper yelled from across the dressing room, as he stood drenched in sweat, naked from the waist up.

"Yeah, Egg, you were well zing tonight." Tea nodded, equally soaked, sucking back a beer.

Burt marched into the dressing room, his blond hair plastered to his face, already down to his underpants and Cuban cowboy boots.

"We rocked it, right?" he shouted, putting up a palm for anyone close to high-five. "I think I defo get Man of the Match, right? I was genius!"

Tea ignored his singer's hand and took a giant swig of beer. Clipper shook his head and continued the battle to get his soaked skinny jeans off. Egg bounced over to Burt and slapped his outstretched hand. Burt studied the guitarist with surprise for a moment.

"You see me snog that girl and then throw her back into the audience? You see how many women wanted my body when I took my top off?"

"Me and Tea think Egg this time," Clipper said. "You've given yourself Man of the Match every night!"

Burt spun on a Cuban heel and stared hard at Egg for a long moment. Gradually, a smile emerged on his ever pouting lips. "OK, I'm down with that. You *were* brilliant," he said, slapping the guitarist on the back. "I had no idea you could jive like that, brother."

Egg nodded shyly and headed for the shower room. As he turned the corner he was confronted with Tyra. She was dressed in denim shorts, her slim, lightly tanned legs once again on show. The checked shirt she wore was tied up in a bow at the front, revealing a perfectly toned stomach. Egg noticed she had her belly button pierced.

Tyra looked thrilled to see him.

"Oh my God. You've no idea how long I've waited for you to let go like that!?"

Egg stared awkwardly and shrugged. "I guess it's not very cool."

"Yes it is! It's cool because letting yourself go is cool!"

"Really?"

"It's like you were a different person out there," she went on. "I haven't enjoyed a gig more in years. IT WAS AWESOME!"

Egg blushed and tried to move past her, but she barred his way. "Look, I know it was a bit awkward last time but I just want you to know, everything's cool."

Egg shrugged. "Cool, it's cool. I don't blame you. I mean, I'm no oil painting."

Tyra pulled a funny face. "What are you talking about? It's got nothing to do with what you look like. I didn't kiss you because of one blatant fact."

"What's that?"

"You have a girlfriend, stoopid."

Egg hung his head.

"Hey look, I'm not trying to guilt-trip you." She put her hand on his arm. "We are cool, Egg. I'm just not into that. I've been on the receiving end of a cheating bastard and it really hurt."

Egg looked up. "And that's not supposed to make me feel bad?"

Tyra chuckled. "Yes, sorry that came out wrong, anyway, I just wanted to say. It's all good and you rocked that party tonight."

Egg relaxed a bit. "They gave me Man of the Match."

"Why do boys equate everything to football? I hate football."

"I hate football more," Egg agreed. "It was unanimous. Even Jack voted for me." He paused and grimaced. "Although to be fair he did vote for himself first."

Tyra burst out laughing. Egg was surprised by the noise for a moment, but it was infectious and soon both were in fits. They paused when Clipper walked past wearing only a towel, and then erupted again.

"What are you two laughing at?" the drummer asked suspiciously.

"Nothing," Egg snorted. Clipper disappeared into the shower block. Egg turned to Tyra and managed to control himself long enough to ask a question. "Hey, you wanna hang out after I have a shower?"

"Will you be naked?" Tyra smirked.

Egg blushed. "No, I mean after I get fully clothed again."

"Sure, as long as you don't try any funny business," Tyra said, patting his arm before disappearing down the corridor.

Jack – 30th November – 06:34 pm – Tour Blog
Gig last night was the nuts! Loved it. You were all amazing. Just read my comrade Clipper's blog. Who is Burt? It's good you all got to see the tour details but he got a right bollocking from our manager. The US tour isn't announced yet. See, I let you into the wonderful world of The RockAteers and our gossip. I've been told not to swear in this blog, but you lot fuckin' love it, don't ya?

By the way, this is the first time I've spoken since all this shit about us being a fake band. For the record, George is a lying dickhead. We wrote all the songs. Anyway you lot don't give a blind feck about that, because you all bought our album by the bucketload and made us all millionaires. We're still number one and we've sold nearly a zillion records.

Can you imagine when we get to Yankee land?
We're gonna blow their star spangled banner off
the flagpole.

@BladeBlueNose – Comment Posted 06:40 pm 30/11
Are you on crack? Are you a narcissist?

@RockAfan – Comment Posted 06:42 pm 30/11
You are the sexiest man alive. Will you marry me? Did you
see me up the front at the Leicester gig?

@PurpleHeart – Comment Posted 06:45 pm 30/11
Is it true that your drummer is a dick weaver?

Egg – 30th November – 08:34pm – Tour Blog
You might not know me but I write and arrange the
songs and basically tell everyone what to play.
If you don't know me you are forgiven. Jack,
our singer, sucks attention like an arrogant
Dyson vacuum cleaner. Anyway if you know my band
I want you all to know three things. 1. I, not
George, write the songs. 2. The thoughts of our
renegade lead singer are his own and not that of
the band's. 3. I really appreciate how much love
you show this band. So thank you and I'm sorry
I don't say hi more often. I'm missing out. One
last thing: big thanks to Tyra, who works on our
social networks, for persuading me to break my
silence. I feel deep catharsis.

Jack – 30th November – 07:18pm – Tour Blog
Message for @BaldBlueBallstwo = I've slept with
over a billion women. You've only slept with your
hand. No, I don't take drugs because my dick is
massive. As for being a narcissist. Some of my
best mates are mixed race.

Message for @RockAfan = Yes I will marry you, and
yes I did see you up the front. You were the well
fit one. I wish I'd had more time after the gig.

Message for @Purpleheart = If you mean is my
drummer gay then yeah and so what? You're
probably gay as well but you don't even know it
yet. Also dick weaver is very uninventive. How
about rump razzler or uphill snorkel hound?

Clipper – 30th November – 09:05 pm – Tour Blog
I am not a dick weaver. I am not a rump razzler.
I am not an uphill snorkeller. I am not gay. I am
out of this band. Goodbye.

Tea – 1st December – 12:00 am – Tour Blog
I wanted to wait till bang on twelve midnight
to post this blog. Nice one, Jack Burt Windsor
Skill or whatever your name is, you really are a
special man. Rest in Peace The RockAteers.

SONG 10 HEADLINES

Jerome and Harry stared down at the newspaper. It was open at the page in question. The crisis meetings seemed to be a weekly occurrence.

"It's like giving a child dynamite and asking them not to set it alight. I just wish you could have consulted me," Jerome said, staring down at the headline gloomily.

LEAD SINGER OUTS DRUMMER: Jack Skill reveals his sticks man is gay in Internet gaffe.

The two men sat in the quiet pub on Ealing Broadway, the Sunday afternoon rush for roast dinner and Premier League football only an hour away.

"How was I supposed to know the idiot was going to 'out' his best friend?"

Jerome put his hand on his chin.

"Erm, let me see? Track record, intuition, instinct."

Harry took a sip of lager.

"Laying the blame on me won't solve our problem."

Jerome sighed.

"Sorry, I just don't understand why this band can't keep their noses clean for one millisecond."

Harry grimaced.

"I'm afraid it's worse than that. Clipper's gone AWOL."

"What?"

"He's not been seen since the show last night."

Jerome glanced at the time on his mobile phone and stared at Harry in alarm.

"But they go on stage in three hours!"

"I'm sick of sending out the search party for one of them every five minutes," Harry said, draining his pint. "You want another?"

Jerome nodded and Harry made for the bar. He picked his phone off the table, scrolled down to the letter C and hit call.

"'Ello," a little voice croaked.

"It's Jerome. Where are you? Are you OK?"

"I'm gay," the tiny voice slurred in response.

Jerome paused, trying to work out how to reply.

"I've left the band," Clipper continued.

"Where are you?"

"I'm at the train station."

"Which one?"

"It's called Redcar."

"Where is that, Clipper?"

Harry returned to the table with two pints of Peroni.

"I came to the seaside."

"Clipper, are you at Redcar train station? I can get Ged to come get you. Stay right there."

"OK, but I've left the band. I'm gay."

"Clipper, it doesn't matter that you're gay, we've been through that. I'm with Harry now and we both agree that it's actually better it's out in the open."

"I have a celebrity footie match next week, it's not better for that!" Clipper garbled. "And it's not better for my dad. What is my nan gonna say?" The phone went dead.

Jerome looked at Harry.

"He's in Redcar. Get on to Ged right away," he said. "Where are they playing tonight?"

"Newcastle."

Jerome redialled Clipper's number, it went straight to answerphone.

Egg - 3rd December
"I love being a drummer. Everyone thinks you're dumb. What they don't realise is that if it weren't for you, their band would suck." Dave Grohl.

I told Harry the blog was a bad idea. I am currently sitting on our tour bus - tour morgue might be a better description. Clipper has the worst hangover of his life and isn't talking to Burt. Burt has failed to grasp why Clipper is so upset. The last comment he made was, "I'm sorry, mate, but you *are* gay!"

Ged drove all the way to Redcar to get him #supertourmanager. Apparently he found him sitting on a bench at the train station dripping wet and babbling about wanting to be gay by the sea. He had a near empty bottle of Jack Daniels in his hand. It was decided that one of the crew members, this bloke called Tony, should step in for the gig. He's about thirty, so looked pretty

weird at sound check. We spent a furious two
hours trying to rehearse him up. Of course Burt
was no help at all and it was left to me and
Tea to go through the set, while Burt was off
probably ruining someone else's life. Clipper
and Ged turned up ten minutes before we were due
to go on stage. Clip looked like shit. Ged made
a point of keeping him away from Burt, but of
course Burt does as he pleases and found the room
Clipper was recovering in and started trying to
apologise. Then Clipper decided he wanted to do
the show, face the public, etc., etc. It wasn't
our best gig, but everyone screamed all the way
through it. It didn't seem to matter that Clip
was almost catatonic and couldn't have found the
rhythm if it attacked him.

Bex isn't coming to meet me until Southampton,
which is in a week, and it sucks. We just
don't seem to be getting on at the moment.
She just keeps repeating the same thing: that
I've realised all my dreams, but I'm still
complaining. I tell her that's a long way from
the truth. I love the gigs and I love making
music but all the bullshit that surrounds this
industry drives me insane. Bex said it didn't
matter about the *Sound City* review and that made
me really pissed off. It's as if she thought I
was ranting on about it or something. Then she
asked me who Tyra was. My heart leapt right into
my throat. I asked her why. She said because I
mentioned her in my tour blog. I told her Tyra
was a mate. Bex asked me if she was pretty. I
told her no, which is a lie.

Birmingham tonight. Tour blog has been cancelled.
Thank hell for that.

Tea — 5th December

My best mate is gay! I'm proper proud of him.
Burt seems sorted since getting back with Crazel.
I'm deliberately not asking him about it, but he
still has his balls so that's a start. I'm not
counting my chickens just yet. We're properly
in that tour bubble again now. We'll have to see
what happens when we get home.

Burt and Clipper are being well moody with each
other, but Egg has come alive on this tour. He
talks to the fans, gives it lots on stage and
he's hanging out with Tyra loads. I don't think
he's messing but there's defo a spark there.
She's great – well sexy and proper funny and she
always looks cool, but if *I* was Egg I wouldn't do
anything that might mess shit up with Bex.

Burt's on it again. The crew stay up partying
with him till all hours but the massive
difference is they're machines. They'll drink
till 4 am, then get up four hours later, unpack
the lorry, set up all the gear, do the sound
check, pack it all down, get lashed and start the
process all over again.

Clipper — 5th December

I thought I would feel better, but all I can
think of is my dad. He's tried to phone a million
times, but I just can't face the conversation.
He doesn't leave messages. The tour is going
amazing. We've been playing great gigs and every
venue is sold out. We're still at number one in
the album charts and "Satellites" is released
for Christmas. Everyone reckons it's gonna be
number one. It seems mad that Egg played it
all those years ago in our school hall. I just

told him that Bex can't make it to Southampton
now. He seemed pretty sad about it but I'm too
emotionally exhausted to have the big Egg/Bex
chat right now. I get to sleep in my own bed
tonight. We leave right after the gig back to
London. I spose I'll be seeing my dad later…

Yusuf won *The Vox*. I'm proper chuffed for him.

Egg regretted not wearing a warmer jacket as he stood watching the building from across the street.

He scanned every face as it came out of the revolving doors. Suddenly he spotted her, a pretty, pale girl with jet-black hair, a bomber jacket and Dr Martins. Egg's heart raced as he set off across the street towards her. Thank God she was alone, he thought, as he trailed along behind her. He caught up and tapped her on the shoulder. She turned and smiled.

"Drusilla Prior?" he asked already reddening.

"Who wants to know?"

"I'm Edward Poacher from The RockAteers. You reviewed our record."

She suddenly looked nervous.

"Look, dude, I dig that you're upset, but it's only one opinion."

"Yes, but it's an opinion that matters to me. You write for the biggest music weekly in the country."

She nodded. "OK, what do you want?"

"To personally invite you to our gig tonight," Egg replied.

"You realise this is pretty spooky, right?"

She turned and started to walk away at a pace. Egg caught up and walked briskly alongside. She turned and faced him.

"Look, I know you're freaked out, but don't be. I'm not angry with you for saying my music is fake. I'm angry at my album being reviewed by your colleague who already loves the band. I want you to give my music a second chance. I want you to watch us tonight, so you can give us a live review that's honest."

She nodded slowly. "Why? You have everything. Your album is number one, you're set to become the biggest band on the planet. You don't need me or *Sound City* to endorse you. You certainly don't need me to like you."

Egg dropped his head and shook his long red fringe. "Because I think you might be right," he mumbled.

"What?" she said, squinting at him. "Wow, dude, you have some serious issues! Let me tell you something: I listened to that song twice, it took me twenty minutes to write the review and then I never ever thought about it again. To be honest, I can't even remember what I said."

Egg flushed with anger. "What?! Don't you realise what effect you have? Don't you realise how much you crushed me and my band? It was our first ever review and I've been reading your magazine since I was nine! I want a second chance. I want you to see how much we believe in what we're doing. That we aren't fakes! After what you've just said, you owe us that much!"

Drusilla's face softened. "Wow, if it means that much to you, I'll come to the gig and review it."

"Really?"

"Yes, but I can't guarantee my editor will print it and I can't promise a good review."

Egg smiled and nodded. "Great, yes, write what you want."

He stuck out his hand and she shook it.

It was the last night of The RockAteers first UK headline tour and Jerome was excited. The Brixton Academy was rammed, the live reviews had been all five stars and people had continued buying the album *Set the Bench High* in their droves. The band had three days off before flying to Dublin to play Malahide Castle for two consecutive sold-out shows. Jerome believed that if you could break a band in a relatively small territory like Ireland, it would be possible to break an artist anywhere. He considered the huge success The RockAteers had gained in Ireland a lucky charm. After Malahide Castle, the band had two shows at Cardiff Arena supporting Karakas and then back to London for a month's writing and recording. Then it was time for the big one, the assault on the USA. He turned, grinned at Harry and raised his bottle of beer. Harry clinked.

"You've done a splendid job, mate." Jerome paused and pointed the nozzle of his beer at Harry. "They're going to win every award going next year, guaranteed."

Harry nodded. "Everything you touch turns to gold, Mr Clincher."

They were standing in the VIP section overlooking the gathering audience. For the past hour they'd been congratulated by every A&R person, live agent, manager and music executive in the business. They'd drunk their way through two bottles of champagne before moving on to beer. Jerome felt like he deserved the praise. He had never worked harder on a band in his life.

He heard the introduction music strike up: a haunting orchestral piece Egg had chosen from Stanley Kubrick's *Space Odyssey*. Jerome was suddenly compelled to see this gig close up. Something he hadn't done for years.

"Come on," he said, giving Harry a slap on the back.

"Where?"

"Down there."

"What are you talking about?"

"Let's get amongst it!" Jerome said passionately. Harry looked horrified. Jerome put an arm around his shoulder. "Come on, mate, you're only thirty, don't be a champagne and strawberries millionaire all your life."

Harry rolled his eyes and followed Jerome down the stairs towards the pit. As the pair reached the ground floor, the heat and atmosphere hit them like a wave. Thousands of people stood, staring expectantly at the stage as the light show and intro music raged. Jerome pushed forwards into the crowd. It was tightly packed and he had to drive hard to get through. He made for the centre, Harry following in his slipstream.

Just as they arrived in a spot Jerome had favoured in his youth, the crowd roared. He looked up. The first RockAteer appeared on stage. Clipper gave a quick wave to the rabid crowd, sat down behind the drum kit and struck up a bass thud. Jerome felt the thump like he was being hit hard on the chest with an open palm.

Tea strutted from stage left, slung his Fender blacktop over his head and stood still and silent.

Jerome glanced at Harry. His friend and colleague gazed back at him with an expectant grin. This is what we do it for, thought Jerome, moments like this. Egg walked on. His head bowed, heading for his guitar. The bass drum continued to toll, the mob buffeted and swayed and Jerome felt a long absent shiver of anticipation roll down his body. Only live music could achieve this feeling.

When Jack Skill stalked on stage a deafening level of noise erupted. The throng bled their lungs dry. Jack gave them a curt wave before strutting over to his microphone. He stood for a moment with his head bowed. Then he looked up and snarled a smile.

"We are The RockAteers," he said in a clear, concise voice, giving the crowd a cool wink. "We hope you came for a riot?"

Wham! Everyone went mental. Clipper clicked his sticks four times and the band struck up their opening tune. The crowd exploded. Mobile phones were thrust in the air and tiny screens captured a few seconds of the teenage superstars, as people jumped rhythmically to the relentless beat. Jerome and Harry let themselves go. They jumped high, dived at one another, knocking into others as they let the music transport them. The songs were taut and angular, catchy and accessible. They were perfect. By the third song, both men were drenched, beaming like children. Screaming into Jerome's ear was the only way Harry could communicate.

"I never do this with any of my artists, it's amazing."

Jerome nodded like a maniac in reply.

After the forth song, Jack Skill engaged the crowd, roaming the stage with decisive boldness.

"I was hoping you lot might indulge us?" he said, stalking up to the edge of the stage and grasping eager outstretched hands. "It's a bit of an Answer and Call thing we do."

He paused to wipe the sweat from his brow and pointed a finger of acknowledgement at Jerome and Harry.

"I wanna find out who's loudest, me or you? You get me?"

The crowd were so ramped up, Jerome realised he could have told them to get naked and they would strip to the bone. Jack waited a moment and then at the top of his lungs he bellowed, "Oi oi."

With two sharp jabs of his arms he conducted the crowd to repeat. "Oi oi," the five thousand shouted back. The noise was shattering.

"That was good, we'll try it again later," Jack told them. "This song was our first single."

Lighters, mobiles and voices sprang up in a vast sing-along, Jerome and Harry joined in, powerless to resist the pop lure of "Golden" – broad grins across stretched mouths. Both men were stunned when Egg came to the front of stage and played to the throng. The quiet ringmaster had found his mojo. His profes-sionalism was astounding. Every backing vocal, every guitar line perfectly executed, but now instead of shoe gazing, he was moving; throwing his guitar around like it was an extension of himself. They were all incredible, Jerome thought, utterly caught up in the moment – just like their crazy, faithful fans.

After "Golden" the band played two upbeat songs back to back and Jerome knew that it was time for the finale, "Satellites". Egg put his guitar down, walked over to the piano and struck up the chords. When Jack's vocals entered the song they were crisp and clear. Arms were flung aloft, lungs were at maximum, and people were happy.

"We've created a monster," Harry shouted in Jerome's ear, just as the song ended.

Jerome nodded, mesmerised. He was absolutely blown away.

"Have you been drinking?" Egg asked, as he towel-dried his sweat-saturated hair.

The smile left Bex's face, replaced by an affronted frown.

"What, are you the gig police? Ain't I allowed a drink?"

Burt and Tea looked at each other.

"Wow, what is your problem?" Egg erupted.

Hurt and surprise flickered across Bex's beautiful face. She cocked her head to one side and angled her jaw forward defiantly.

"Well, clearly *you* are, Egg!"

"We'll leave you to it," Tea said, grabbing Burt's arm.

"Hang on a minute, I'm not going anywhere. This is my dressing room and things are just getting interesting," Burt said, with a grin.

"Get out!" Egg screamed.

Tea pulled Burt out of the room and slammed the door.

Bex fixed Egg with a cool hard stare.

"Don't you start on me in front of the band."

Egg frowned and held his palms out.

"I started on YOU? I didn't do anything!"

"Yes you did. And it's not what you've done, it's what you haven't done," Bex snapped. "We haven't had sex in a month. When I see you, all you do is talk about yourself, how *you* feel, what the band is doing or how annoying it all is. You've become a miserable bastard and I can't deal with it anymore."

"I've tried to get close to you, but you're all cold and anyway, you don't love me so what am I supposed to do?"

"WILL YOU STOP GOING ON ABOUT ME NOT LOVING YOU!" she shouted. "I haven't been cold at all. What the hell you on about?! I've been busy doing my own thing. But you wouldn't care about what my thing is, because all you're interested in is YOURSELF."

"So what are you trying to say?"

Clipper walked into the dressing room nude, save for a towel around his waist. He took one look at the screaming couple and disappeared again.

"I'm trying to say exactly what I already said. You've changed and I don't want to be around what you've become."

"I see! … So you're splitting up with me?"

"Is that what you want?"

"No, of course not, but you're such a bitch sometimes. I'm going through some bad stuff as well, you know."

Bex stared, her mouth tight.

"Let's ignore the fact you just called me a bitch for a second and pause to examine poor little Egg's life. You're in a massive

178

band. You write amazing songs, and judging by tonight's performance you've totally come out of your shell. Egg, you are living the dream. All I want is for you to enjoy it, but you seem incapable of doing that."

Bex paused and crossed her arms.

"You really liked my performance tonight?" Egg said with wide eyes.

"Aghhhh," Bex shrieked. "See, that's what I'm talking about – your ego. Do you even know what I have been busy doing?"

"No!"

"I've been getting singing lessons. Turns out I'm good, just like my dad always told me."

"Wow, that's great."

"And I made it through the open auditions of *The Vox*. I'm going on the show next year."

Egg frowned. "What are you talking about? *The Vox* is mindless toss!"

"See, that's the support I get from you. I'm leaving."

Bex walked to the door, stopped and turned around to face him again.

"You go on about Burt being an egomaniac all the time, but you're just as egotistical now. You might hide it behind that moody muso disguise, but it's there, like a giant spot on the end of your nose."

"Don't you dare compare me to Burt."

"Great, that's just great. I tell you the truth in the hope you might actually listen and all you can focus on is Burt!" Bex left the room, slamming the door behind her.

Egg – 10th December
Bex and I had the most horrible row backstage. It feels so strange sitting here alone after playing the biggest and best gig of my life. My ears are ringing and my heart is broken. I suppose it's why people in bands go off with fan-girls all the time, to counteract the loneliness. It's ironic but I feel constantly alone on tour, yet I'm always surrounded by people.

One minute I'm in front of thousands of people, getting more adulation than any man should know what to do with, the next I'm sitting alone pining for a girl who has just told me I'm boring, moody and that I've changed irreversibly. It would seem success really isn't all it's cracked up to be. I was right all along.

What the hell is she going on about? *The Vox*? It's a kids' show. Why is she trying to do something that I'm doing? It doesn't make any sense.

I texted Tyra to see if she wanted to come over for a beer; she's on her way in a cab.

I wonder what Drusilla made of the gig. She must have liked it, surely!!

Clipper – 10th December
My old man came to see the gig with my mum. I haven't seen him since I got outed by Burt. I hate that word. Outed. It sounds like I've done something wrong. When I saw my dad after the gig

I was so scared I just burst into tears. He ran
over to me and just started hugging me. Then he
started crying too and kept saying, "I love you,
son, I don't care who you like. I just want you
to be happy!"

My mum was watching and she started crying. The
three of us talked for about an hour backstage
and all got a bit pissed, it was such a massive
relief. Although, they're not overly sure my nan
is gonna accept it as calmly.

When they left I went back into our dressing room
and was confronted by World War Three.

"Wow, your band is so awesome. The way you play that guitar is
sooooo cool," Patience or Faith said.

"Actually it's a bass," Tea replied with a dashing smile.
"You're Patience, right?"

"Faith," she replied, fluttering her eyelashes.

The twenty-one-year-old models were twin sisters. They wore
short, skintight black dresses, their hair identical: straightened
and platinum blond. Tea's plan was to keep them away from Burt
and then continue to keep them away from Burt. The deserted
venue was a good place to do that.

"I can't get over that I'm actually backstage at a RockAteers
gig. It's amazing," Patience said, gazing up at the stage as the
crew packed away the gear.

"Yeah I know, it's CRAZY. I still can't believe that guy came up to us and gave us backstage passes," Faith said.

"Yeah right, how come he just like, gave them to us?" Patience said.

Tea wasn't about to reveal that Burt had spent a good while peeping through the curtain behind the stage and picked ten girls for Ged to give passes to.

"Hey, you're a guy!" Faith said.

"I sure am," Tea replied, enchanted.

"Patience and I are thinking of getting boob jobs. What d'you reckon?" Faith said in her posh accent.

Tea coughed in surprise.

"They look pretty fine to me, ladies."

Suddenly Patience unhooked the straps of her little black dress and pulled it down over her chest.

"What do you think? Bigger, right? I can tell by the way you're staring at them you think they should be bigger."

Patience sounded in genuine distress.

"Babes, you're perfect. Look at my bee stings, they're the ones that need serious help," Faith whined, pulling her dress down so it bunched just below her ribs and exposed her entire chest.

Tea stared from breast to breast. They all looked exactly the same to him. This was genuinely the best situation he had ever found himself in.

"Girls, I'm titmatised," he said, grinning. "I think all four are the perfect size. My advice is don't touch any of them."

Both girls giggled. "Titmatised, oh, Tea, that is soooo funny."

Tea grinned along with them, glancing over his shoulder to

check the area was still Burt-free. There, standing in the wings slightly hesitantly he spotted Bex. She had obviously seen Tea, but decided not to interrupt. Tea saw her check her watch and start to move away.

"Hey, Bex!"

She spun back around.

"Sorry, girls."

Faith and Patience were pulling their dresses up. Tea placed a hand on both their bare arms.

"Listen. It was great talking to you but I've gotta jet, like, right now... Come to another show, yeah? We can continue this awesome discussion."

The twins glanced over at Bex, seemed to accept defeat and waved goodbye. Tea hurried over and strolled alongside.

"I wondered if you fancied coming with us, but you looked a bit, er, busy," Bex said, as Tea followed her out of the venue.

"They were twins," Tea told her.

"I saw that," Bex replied, with an amused smile.

They reached the wintery outside and Tea spotted Clipper in the back of a taxi. Bex climbed in and left the door open.

"Where we heading?" Tea said.

"Karaoke!" She waved for him to get in the car. "Get in."

Tea shrugged and jumped in.

"That was SUCH an abuse of power, Tea!" Bex said, as the cab moved off.

"What?! I'm totally innocent. Burt was the one that invited them backstage. I was just being polite." He flashed her a smile. "Weird thing is it keeps happening to me. Girls don't seem to be able to keep their clothes on around me?"

Clipper groaned.

"Well, Mr Twining, I can assure you I will be keeping my clothes on for the entire evening," Bex said. "Despite being very drunk already," she added with a wink.

The threesome laughed and joked all the way to Oxford Street.

"We're here," Bex said, leaping from the taxi, as Clipper fished in his pocket to pay.

They walked into a restaurant, flashed their IDs and were shown downstairs by two huge bouncers in tuxedos. At the bottom of the steep steps they arrived in a lively, dimly lit basement. The walls were lined with secluded booths. In the centre of the room was a dance floor and behind that a tiny stage with a huge screen on the back wall. On stage was a young man with skintight jeans, loafers, no socks, Michael Caine glasses and a kitchen clock round his neck. He was attempting to sing "My Way" by Frank Sinatra.

Tea and Bex took the last empty booth.

"Let's all have a cocktail, yeah?" Clipper said. "I'm buying. How about I surprise you?"

Tea and Bex nodded and Clipper went off towards the bar.

"I'm so glad he's all right," Bex said to Tea. "Did you see him with his folks?"

Tea nodded. "His old man is a proper nice fella, his mum's lovely too. It was always gonna work out OK." He looked around the bar.

"Nice place," he said. "You come here often."

Bex grinned. "Few times. You like?"

"It's cool. So you gonna tell me why you dragged me away from two of the fittest girls I've ever seen in my life?"

"You're remembering it all wrong, Tea. You dragged yourself away from two pairs of tits."

Before Tea could respond, Frank Sinatra had finished. Bex looked at the DJ and smiled. He waved her over.

"I'm up. Put my name down via text," she said, already on her feet. Before Tea could answer she was on her way to the stage.

Clipper returned to the table with a tray of ostentatious-looking cocktails and sat down. The intro to "Back to Black" by Amy Winehouse started up. Bex stood still, her head down, one hand on the microphone. As soon as she started to sing, the thirty or so people in the place fell silent. Tea felt his mouth drop open. When he glanced at Clipper he was grinning and giving little shakes of his head. After four mesmerising minutes, Bex finished and the place erupted. Clipper and Tea clapped until their hands hurt, glancing at each other and laughing in amazement.

Bex returned to the table, gave a little curtsy, hugged Clipper and sat down between him and Tea.

"When did you... I mean how did you...?" Tea couldn't find the right question.

She glanced at Clipper to her right, smiled and without warning turned and kissed Tea long and hard on the lips. Tea returned the kiss hungrily. After a few moments he pulled away and looked around nervously at Clipper.

Clipper sat staring wide-eyed, not at the two of them, but at something on the other side of the room.

"What is it?" Tea asked, over the din of a tone-deaf guy singing Tom Jones's "Delilah".

"George Graves is over there," Clipper replied, without breaking his stare.

Tea followed Clipper's gaze to a booth on the other side of the basement. Sure enough there was George, and he had a companion. Suddenly the girl George was with stared right at them, stood up and started to make her way over.

"It's bloody Sophia from Big Tone Records," Clipper hissed.

Before they could say another word, she was standing over the table. Sophia had her hair pinned up. She looked as prim as ever in a dark pencil skirt and silk blouse. She smiled down at Bex.

"I thought you were extraordinary. Really, really great," she gushed.

Bex raised an eyebrow.

"Thank you, I think your choice of men is pretty extraordinary," she replied, nodding towards George.

Sophia ignored the sarcasm and handed Bex her card.

"You're stunning, you obviously have bags of charisma and you're the best singer I've heard in a long time. Seems like you're dating a RockAteer too." She nodded towards Tea. "The possibilities are endless."

With that Sophia turned and walked back to her table. George stood up, kissed her on the lips and the pair made their way towards the exit.

"That little bastard," Clipper hissed, getting up and lurching after them. Tea clambered over Bex and hurled himself after his friend. Just before Clipper could reach George, Tea managed to grab him around the waist. He was dragged two metres before the drummer ground to a halt.

"It's NOT worth it," Tea hissed in his ear. "Imagine the papers if you smack him!"

George turned, Sophia's arm hooked into his. "You ladies having a bum party?" he sneered.

Tea let go of Clipper, skipped around him and planted a long-range haymaker on George's ear. George fell backwards, dragging Sophia down with him. In a flash, Tea turned and pushed a dumbfounded Clipper back towards their booth.

"Grab Bex and let's jet," he yelled. "Did you see the size of the bouncers upstairs?"

Bex was already on her feet. Clipper took her by the arm, pulled her up the stairs and out into the street. Tea followed behind.

"Keep going," Tea shouted. "Let's get round the corner."

They dashed up the pavement. Suddenly, as he ran, Tea burst out laughing. Bex joined in. They all ducked around a corner and stopped, doubled over, breathing hard. Clipper stood and looked back at the other two, his face full of fury.

Tea stopped laughing and put a hand on his drummer's shoulder. "Don't worry, mate. It was me who smacked him and I'm glad I did."

Clipper shook his head. "I don't give a shit about you hitting George," he said.

"What's wrong, Clip?" Bex asked softly.

Clipper looked at her sternly.

"I saw you, that's what's wrong," he hissed. "How could you do that to Egg?"

There was no trace of fun now, as Bex and Tea stared back at Clipper.

"I saw you kiss and I think it's proper snide." Clipper shook his head. "I'm going home."

He turned and walked off up the street, leaving Tea and Bex to stare at each other guiltily on the dark, Soho corner.

SONG 11 CRACKED

Tea — 11th December
Me and Bex spent all last night on the lash,
drinking tequila in this little bar in Soho. All
we did was talk and snog. The bar closed at 4 am
and I invited her to my gaff. Luckily she said
no. It was like a dream being with her. Problem
is, I think it might be followed by a proper
nightmare. I woke up this morning smiling. Even
though I know it's the wrongest thing I ever did
in my life.

I keep asking myself why I did it? It was a mix
of stuff. I was proper high on adrenalin after
the gig. Seeing her sing was a proper turn-on too.
I also think I was mental randy from seeing the
identical tits. All this Lenny-Hazel-Burt thing
has been stressing me out massively. I realise now
that I've fancied Bex for a long time.

I can't shake the feeling that I've just wrecked
my band. We play some castle in Dublin in two
days: a bloody castle! I'm hoping I've figured it
all out by the time I get to Ireland.

I can't believe I hit George. I got him real good
too. He deserved it.

Burt asked the cab driver to turn into the drive. The night before had lasted until morning. He'd fully intended to take it easy, but the gig had been too much fun and the aftershow party had presented too many temptations. The excesses were hitting him hard now. He eased himself out of the Mercedes. His hair covered most of his face and sunglasses shielded his eyes from the wintry December sun.

"It's on account, yeah?" he asked the driver.

"Yes, sir."

Burt greeted the paparazzi with an unenthusiastic wave and shuffled towards the house.

"I'm going in my front door, lads, what's interesting about that?" he muttered to himself, ignoring the barrage of questions and requests for him to turn around.

Burt entered the house and immediately sensed something was off. There was a smell he didn't recognise: dodgy aftershave. He went directly to the kitchen. As soon as he entered the room he pulled up, horrified. There, sitting at his family table, was Lenny Brown. He turned his thickset frame and grinned. He looked like a cliché of every London gangster Burt had ever seen on TV. Jet-black hair, slicked to the scalp, a sovereign on every finger, eyes close-set, a startling, turquoise colour. The blood drained from Burt's face and a cold shock swept over his entire body. Hazel greeted him as she busied herself over the stove.

"Hello, I thought it was about time I come round and introduced myself." He winked. "I'm Lenny, Hazel's dad. Come sit down. Haze just browned up some eggs and bacon for us. There's plenty."

Burt rushed out of the room, down the hall and stopped at the foot of the stairs. He bent over and took long, deep breaths.

"What's the matter?" Hazel asked worriedly from behind him.

"What's he doing here?" Burt asked.

"He's my dad. He came round to see his grandson," she replied shakily.

"OK, but you should have told me. It's a shock."

"Why? You've never even met him."

Burt turned and stared at her. "He said he'd never met me?"

"He didn't need to. I know you've never met. Why would you have?"

Burt nodded. Something about her not knowing gave him some relief. Lenny hadn't told her for a reason. Blackmailing him into marrying her wouldn't go down well and Lenny knew it. Could he use this to his advantage, somehow?

"Come on, let me introduce you."

"No no no. I was with the lads all night. I need to crash. Later. I promise."

Burt pushed past her, rushed upstairs into his room and dived under his Sanderson duvet.

He lay there, trying not to sleep, but found its lure impossible to resist.

Burt was standing on the stage of an arena, alone. Stretching out before him was the empty auditorium. He heard a high-pitched whistle and then, from every entrance streamed identical men in white coats. Each was carrying a meat cleaver. They rushed towards the barrier in front of the stage and stopped. As they came closer Burt saw their blood-spattered aprons. They continued to pour in. Within seconds, the entire floor space was filled. The men stared up at him, grim and expectant. Suddenly they thrust their cleavers in the air and began a low rumbling chant.

"We're gonna chop your balls off, we're gonna chop your balls off."

The men's faces grew more menacing and twisted, as the chant grew louder. They thrust their cleavers in the air as they recited the line, again and again. Burt was rooted to the spot, unable to run, staring down at the crowd and clutching his mic stand. Suddenly from behind him he saw shapes, then a moment later an intense pain erupted at the base of his back. He woke with a start.

It was still light outside. It took a few moments for his eyes to finally focus. There, sitting in the armchair opposite the bed, was Lenny.

"Big night?" Lenny asked casually.

"What are you doing in here?"

"Haze went for a nap. Sleep when the baby sleeps, that's the key to parenthood."

"What do you want?"

Lenny crossed his legs and looked out of the window. "I wanna know if you intend to betray our agreement. Haze hasn't had a marriage proposal yet?"

"We're living together! Isn't that enough?"

Lenny turned from the window and stared at Burt. His icy eyes danced madly, striking added fear into Burt's already terrified haze.

"No, Bertram, that is not enough. We had a deal. You marry my daughter and make my grandson legit."

Burt started to get out of the bed. Fast as a whip, Lenny flew at him, his knee landing heavily on Burt's chest. His hand closed around Burt's mouth before he could scream, the noise disappearing into Lenny's palm. His other hand was fastened around Burt's neck, and it began to squeeze.

"You gonna make good on our deal?" he hissed. "Or do I stay in this house until you do?"

Burt nodded violently, his eyes darting from side to side.

"Good boy."

Lenny slapped him lightly on the cheek, climbed off the bed and left the room.

Burt sat up and failed to stop himself from shaking. He needed Millie, but she was the last person he wanted to drag into this waking nightmare.

"I want two things from you, Burt."

Burt nodded.

"I want you to love our child and I never want you to do drugs in front of either of us."

Burt nodded.

"I'm not naive, I realise you will shag other women and you will do drugs. It's just the way things are. I just don't want drugs to come into our home. Do you understand?"

Burt nodded again.

"OK, then, well I'll consider your proposal," she said seriously.

"What do you mean, you'll consider it? You've got to marry me!"

"Oh do I?" Hazel replied, narrowing her eyes. "And why's that exactly? Because you're a big rock star, or because me and Baby Burt are desperate?"

"Of course not. Because we all love each other and the sooner we're a family the better."

"I want time to think about it."

"How much time?"

"Two months."

"That's ridiculous!"

"I want to find out if it will work between us."

"Your dad is keen we get hitched. Don't you want to make him happy?"

She nodded.

"He's very traditional, but this isn't his decision. It's mine."

Burt put his head in his hands, got up and left the room.

Burt – 17th December
Lenny threatened me in my own bed so I asked
Hazel to marry me and then the mental bitch said
she wanted to think about it. FOR TWO MONTHS!!?

We fly to Dublin today and I'm going to miss Baby
Burt massively. But I will not miss Lenny the
Bastard. I've never been so relieved in my life
as when I heard the front door slam and knew
he'd gone. I still can't believe Double B is
my kid. He is still so tiny. Sometimes I just

stare at him when he's lying in his cot in total
amazement. In some ways, the last few days have
been the best of my life. I don't love Hazel,
but I really, really love Double B. Sometimes I
think he smiles at me, but Hazel reckons it's
just wind. He doesn't cry that much. He's a great
kid. It's a pity both Baby B's grandfathers are
psychopaths. Him and Millie are the best things
on the earth. They're all I need.

Lenny keeps asking me all about the band and the
music industry. I stupidly said I'd intro him to
Jerome or Harry. Big mistake. Now he keeps asking
for their phone numbers.

Hazel loves listening to our album and goes on
about how amazing I am. Now I know where she gets
all her crazelness from.

I had a threesome with these twin models called
Patience and Faith a couple of nights ago. They
were so fit I thought my balls would explode.
After the orgy I told them if they had slightly
bigger tits they'd be my perfect woman.

I had another well scary dream. All these
butchers came after me at a gig. The strangest
thing was they were all identical, and they
weren't Lenny. They all had my dad's face.

Sir Wilson Cloom knew she was a megastar from the moment
she walked into the office. Within seconds of her being there it

became essential to sign her to his label. He'd missed out on The RockAteers. He wouldn't miss out on her too. That she sat so serenely, so seemingly unimpressed, made Wilson want her all the more. In addition she was Egg RockAteer's girlfriend, and according to the newspapers, she was the reason for Jack Skill's attempted suicide.

When Sophia had told him all about her, she had focused on her incredible voice, but honestly, Cloom knew with looks like hers she could conquer the world with an average voice. The thick jet-black hair, remarkable green eyes and the flawless skin – it was a breathtaking combination. He cocked his head and studied her face again. A mix of Jennifer Lopez, Beyoncé and Cheryl Cole, he thought, only younger.

"Tell me what you don't like about yourself?" he asked, deploying his best broadcast smile.

Bex stared at him blankly. The response fazed Cloom.

"Sophia tells me you're an amazing singer and said we should mee—"

Before Cloom could continue, Bex stood up and began to sing. Wilson sat back in his chair and watched, spellbound, as she belted out the verse and chorus of "Satellites" by The RockAteers.

Cloom had seen a million singers audition, but he had never seen anything like this. Her voice was fully formed, confident and powerful, her tone rich and silky with a bucketful of sex appeal. Cloom suddenly craved a large roast dinner, with all the trimmings.

Bex finished and calmly sat back down. Nerves weren't going to be a problem for this one, Cloom thought.

"You're tremendous!" he boomed, clapping his hands.

"Thank you," Bex replied.

Cloom controlled his excitement and tried to focus.

"So, why are you here? What do you want?"

"I want a record deal," she replied, cracking a smile for the first time since arriving.

Cloom was spellbound; he could bathe in the light of that smile all day.

"Where do I sign?" Cloom said, with a genuine chuckle.

Sophia broke into snorting laughter. Cloom raised a hand and she stopped immediately, grinning nervously at her boss.

"I want the right deal, something artist friendly. I wanna choose the songs that go on my album. I wanna choose the direction musically and stylistically I go in," Bex said.

She gave Cloom a hard stare.

"Forgive my suspicious nature, but with your talent, why has it taken this long to look for a record deal?" he asked.

"Let's just say something awakened in me after seeing the boys succeed."

"And you want me to make your dreams come true?" he said.

Bex shook her head and grimaced.

"I think I'll make my own dreams come true."

"I see, well then…" He paused to extend a hand. "Let's do it."

"Great, but there's one further thing you have to agree to or I'm out of here."

Cloom cocked his head to the side and showed her his palms.

"Tell me. I'll do anything you want if it means you sign with me."

Bex took a deep breath.

Clipper – 20th December
I've just had the best three days of my life.
Ireland, the Irish and the whacking great castles
are the only place to be. I met a boy. Not just
any boy. His name is Tomaltach. It's a stoopid
name, but he's called Tom for short. He's a
bloody Laird (Lord in Celtic) and is nineteen
(but seems older), has green eyes, pale skin, is
tall and athletic looking.

He saw us play the first night at the castle and
lives in another castle down the road. I didn't
ask him how he got backstage to talk to me, I
suppose it's because he owns the castle next
door. After the gig we got drunk and went for a
walk around the grounds. We found a secluded spot
and talked for ages. Then we kissed and it was
amazing. I am so glad my first kiss was with him.
When we said goodbye we exchanged details. It was
the best night of my life.

I'm not pissed off with Bex anymore. I can't stay
angry at her for long. I rung her and she asked
me if I was in love, because I sounded as if I
was. I told her yes and she said it was fitting
that my first love was a gay Lord. We laughed our
arses off.

I'm on the plane now and I miss Tom already. I
want him to visit over Christmas, but he says he
hasn't got the dough.

I've avoided Tea over the last few days.
(Although he's asleep next to me on the plane
with his headphones blaring. How do you manage

that, fella?) I didn't ask Bex about it when I
spoke to her on the phone. I just don't have the
space for such a head fuck at the moment. I'm
angrier at Tea than Bex. He must know that if
this got out Egg would leave the band and then
it would all be over. Egg already seems pissed
off the whole time and I have a stone in my belly
every time I see him, knowing what I do. Who
would write the songs? He does chat about Tyra a
fair bit and I know they text each other a lot.

When I get back to London, I'm going to go and
talk to Jerome about it all.

Egg - 21st December
I'm home. Thank God. I have exactly six weeks
to recover before the next tour starts. We only
have four rehearsals before we fly to Los Angeles.
That gives me a while to repair my head. I told
the band after the last Cardiff Arena show that
I didn't want to hear from them in that time.
I tried to soften the blow with an "it's not
you, it's me". It was pointless of course. Burt
immediately took offence.

According to my call count I've left fourteen
messages on Bex's answer phone. The first message
said, "I love you." By the fourth call I'd
changed direction. "If you want to split up
then you need to say it because I'm not going
to say it." By the seventh call I was all over
the place. "I can change, I will change." On my
twelfth and final call I drew a line and told her,
"OK, if you won't phone me back I'm going to make
a decision. We are officially over." I hung up and
only managed to wait five minutes before I called
her for the thirteenth time. "I didn't mean to
say we are over but I just really need to talk."

199

I called a fourteenth time but the inbox was
full. Despair. All I could think about was how
unlucky thirteen is.

I got a royalty statement from the publishing
company the other day and my projected wealth
is astounding.

✪

The A&R man put his arm round Clipper and took the selfie.

Clipper had spent almost half an hour in the plush foyer for the
impromptu meet and greet. It seemed even the music industry's
elite loved The RockAteers. Clipper could sign autographs and
put his arm around people for pictures all day long. He never got
tired. He loved it.

He glanced at the huge metallic clock behind the reception.
"Gotta jet, lovely to meet you all," he said with a wave, before
leaving the lobby and heading for the lifts.

"I heard you got delayed?" Jerome said, when he reached the
headquarters of Fictitious Records.

Clipper smiled back and the pair embraced.

"All part of The Rockateers' guaranteed service," Clipper
replied. He followed Jerome into the glass-fronted conference
room and took a seat in his usual chair. A girl Clipper didn't recognise popped her head around the door.

"Cuppa, anyone?" she asked smiling.

"Tea, please, sugar and milk," Clipper said, with a smile.

Jerome asked for coffee and she disappeared.

"New?" Clipper asked.

"We've employed two extra staff just to keep up with The RockAteers' business."

"You're kidding me?"

"I'm not! A number one album that stays there for six weeks has consequences. I got the new sales figures this morning. One million records sold."

Jerome reached over and clapped him on the shoulder. "You're officially one of the biggest breakthrough bands in the history of mankind. You've beaten everyone."

"The Beatles?"

"Ke$ha's 'Tik Tok' single sold more copies than any Beatles single. It's crazy!"

"That doesn't make any sense."

"It doesn't have to, Clipper, you've sold a million records in the UK alone. It's huge."

The new member of staff entered the room with Clipper's tea and disappeared again.

"So, you called the meet, tell me what's on your mind?" Jerome asked.

Clipper told Jerome about Bex and Tea. "I'm worried it might end the band if Egg finds out," he finished.

"Firstly, I want to say that it's cool you came to me with this," Jerome said, his usual affable smile replaced by a troubled look. "But I can't see how I can help. If I confront Tea, he'd be well within his rights to tell me to piss off and of course I can hardly confront Bex."

"But you know her dad?"

"I can't go to her dad with this. What would I say?"

"You could tell the truth, say that she's going to split the band up if she goes straight from Egg to Tea."

"Look, I understand you're worried, but I really think the best thing we can do is monitor the situation. I mean it's not like Bex is going to America with you, is it?"

Clipper took a sip of hot tea and considered this for a moment. He nodded slowly.

"Great." Jerome glanced at his watch. "Sorry to be a pain, but you were half an hour late and I've a meeting upstairs that started five minutes ago."

"No problem, one more quick thing: I saw George with Sophia, the girl that went out with Burt and works for The Cloominater. They're a couple."

Clipper noted the flash of alarm on Jerome's face.

"It seemed too much of a coincidence. So I thought I better tell you."

"Really good to know. Leave it with me," Jerome said, before shaking him by the hand and heading out of the room.

As Clipper tried to leave the building through the lobby, he saw right away that it had become even busier. He spent another hour posing for pictures and chatting.

Egg – 23rd December
I'm back at Mum and Dad's until Boxing Day. It's so calming to be here. I was going stir crazy

in my flat on my own. My dad and I watched *The 40 Year Old Virgin* last night and laughed all the way through it. Laughter is very contagious, especially when my dad laughs. I love old films. Mum has chilled out a bit more. It's like now I'm not there, she doesn't have to worry about me as much and she's relaxed. She and Dad seem happier too. She even hugged me the other day. I'm glad, I need all the hugs I can get right now.

Clipper – 24th December
Me, Mum and Dad were watching some crissy movie with Meg Ryan and Tom Hanks last night when my mum said, "Oh, don't they make a lovely couple." Then she clamped her hand over her mouth, looked at me and said. "But it could just as easily be two men finding love."

I stared at her, wondering if I should tell her it was the stupidest thing I ever heard, but then suddenly my dad started laughing and that made me crack up. "No point walking on eggshells round him," I overheard my dad tell her later.

We have a five bird roast dinner for Christmas Day tomorrow. All the trimmings. Including Yorkshire puds.

I love Christmas. I wish Tom was here too.

Tea – 25th December
My Uncle Frank is awesome, but I really wish he didn't play his Frank Sinatra records all the way through the day. Also, if he says he was named after the crooner one more time I'm going to hang myself. Mum made a proper nice dinner. I paid for the bird. She loves her new flat. She's so proud

of it. I love her so much and now I can give her
what she deserves after all these years. I think
Christmas is the business because you are forced
to make time for your mum.

Burt watched as his breath danced in wisps against the backdrop
of the vast, frozen park. The city of London was blanketed in a
Christmas hush. High Bench was silent and still.

Burt glanced at his watch; he knew he couldn't put it off any
longer. Millie and his mum would be there now, so he needed to
get back home. He hoped and prayed Lenny had other commit-
ments today, but he wasn't counting on it.

He entered the house and the smell of turkey roast filled his
nostrils, inducing happy memories. Burt checked himself in the
hallway mirror, as Millie stuck her head around the door.

"Yay! You're back!" She shook her head. "You're such a
poser!"

She ran up, hugged him and dragged him into the warm
kitchen. A quick scan of the room turned up a Lenny-free zone.
Burt smiled. The tree Hazel had spent hours decorating now had
a mountain of gifts under it.

"Presents!" Millie announced, holding her arms out with a
flourish. His mother approached. She was wearing a dark,
floral-patterned trouser suit, which Burt had seen on the cover of
Vogue the week before, and pointed, black patent heels.

"Darling," she said, performing an air kiss. Burt thought he heard the tiniest hint of warmth. "There's something for you under the tree."

Claudia waved a hand dismissively towards the pile and tucked an errant strand of platinum-blonde hair back behind her ear.

Before Burt could wonder why his mother was being remotely nice, a man entered the room from the hall. He was tall and handsome, wearing a suit. He looked around fifty.

"James, this is Martin," his mother said. The man held out a hand to Burt, smiling.

"So good to meet you," he said, in an accent Burt thought could be German.

Burt shook the hand.

"Hi, and who are you then?" He felt Millie dig him in the ribs.

"I'm your mother's friend," Martin said in a friendly tone. Tall, silver hair, expensive shoes, European and obviously loaded. His mother certainly had a type, Burt thought.

"He's all right," Millie said brightly, in a very loud whisper. Burt looked around at his mum, who was knocking back a glass of champagne.

"Anyone's better than the last guy she bought into this house," he said loudly.

"How did you meet Mum, then?" Millie asked.

The man was still smiling. "I was flying the plane she was riding on."

"Was it a private jet?" Millie demanded.

"No, it was a scheduled flight."

"How come you're not with your family, then?" Burt asked.

"I was with my daughters yesterday. In Germany the 24th is

the most important day, so I thought today I would join your mother for a short time."

"You could have brought your daughters round here." Burt grinned.

Martin laughed. "I don't think I'll be bringing my daughters to meet you, James. You are well known in my country. In Germany we call your kind *Schürzenjäger*."

Millie let out a laugh. Burt looked confused. He looked over at his mother, who gave him a curt smile, followed by a withering look.

"Come on, it's presents time," Millie said excitedly.

Burt sat on the sofa as his sister knelt by the mound of presents. She handed him two neatly wrapped gifts.

"I really hope you like them. What do you give the boy who has everything?" she said.

Burt unwrapped a *Sons of Anarchy* box set and a Jimi Hendrix T-shirt from her.

"I love them, Mills." He smiled and pointed at the pile. "The blue one and that big one are from me."

Millie was thrilled with the foam pickaxe Burt had picked up for her and shrieked when she unwrapped the MacBook Air.

Martin was cool and quite possibly, Burt speculated, responsible for his mum not acting like a total witch for the first time in years. It was impossible not to like him, and when Burt found out what *Schürzenjäger* meant in English, Burt liked him all the more. After three glasses of champagne, the third of which Burt had to get Millie to fill when Hazel wasn't looking, he was settling into the day nicely. Still no Lenny. He sat with Millie, playing Xbox and listening to his mum chat to Hazel and Martin in the kitchen. Hazel had the dinner under control and Claudia seemed to actually be enjoying herself.

Hazel checked upstairs.

"Baby Burt's still asleep," she told them. "Shall we eat?"

Then the front door slammed shut and a moment later, Lenny Brown entered the room. Burt felt the smile slip from his face.

Burt – 25th December

I am currently hiding in the bathroom upstairs.
Lenny is back in my house on Christmas bloody
Day. It was all going good 'til the bastard
arrived. Hazel, Millie, my mum, her new fella
and Lenny are all sitting round the same bloody
table, what an absolute disaster.

My mum asked Lenny what he did for a living.
Lenny said he was a debt collector and then he
said we should raise a glass to the newly engaged
couple. My eyeballs nearly fell out of their
sockets. Hazel obviously hasn't told him she
wanted to think about it.

Mum asked when the big date was and Hazel told
her it's when I get back from touring America.
She has checked my schedule and thought the
fifteenth of March might suit us. "Do you really,
Hazel?" is what I wanted to scream into her face,
but I glanced at Lenny and he made his fingers
like scissors and mouthed the words "Snip, snip."
So I just nodded, and now I'm getting married on
the fifteenth of March. I looked the day up on the

web. To see if there were any natural disasters
scheduled for that date and I found out that it
was the day Julius Caesar was stabbed and killed
by loads of his mates. If that isn't a bloody
sign then I don't know what is.

Mum and Millie were pretty excited. In fact
Hazel, Millie and Mum talked about it the whole
rest of the dinner and then started looking
on the Internet at gear I might wear on the
day. Whilst they chatted, Lenny just looked up
occasionally and gave me this horrible grin. Then
he came over, put his arm round me and said I'd
look good in a shiny cream suit, like something
Elton John would have worn at his wedding – the
one where he married a bloke. Then my mum and
Crazel actually agreed! I looked at Millie and
she was laughing so much behind her hands she was
starting to cry. For a second I nearly joined
in, but I'm not sure the laughter wouldn't have
turned into a different kind of tears.

I love Double B, but I'm not sure I can do this
anymore. The last few weeks since I came back
from tour have been awful. Lenny shows up all the
time and just sits on my sofa. Once he even wore
my Mark Jacobs slippers to watch *Countdown*. I
properly wanted to kill him then. It's like I'm
trapped in a nightmare. The problem is, I have no
idea how to get out of it.

✪

SONG 12 SHOWDOWN

Jerome stood outside the Radio One Building on Clipstone Street in the heart of London's West End. He was having a rather uncharacteristic attack of nerves. Thoughts of Sir Wilson Cloom had consumed him over the Christmas and New Year Holiday. It was a year since Jerome had told Cloom he would expose his dirty tricks if he continued in his quest to destroy The RockAteers. He wondered how much Cloom had paid George to lie. Each time he went over it, he came to the same conclusion. The Cloominater, as the band called him, could not be allowed to continue. He had to be stopped, once and for all. Jerome was about to deliver the decisive blow.

Jerome entered the building and saw The RockAteers standing in the small lobby.

"What are you doin' here?" Burt asked, with a frown.

"I've come to watch my investment being interviewed," Jerome replied jauntily. "Make sure you're getting all the right plugs in."

Egg and Tea looked at each other. Before any of them could question it further, a cool-looking girl in a cropped tartan jacket came out and presented herself.

"Hi, guys, I'm Sam, Rona Cottefer's assistant, follow me and I will show you through."

They followed her through the turnstyles, a security door and up a wide corridor. Sam turned and smiled.

"Rona is a huge fan; she came to see you at Brixton Academy. She loved it…" She paused, her smile disappearing for a moment. "…but she wasn't allowed backstage."

"We don't let anyone backstage, love," Burt said flatly.

"You let Dave Berry from Capital FM backstage," she said.

"How do you know that?" Burt replied.

"Rona and Dave are friends."

"Oh yeah!" Burt exclaimed. "I remember now. I let Dave backstage because I wanted to meet the well-fit bird he was with."

"And we've been on his show a couple of times and he's a lovely fella," Clipper added.

"Don't you fancy Rona?" Sam asked Burt with a smirk, as they passed through an open plan office full of people.

"I heard she fancies *me*," Burt said loudly, causing people to look up from behind their desks. "I certainly wouldn't kick her out of bed."

"Really," Sam said.

They passed through a door marked "Studios".

"Make yourselves at home," Sam told them. "Would you like any refreshments?"

Clipper nodded cheerily. "Tea – sugar, milk, please."

"Have you got an orange juice?" Tea asked.

"Water for me," Egg said.

"Coffee, how it comes," Jerome asked.

"A litre of café frappé, with truffle foam and chocolate shavings, please," Burt paused. "But they gotta be Green & Blacks shavings, you get me?"

"I'll see what I can do," Sam said, raising an eyebrow before departing the room.

"Can you stop being a dildo, Burt?" Tea asked. "We're at Radio One!"

Burt grinned and held his hands up. "I'm just tryna to have a laugh."

There was silence for a few moments before Clipper spoke.

"So, tell us why you're really here then?" he asked Jerome.

"I want to prove your innocence."

"I don't follow you?" Clipper replied.

"That's coz he's talking in riddles," Tea said.

"I'm ninety-nine per cent certain the Cloominater manipulated George into accusing you all of being fakes," Jerome said plainly.

"I knew it!" Clipper exclaimed.

"How the hell do you know that?" Burt asked.

Egg was looking concerned.

"What's that got to do with you coming to our radio session though?" Tea asked.

Sam came back with the drinks.

"Great," Tea said with an engaging smile, as he lifted the orange juice from the tray. "Thank you."

"You guys want to meet Rona then?" she said, after they'd taken their drinks. Jerome noted Burt's affront at being handed a non-frappé with no truffle foam or Green & Blacks chocolate shavings and hoped he would keep his mouth shut.

They were led through more corridors, past studios and offices until they were confronted by the familiar face of Rona Cottefer.

"Hi, guys, I'm Rona, so lovely you could come do the show,"

she said, shaking Clipper's hand first. She turned to Jerome and whooped. "What are you doing here, my darlin'? How lovely to see you!" They exchanged cheek kisses.

"I missed you, what can I say."

Rona gave him a searching look. Jerome smiled back, but said nothing more.

"OK, look, we're on in five, so I'll see you in the studio in a second."

She nodded politely at her assistant.

"Sam will look after you."

"When the green light comes on we'll go inside. If you could pair up, we only have three microphones. We have plenty of headphones though," Sam informed the group.

Jerome watched through the thick glass as Rona chatted away and introduced "Golden". The song reached the final chorus and they were being ushered inside. He hung back deliberately so he wouldn't have to share a microphone, took a deep breath and entered the studio. The band stood in pairs around a wide circular table, foam microphones on stalks facing them. Jerome made his way over to the remaining mic, picked up the headphones and slipped them over his ears. The song finished. Rona, who was sitting opposite, nudged a fader and began to talk.

"That was 'Golden', and as if by magic we have the guys behind that song right here in the studio. Hello, RockAteers, how the devil are you?" she said enthusiastically.

There was a ripple of greetings.

"Great to have you with us," she said. "It's been an amazing year for you, number one single, fastest-selling album and wall-to-wall

212

sold-out shows across Europe. What's been the highlight?"

"Being here with you, Rona," Burt said casually. "And of course all the girls."

"Seriously, what's really stood out?"

"We did a couple of gigs in Dublin, in this castle, it was amazing," Clipper said brightly.

"You liked those gigs for a totally different reason though, Clip," Burt said.

Clipper blushed.

"Do tell? I'm sure the Radio One listeners would love to get the inside track."

"He's talking bollocks, Rona," Tea intervened.

Rona coughed. "I think what he meant to say was baloney, listeners."

She paused to give Tea a disapproving look.

"And I see you've brought your talismanic label boss Jerome Clincher with you. To what do we owe the pleasure?"

"He gate-crashed, Rona!" Burt said, with a grin.

"Thanks for that, Jack, I love you too," Jerome said. "Hi, Rona, I did come for a specific reason."

He paused.

"I sense an exclusive?" Rona smiled.

"Well, yes, I suppose it is."

Jerome took a deep breath, he knew it was now or never.

"I wanted to end the ridiculous rumours circling in the press that The RockAteers don't write their own songs."

"I don't think we need to do that live on air do we, Jerome?" Egg said nervously, covering the microphone with a hand.

Jerome continued with authority.

"I just want to set the record straight and give the public a little more perspective than they're currently offered in the papers," he told Rona. "From the start of their career, The RockAteers have been dogged by a very powerful enemy and it's this individual who has engineered these ludicrous claims."

"Can you tell us who this person is?" the presenter asked cautiously. "Do you have proof?"

"I have indisputable evidence of his dealings. He knows who he is and I want to publicly challenge him to a discussion live on national television. I've already spoken to *Good Morning Britain* and they've agreed to cover it. So if he accepts, Sir Wilson Cloom and I will come face to face in that arena and people can determine who the real fake is."

Jerome scanned the studio and saw the flabbergasted faces. Had he just made the boldest and most decisive move of his entire career or taken the worst decision of his life?

"OK, erm, I'm not sure I know how to follow that," Rona said. "So I'm going to play a song and we'll continue speaking with the band when we come back."

The opening bars to "Satellites" struck up and Rona turned to Jerome. "Thanks for the exclusive, darlin', but you could have mentioned you were going to do that," she said with a smile.

"I'm sorry, you might've stopped me."

"You're always nagging me about media attention," Burt said. "And then you go and do that!"

"For once I agree with Burt," Egg said, standing up. "I really can't believe you just did that without consulting us."

He tore off his headphones, threw them on the table and stormed out of the studio.

"Who's Burt?" Rona asked.

Harry stared at The RockAteers' Twitter feed in dismay. He read it back again. Just in case.

@TheRockAteers Our manager said to use Twitter more so here I am. Our label boss "The Clinch" goes up against "Cloominater" next week. #punchupliveonair. Ja

@TheRockAteers You only get a few words on this ball ache of a thing. I am not Ja, I am Jack Skill. Follow me NOW! U snivelling cum dogs.

Maybe digital marketing wasn't meant to be part of the band's repertoire? After the tour blog debacle Harry had asked himself many times if it was a good idea to ask the band to go on line and "socially network". The fans craved contact with the artist so he'd decided, against his better judgement, to give it another go. He ran the line "Follow me you snivelling cum dogs" over in his head a few more times. What was a "cum dog" exactly?

The simple fact was that since the comment went up, the hit

rate on the Twitter account had surged. @TheRockAteers were top of the worldwide trending list for the day and had gained sixty thousand new followers in an hour. Was Harry out of touch? Is that what the kids wanted, to be called "cum dogs"? He decided to give up trying to work out what it all meant and started to reminisce about his time as a tea boy for a big music management firm in the late 90s/early 2000s. No one had heard of Twitter or Facebook. Back then, mobiles were as big as bricks, CDs were bought in their millions and major labels still made bucketloads of money. Harry understood the new climate of course, it was part of his job to keep abreast of innovative marketing tools and the latest music-related applications or gadgets. He just longed for an artist to come along with an air of mystery. He had resisted constant suggestions from colleagues to get a Twitter account himself. What would he write?

@Harry_Branch I just had a bath. It was just a little bit too hot!

Or

@Harry_Branch I had to placate one of my overpaid, pampered artists today because they're flying first class instead of private jet. What a snivelling cum dog!

How Harry had survived this long as Jack Skill's manager was beyond him. He'd rung him that morning to find out if everything was OK, explained the set-up for the trip over to the USA and asked if he might put a personal message on Twitter. That's when the now all too familiar "Burt rage" ensued.

"We've been at number one longer than Adele and you book us on a poxy normal flight? Where's the perks, Harry? Where's the private jet? Things really can't go on like this. You will find yourself jobless if you don't buck your ideas up."

Harry so badly wanted to answer with: You've been famous for five minutes. Instead, he assured Burt of a pleasurable flight and managed to get off the phone. He contemplated resigning as the band's manager on a daily basis, but he stayed because he genuinely believed The RockAteers could go on to become a truly important band. He was a fan. So he took deep breaths and convinced himself that things would get better.

Harry's desk phone rang.

"Jack Skill's father is on the line and he wants to discuss something urgent with you," his PA informed him.

"Put him through, Harriet."

The phone clicked.

"Hi, it's Harry Branch, what can I do for you?"

"Lenny Brown 'ere," came a growling East End voice. "I will come right to the point, Mr Branch." He paused. "I've got a hundred K in cash sitting here for ya."

"Erm, OK. Sorry, I don't follow?"

"I'm buying a slice of The RockAteers' action." Lenny paused. "We'd be partners."

Harry was silent for a few moments.

"Sorry, my PA said you were Jack's father?"

"In-law."

"Jack's not married."

"He will be in a few weeks, to my daughter."

"Right, OK. Well anyway, look, I'm sorry but I think you have the wrong end of the stick. I don't require a partner. We're financially secure and we simply don't have a slice of the action to give away."

"No, I think it's you that's got the wrong end of the stick, Mr Branch. I'm not asking. If you don't cut me in then I will be forced to stop Burt undertaking any further activities."

"Sorry, are you blackmailing me?" Harry tried to keep his voice steady, but alarm bells were ringing.

"No, if I was blackmailing you, I'd be asking *you* for a hundred grand. I'm an investor looking to invest. All I ask for in return is a tiny ten per cent."

"Look. Thank you so much for the call but I really can't help you."

"You can help me, Mr Branch, and you will help."

"OK, I'm hanging up now, I wish you all the best and am very sorry I can't help."

"Look me up, Mr Branch. Ask around, I think you'll soon change your tune." Lenny laughed suddenly, a low, cruel chuckle that chilled Harry to the bone. "Change your tune, see. I made a funny!"

The phone went dead.

Harry sat silently for a long time. He didn't have to look Lenny up, he knew exactly who he was. Maybe it really was time to sever all ties to The RockAteers?

Tea - 9th January

Harry just belled me up. Lenny phoned him and threatened him. He wants a cut of his management firm. WTF? He sounded proper shaken up. I got off the phone and belled my uncle.

Fuck knows why but he was on the south coast, somewhere called Bognor. He told me not to talk on the phone and said he will call me when he gets back tomorrow morning. Sometimes I wonder if he's not some type of cockney spy.

Egg - 10th January

I haven't answered any of Jerome's calls for almost a week. I haven't answered anyone's calls. People have no idea how strongly I feel about not being a pantomime act. What the hell was he thinking? Every tabloid in the land has splashed the story.

They are calling the event "Clinch Vs. Cloominator". Harry left me a message saying and I quote, "Sales have gone through the roof again because of this exposure." I wanted to jump off a bridge. I just want my life back. When are this lot going to understand that it's not just about the sales? It's about longevity and integrity.

Added to the latest shit storm, Burt has gone Twitter crazy. The same man that rang Sainsbury's and complained that the frozen pizza he bought had no topping, only to turn it over thirty minutes later and discover that he was looking at the pizza the wrong way up, is in charge of our Twitter account. The strangest and most depressing thing about his tweets is the fans go mad for them. He posted a semi-nude selfie posing in the mirror and it had twelve thousand retweets in an hour. I despair.

I still haven't heard from Bex. I had to delete
her number so I wouldn't phone her anymore.
Then I had to delete all her texts because I was
so tempted to reinstate her number. In the end
I ended up deleting everything from my phone,
pictures and all. Then I deleted my email account
so I wouldn't be tempted to email her. Bollocks
to her, if she doesn't even have the common
decency to talk to me and sort this out.

The only good news is Drusilla Prior actually
wrote us a live review. She gave us 6/10. My
favourite quote – "The RockAteers live show is
better than staying in and watching *EastEnders*.
To my utter surprise I half enjoyed myself."

I wrote a song called "Pantomime". I would prefer
to be thought of as a fake than a pantomime… Hang
on, my phone is going. It's Bex!

They walked up the slope towards High Bench side by side. Bex
felt compelled to take Tea's hand but resisted and instead let her
fingers brush lightly against his, occasionally nudging him with
her shoulder as they walked.

Being with Tea was a revelation. He really listened to what
she said, like Egg used to. He asked her questions and genuinely
wanted to know the answer. He didn't complain about anything.
He was handsome, gentle and quietly intelligent. He also turned
her on like no other boy ever had. The fact that it was so horribly

complicated was always in her thoughts.

"You know I swear this hill gets steeper every time," Tea said, breathlessly.

Bex laughed. "Old man!"

Tea scowled at her. "What you chatting about? I'm in my prime."

"Nineteen is nearly twenty. That's old," Bex replied with a grin, shifting her weight and lightly barging him so he missed a step.

"Age is perception and anyway, I only just turned nineteen," Tea flirted back.

They reached High Bench and sat down next to one another. Bex stared at him, smiled and shuffled up the seat so they were touching. Tea stared back at her, his dark hazel eyes and coffee-coloured skin seeming to glow against the background of the frosty park. She leaned in and kissed his full lips.

They remained close, their cheeks touching as they gazed out at the wintery view.

Bex took a deep breath.

"I'm going to sign with Big Tone Records," she said nervously.

Tea pulled away and stared at her.

"You gonna do what?"

"The Cloominator loves my voice and offered me a deal."

"But, but, he's like our number-one enemy. He's trying to stitch us up again. You know that!"

She shook her head.

"That won't happen."

"But you don't have any songs?"

"I have a good voice. The rest will be provided."

Bex reached over and took his hand. Tea pulled away.

"This is proper weird, Bex. Don't you see that?"

He stood up and shook his head.

"I don't just mean you signing for Cloom, I mean us. If we don't stop this we will always regret it, and it will probably be the end of my band."

Bex watched as he walked away.

"I told Egg yesterday I wanted to split up for good."

Tea continued on down the hill.

"I want to be with YOU," she shouted after him.

Tea didn't look back.

SONG 13 SHOTGUN BLOGGER

Tea - 12th January
Clipper came round my new gaff this afternoon.
The truths came flying out of us both. I told him
about Bex splitting up with Egg and he sat in my
wicked new leather armchair and looked all doom
and gloom. I also told him about Bex wanting to
sign with The Cloominater, but he already knew
that and said that she was an amazing singer and
she had to follow her own path.

Once that was done, Clip told me he's invited his
Irish "friend" over and asked me if I thought he
should sleep with him.

It kind of hit me like a brick in the face. We've
never talked about his gayness before, so it was a
shock. I just couldn't think about this posh lad
clambering all over my mate! So I told him to do
what he liked and it wasn't any of my business.

I looked up and he was storming out in a huff. I
felt bad about it, but I'm not exactly sure what
I said wrong. I've texted and rung him all day. I
will keep trying.

Been thinking about Bex all the time since I
left her up on High Bench. I think I might be
falling hard.

★

Burt swam through the crowd of photographers on the corner of
Bethnal Green Road and entered the members' bar.

"I'm Jack Skill, I'm not a member but I'm getting hounded.
Please will you shelter me from those bastards outside?" he told
the pretty receptionist.

She smiled. "I'm a big fan, Mr Skill. Can I take your coat?"

Burt looked down at the ostentatious, fake polar bear coat,
looked up again and shook his head.

"This coat needs to be seen, it cost me mucho dinero and
anyway, I'm still freezing."

The girl nodded and showed him inside.

Burt strode into the lounge and stood for a moment to take the
place in: wood, glass and media folk. It wasn't his taste but it
smelled of money. A waiter immediately approached him.

"Can I get you anything, sir."

"You have a pool table in the place, yeah?"

"Second floor, sir, can I get you a drink sent up?"

"Sex on the Beach."

Unfazed, the waiter nodded and moved away.

As Burt made his way through the lounge he spotted someone he recognised, sitting alone in a corner tapping away on his
laptop. Burt went over.

"Sorry to interrupt, but I'm a big fan. You wanna shoot some
pool? I mean billiards?" Burt said grinning down at Jet O'Lared,
Hollywood actor and front man in the band Capote.

The slight, finely featured man fumbled for a response, his

eyes darting around as if searching for help.

"Oh, hey dude, er…"

"I'm Jack Skill," Burt said.

"Have we met? I'm sorry, I just have no idea who you are," Jet said.

Burt scowled. "No, we haven't met, but I'm the lead singer of The RockAteers. We're massive over here and I'm asking you, my American cousin, if you would like a game of billiards. No need to get all dickish about it!"

Jet smiled broadly, revealing two perfect rows of American teeth, and held out a hand.

"Man, I'm so sorry. You walked up in that insane coat and I thought you were a crackhead. Course I know The RockAteers. Wow, my manager played me 'Satellites'. What a song!"

Burt stared down at his coat.

"This coat isn't insane, it's fake polar bear."

"If you say so, man," Jet said, getting up. "Let's play some goddamn pool."

Burt nodded and the pair started towards the stairs.

"You just gonna leave your laptop sitting there?" Burt asked, as they made their way up the stairs.

"We come to these places to feel safe, right? It's a nice feeling to leave your shit somewhere and feel pretty sure it's gonna be there when you get back. Besides, in the unlikely event it is stolen I have everything backed up and I have the money to buy a new one."

"You wanna bump before we play?" Burt asked, as they walked past the toilets.

"No thanks, dude, I gave that shit up a long time ago."

"Why?"

"Playing junkies in two movies required me to do my research. Spending time with addicts convinces a man to stay clean."

Burt shrugged.

The pair arrived in the pool room. Rich velvet drapes adorned the windows and plush sofas hugged the walls. In the centre of the room was an ornate pool table. Two tall, beautiful, exquisitely dressed women were already playing, a blonde and a brunette. This was one fantastic club, Burt thought. It was the kind of club James Bond would hang out in.

"You boys want a game?" asked the blonde. She was wearing skintight leather trousers and killer red heels, her hair a peroxide mane.

"Jesus bloody Christ! You're Catalina bloody Summers," Burt cried, gazing at her famous figure.

"I am. And you are Jack bloody Skill," she winked, seductively.

"I've been perving at pictures of you since I was a kid," he gushed.

"Hey, I'm Jet, don't mind him," the American said, stepping forward. "The polar bear he's wearing froze his manners."

The foursome introduced themselves. Catalina's friend, Bryce, turned out to be her stylist and best friend.

"Doubles?" Burt suggested, stepping towards Catalina and grabbing her hand. "You and me against Jet and Bryce, yeah?"

Jet smiled at Bryce and nodded. "We can be team 'awesome name' right?"

They began to play and it was obvious right away the girls were no slouches.

"You know, Jack, I came to see you at Brixton Academy," Catalina said, as she lined up her shot.

"Cool!" he said marvelling at her toned figure as she leant over the table.

"Yeah, you didn't let anyone backstage to say hi."

She smashed the white ball and potted a red.

"Oh, yes, sorry. We didn't let anyone back on that one."

"You let Dave Berry back?" she said, lining up her second shot.

Burt rolled his eyes.

"Oh right, really, I heard a rumour he was backstage, no idea how he got there though."

"You know I love your record, right? I play it all the time."

"You do?"

"Yes. I do. We have so much in common, you like pool, I like pool."

She turned and winked at him before potting another red.

"You like my band, I like my band," Burt flirted back. "We should get married!"

"I read in the paper you were doing that already? In March?" Bryce interjected.

Burt – 14th January
Catalina Summers in the flesh is overwhelming. #herbodyisarocketshipiwanttorideon I realise she's a supermodel, but she was in such good nick, for someone old, I mean. Thirty-five and she looks like she's eighteen. Well, maybe not. I think I was a bit starstruck.

Anyway, one thing led to another and all of a
sudden we ended up back at her place at
5 o'clock. What a gaff! Primrose Hill is
boomtown. Sod Blackheath, I'm buying a place on
the hill. She's a wildcat in the sack. After
finding out that my marriage plans are all over
the papers I needed it.

When I got home this afternoon who greeted me at
the door? Lenny with an iron fist in my eye. I'm
going on tour in a week and I've got a black eye
the size of a golf ball hanging off my face. He
didn't even say anything before he hit me either,
he just smashed me with his big cabbage fist. I,
of course, go down like a sack of shit and while
I'm on the floor he throws a newspaper at me. I
read the headline "Jack the Rat's at it again"
and there I am, all large as life coming out
of Shoreditch House, late afternoon, arm in arm
with Miss Summers. I read the opening paragraph,
just to check how bad the damage actually is. I
discover pretty early on it's pretty bad.

"Catalina Summers enjoyed a wild sex romp with
rock 'n' roll love rat Jack Skill last night.
Introduced by actor/singer Jet O'Lared, the
pair partied at well-known celebrity hang-out
Shoreditch House. They consumed multiple bottles
of champagne before heading back to Cat's North
London pad. Catalina, old enough to be his
mother, refused to comment on what went on behind
closed doors. If past evidence is anything to go
by however, the model, famed for her appetite for
teenage rock stars…"

When Lenny told me that Hazel had seen it and
cried, I did feel pretty bad. Then he said that
next time I wouldn't just get away with a slap,

he would insert a wine bottle up my rectum. I
believe the mental bastard too.

When I saw Hazel, I did some big style
apologising. I promised never to do it again.
Weird thing was Hazel didn't actually seem that
arsed. She was more worried about my swollen eye
and went and got me an ice pack, cooked me dinner
and gave me a head message. #cakeandeatit

Catalina wants to see me again. I still can't
figure how to wriggle out of getting married. I
absolutely need to keep hold of my knackers.
People can't get enough of them.

The café in Elephant and Castle was packed. Tea looked across
the table at his uncle and a surge of pride, respect and warmth
welled up inside him. When his father had left him and his
mother alone and penniless, Frank had been there. When Tea had
told him he wanted to make his life in music, instead of advising
him against it, or laughing at him, he had supported him whole-
heartedly. Now, after explaining Lenny was trying to blackmail
Harry, he stared back with a level, unruffled gaze. Tea breathed a
sigh of relief. Uncle Frank was a man to be relied on.

"Go to America and when you get back it will be taken care of,
don't think about it no more," Frank said calmly. "Just make sure
those septic tanks love yah."

"What are you going to do?" Tea asked.

Frank lit a cigarette with his bandaged hand and took a deep lug.

"That's for me to know, boy."

Burt — 16th January

I was always the most popular kid at school. The LBC was the gang everyone wanted to be in and I was the leader. I suppose it was a foregone conclusion I'd be famous. I used to watch interviews with people who were being hounded by the paparazzi and think, "Stop complaining." Now I realise having ten grown men outside your house all day, pointing lenses at you every time you leave, is pretty shit.

Everyone isn't best pleased with me about the whole "being in the papers" thing. Again. Harry called me up to ask me loads of weird questions about Lenny, told me he was worried about my consumption of drink and drugs and said that I needed to watch my every move. Getting snapped coming outside a members' bar with a famous socialite/ligger/model isn't clever.

I can't stop thinking about my night with Catalina. We proper talked a lot. I told her all about Double B, we talked about her daughter, who is nearly seventeen, which freaked me the hell out. Apparently she really fancies me. I can't stop thinking about that either.

Burt hurtled into the kitchen and skidded to a sock-wearing halt. How many times would he be confronted with Lenny in his own house? He'd needed an urgent food fix from the fridge but he didn't feel hungry anymore. It was unbearable. Every time he turned a corner, Lenny was there. He stayed over, he watched television in the lounge, he ate whatever he wanted from Burt's fridge.

"Come in, boy, I wanna talk to you," Lenny said, without turning.

"Can't, gotta get going. I'm late for rehearsal; we leave for America in a week."

Lenny jerked his head around and stared at Burt.

"Sit down or I'll make yah."

Burt hung his head, shuffled over to the table and took a seat.

"I wanna chat business," Lenny stated, crossing his arms. "I'm gonna be a shareholder in your band. I need your support on that, after all, we're family now."

Burt sat in the chair and shook his head with incomprehension.

"I don't understand, how are you involved in my band?"

"I had a chat with Harry. We're gonna partner up on the management side of things. Ten per cent each."

He pointed at his future son-in-law and narrowed his eyes.

"You're gonna rubber-stamp it. Make sure it all goes smooth."

Burt stared at him and slowly shook his head.

"I can't do that."

Lenny flashed his palm and cuffed Burt hard around the ear.

"You can and you will. You druggy prick!"

Burt put a hand to his bludgeoned ear and stared at the floor.

"How do you even know I do drugs?"

"I'm the biggest wholesaler in South London and I supply your dealer. When you gonna get it? I take a special interest in you, Burt Windsor."

He paused, reached over and pinched Burt's chin roughly, forcing him to look up.

"For example, I know your sister lives in dorm number seven in that posh school of hers."

Burt yanked his head away and leapt at Lenny. The gangster was too quick, caught Burt by the throat and squeezed hard. With his other hand, he took him by the belt and flung him across the dining table, sending him skidding over the surface and crashing on to the stone tiled floor. Lenny walked casually over to where Burt lay prostrate, knelt on his chest, took him by the throat again and lowered his face so their noses were touching. The pressure on his windpipe and diaphragm combined with Lenny's dog breath forced Burt to gag.

"You make sure the deal with Harry goes through, boy," Lenny hissed, spraying Burt's face. "Or I'm personally going up to Scotland to deal with your little sister."

"What are you doing?" a voice shrieked.

They turned to see Hazel, framed by the kitchen door, rooted to the spot, Double B in her arms.

Burt – 17th January
I'm proper scared now. I can't go on like this.
It's not funny anymore. Millie never hurt anyone.

I can't sleep. I don't know what to do. I think I have to give in. I texted Millie, asking what the number of her dorm is. It is seven!!! How does Lenny know that?

If only Hazel had overheard what her dad said to me. When I told her she didn't believe me. Five minutes later I was begging her not to tell her dad I accused him.

Every way I look at this, there is only one solution. Lenny becomes our manager.

Clipper – 19th January
What a pucker weekend! I have just waved Tom off from the airport. I wasn't definitely sure if I was in love with him when we were in Ireland, but I'm sure now. He sent me a text from the plane saying thanks for the best weekend of his life and that he will pay for everything next time.

I am going to phone Tea tonight. I overreacted. I just thought he was being judgemental.

It's Jerome and The Cloominater's showdown tomorrow; it's been proper hyped by the papers.

I will be in LA soon soaking up the sun. Tom told me he's been there and it's well zing. I wish he was coming with us but I'm not sure what the other guys would say – after all, we do have a ban on girlfriends. I am pretty sure that stretches to boyfriends too.

The showdown had bumped news of war, politics and natural disaster off the front pages. Column inches had turned into column miles. Every fact, every fiction and every detail had been unearthed, scrutinised and written about the contenders. The face-off dubbed "Clinch Vs. Cloominator" had trended world-wide on Twitter. The story had become a monster and Jerome Clincher its Frankenstein.

Jerome stared into the mirror as make-up was applied to his nose and cheeks.

"To stop shine," the make-up woman said gently.

Jerome nodded.

Why had Sir Wilson Cloom agreed to the showdown quite so readily? If he knew something Jerome didn't, this could turn into a nightmare, possibly even career suicide. The fact remained: Jerome did not have proof of George and Sophia's link to Cloom, and that left him extremely exposed. The RockAteers had given him the nickname, Cloominater, for a reason. Like the cyborg in *Terminator*, Wilson was ruthless, relentless and just about unstoppable. In about five minutes Jerome would face him and find out, once and for all, if he had tested the music mogul one too many times.

A familiar face peered around the dressing-room door.

Jerome returned the smile with a cheerfulness he did not feel.

"Hi, I'm Ben Kelly," the TV host said.

"Mr Kelly, hello to you!"

"You all set?" Ben said. "It's certainly been hyped enough, we're expecting our highest viewing figures in years."

Jerome's eyes widened. "Super."

Ben nodded and disappeared. A man with a clipboard appeared in his place.

"Ready, Mr Clincher?"

Jerome nodded and made his way slowly out of the dressing room. They passed through the heavy door marked "Studio". Waiting on the sofa opposite Ben Kelly and his co-host Rachael McSwiggan was Wilson Cloom: hair an unnatural shade of brown, his face showing the unmistakable signs of a surgeon's touch. He wore the usual faded jeans and cream cashmere jumper. He looked relaxed, too relaxed.

"We are just in a commercial break," the producer told Jerome.

Jerome stepped over wires, negotiated the cameras and made it to the sofa. Cloom did not acknowledge him.

"Hi, I'm Rachael, how are you?" the bubbly presenter said, holding out her hand.

Jerome took it, smiled and took his place on the unexpectedly uncomfortable sofa, next to his arch-enemy.

"Nothing below the belt, let's make this a clean fight," Ben said brightly.

Cloom scoffed. Jerome managed a thin smile, whilst a man attached a tiny microphone to his collar. He slipped his hand into his jacket pocket and touched his iPhone. If he was going to win this showdown, whatever Cloom might throw at him, it was the incriminating audio evidence stored literally within his grasp. The recording, now an MP3 file on his phone, could see him emerge triumphant. The floor manager counted down.

"Welcome back, so the one you've all been waiting for, the main event, a story that hasn't been out of the papers since Jerome

Clincher, the man behind a host of successful music artists, challenged Sir Wilson Cloom to a public showdown. Gentlemen, hello."

The cameras were on them. Jerome felt his unease growing by the second.

"So if I can come to you first, Jerome. You have accused Sir Wilson of manipulating a gentleman called George Graves into claiming he wrote all the songs for one of your acts, The RockAteers. Is that correct?"

"It is."

"Do you have proof?"

"Well … I have proof of a sort … yes."

"OK, would you like to share that with us?"

Jerome swallowed.

"I'd prefer to ask Wilson if he'd like to confess first?"

"Sir Wilson?" Ben asked, the camera switching to a close-up of the music mogul.

Cloom spoke calmly in response, as Jerome eyed him suspiciously.

"Benjamin, I would like to publicly say that since I was so uncouthly accused on national radio by this man," Cloom jabbed his index finger towards Jerome, "I have looked into this matter very seriously."

Jerome watched as Sir Wilson's face transformed from indignity to sorrow.

"Please go on," Ben said.

"I regret to inform the watching public that Jerome is absolutely right. The RockAteers have been the victim of a cruel fraud."

Cloom paused to maximise impact. Jerome gritted his teeth.

"I questioned my employees extensively and discovered that one of my junior A&R girls, I won't publicly humiliate her by saying her name, has been carrying on with Mr George Graves for some months now. I can now reveal the pair plotted this outrageous scam completely of their own accord and that I am not implicated in any way."

Jerome suddenly realised, in all the scenarios he had played out in his mind, he hadn't considered this outcome. He glared at Sir Wilson in enraged bewilderment. He wanted to say something, but was so blind-sided by Cloom's confession, he felt numb. What could have caused Cloom to back down so completely and feed his bright, loyal and talented A&R girl to the wolves?

"What do you think was the motivation behind the swindle?" Ben asked Cloom.

Jerome tried to focus.

"It seems the guilty parties have been spurned by The RockAteers in one way or another."

Cloom paused and glanced at Jerome.

"I discovered my employee had an affair with Jack Skill last year, and as we already know George Graves was a close school friend. Both claim to have been dropped by Jack when the band started to become big. They obviously took it to heart. Revenge is a powerful motive."

"Jerome, do you want to comment on what Sir Cloom has just revealed?" Rachael McSwiggan asked.

Cloom wasn't finished.

"Before Jerome answers that, Rachael, I agreed to come on the show today because I wanted to say publicly that I am sorry. I have terminated or should I say Cloominated the employee's contract."

Wilson turned to camera, winked and flashed a toothy white grin.

"I have also informed the newspaper that broke the story."

"How did the newspaper respond?" Ben asked.

"They've handed the matter over to their legal team. I can only assume both George Graves and my ex-employee are in for an extremely bumpy ride over the next few months."

Sir Cloom turned to Jerome, gave him a sincere smile and offered his hand.

"The newspaper has said they will print a full retraction and apology in tomorrow's early addition. I assure you I had nothing to do with this stink, but I must accept responsibility for my former employee. Can you accept my apology, Jerome?"

Jerome ignored the hand. He didn't have proof that Cloom was involved in the George Graves affair, but in his pocket, he did have evidence Cloom had tried to ruin The RockAteers a year before. Doubt weighed heavy, was the tape recording enough?

"Much has been made of your comment on Radio One. You said a year ago before you signed The RockAteers that Sir Wilson did something untoward?"

Jerome was startled by the question. Was Ben Kelly a mind-reader? He fiddled with the iPhone in his pocket again. Wilson had connived to destroy a tour Jerome had set up with The Desert Kings and he had the recorded proof, but now it somehow felt flimsy and inconsequential. It could be argued Sir Wilson was merely being a strong-willed businessman. Finally, Jerome looked up and faced Cloom.

"In light of the admittance of responsibility and the apology I am prepared to accept and move past all this," Jerome said, withdrawing his hand from his jacket pocket.

"So you don't have proof that Sir Wilson was involved in anything untoward a year ago?" Ben pressed.

"I'm just pleased my band, The RockAteers, have at last been cleared of these accusations and I can go back to being part of a project I am immensely proud of."

Jerome stared into the middle distance. He heard Ben Kelly wrap up and throw to the news. Without looking up, he pulled the microphone from his chest, got up and left the studio. He knew Sir Wilson Cloom would come at him again and that the war was far from over. He made it outside and took a long deep breath of fresh air. Next time he would be better prepared.

Egg - 19th January (Blog on The RockAteers Website) Part 1
Dear Everyone,

I wanted to respond to everything that has been going on recently. I am asked so often to talk about the soap opera that surrounds this band and I always decline because I feel we should be judged on the music we produce not the circus that surrounds and enslaves us. Now I've been vindicated and validated as the real songwriter in The RockAteers I thought I might say a few words.

It might come as a surprise, but what we the band tell you, the listener, is almost always what you want to hear. The truth can be very different. "We went on tour and the crowd were amazing." "We got a number one record, thanks to everyone who bought it."

Basically, it's all fake! People like Sir Wilson Cloom manipulate the public. Here's how it really works: we make a record and our label and sales team promote the hell out of it. We are the product and have no say in how we are sold.

Our album review in *Sound City* was bogus. Our label deliberately sent it to a reviewer who was already sympathetic to the band.

Artists are afraid of speaking out for fear of career damage. So, where is the next evangelical self-righteous rock 'n' roll star gonna come from? There are loads of musicians that are obviously sharp enough but they all seem reluctant to climb up on the soapbox. I don't blame them. The press in this country would flay their flesh and bonfire their bones. People want their family to be comfortable; they want five stars in Q magazine and a Grammy award. Ex-punks selling cheese!?

Don't suggest my idiotic singer, Jack Skill, will speak out. I can guarantee he doesn't agree with a word of any of this. Society applauds greed and celebrity in all its horrible facelessness. We reward ruthless tyranny and until we tear down the corrupt system people will continue to sell their own grandmother for a shot at the capitalist dream.

I asked my lead singer why he didn't get nervous before going on stage. He told me he thinks about how massive the universe is and how there are billions of stars and how he is just a tiny spec on the earth and so this music shit really doesn't matter all that much.

If this is what stops Jack Skill feeling nervous then Hope remains. If we can somehow instil the ethos that we don't all have to follow trends like lemmings, that there are bigger things at stake, we just might have a chance.

Edward "Egg" Poacher. Lead Guitarist with The RockAteers.

Bex left the second meeting with Wilson Cloom and her lawyer on cloud nine. As she walked alone down the corridors of Big Tone Records she allowed herself a rare moment of pure elation. Is this what it felt like to win the lottery? she thought. Cloom had agreed to a £500,000 advance. Suddenly Bex couldn't contain the excitement and skipped high, punching the air.

She landed, the joy vanishing as she remembered her situation. She had spoken to Tea on the phone that morning. He seemed preoccupied with something, but she could tell he was pleased to hear from her. She told him she understood why he was so confused about it all, because she was too.

As she came out of the building and on to the street she was completely consumed with thoughts of Egg and Tea and failed to hear her name being called. She felt a tug on her sleeve and turned to face a girl of around twenty, with red hair cut into a blunt bob and a pretty smile. She was dressed like a punk and she looked cool.

"I'm so sorry to bother you, but you're Egg's friend, right?" said the girl. "I'm Tyra, I'm his friend. I work at his label."

"Right," Bex said suspiciously. The girl wore denim hot pants and fishnets with a tight gingham shirt: a vintage ensemble. She really was unusually pretty.

"Look, I just wanted a few seconds of your time?"

Bex shrugged.

"What can I do for you?"

"Thing is, he's really pining for you and I, well I've been picking up the pieces for a while now."

Bex frowned and narrowed her eyes. Was this girl seriously doing this?

"What do you want me to do about it?" Bex said. "Me and Egg split up."

"Yeah I know, that's why he's so cut up."

Bex kissed her teeth. "You know you're partly to blame for me dumping him?"

Tyra blushed and looked at her shoes. "I didn't know you knew about that. Egg doesn't know that you know."

"I've known about it for a month."

Bex moved to walk on, then turned back.

"Look, I know you didn't do anything and I'm sure you're really nice." Her face softened. "He's all yours. You'd make a nice couple. I don't want him anymore."

Tyra looked confused.

"But I don't…"

Bex turned and headed for the Tube.

Egg – 20th January (Blog on The RockAteers Website) Part 2
Dear Everyone,

Thank you ever so much for your many responses to my blog. Huge appreciation especially to John and Randy from Liverpool who said that I was a pretentious fuckwit and that I was using words no one understands for absolutely no reason apart from to hide the fact that I was actually saying absolutely nothing. I wasn't deliberately trying to "be a twat", Chris from Ipswich. Brett, no I don't wank myself off to the *Communist Times*. It seems there are more Team Burt fans than Team Egg fans out there. I don't really think you read my blog properly, any of you. A lot of you said that you agree with Jack, that I should shut up and play. Loads of you said I was preaching. OK! I will shut up and play, but before I go, one more thing…

I feel positive that you, the public, should be more logical, controlled and adult (especially you, Linda from Solihull) about what artists you get into. Don't get me wrong, I don't advocate we turn music into a marathon of political songs, where everyone bemoans the wreckage of our culture and the state of the government. Rather

I would love to see it reflect occasionally the hard, unyielding realities of the world in which we live. Surely there is room for "Yellow", "Wonderwall" and "Imagine". All three are classics, all three are about Love, but only one is about something more. I wrote "Satellites" and it's about personal tragedy and love. You the people will decide if it enters the pantheon of those aforementioned classics. I might have put it under your nose, but it's you that chooses what will grow evergreen. That's called responsibility, Cara from Peckham!

Which leads us full circle back to the lies. On the album sleeve it says all songs written by The RockAteers. That's a lie. I wrote them. All of them. Why can't I just say that? Why do people in the band have such big egos? I made art, shouldn't I be allowed to say it's mine?

In conclusion, I urge you with all my soul to rise up against the suited man and shout from the highest mountain. "It is not good enough and we are going to do something about it."

Of course, judging by the backlash this is most unlikely.

Fuck you very much!

Edward "Egg" Poacher. Lead Guitarist with The RockAteers.

"That was quite a blog you wrote yesterday," Jerome told Egg over the phone as he sat at his desk, the handset resting between his ear and shoulder. "You certainly seemed to offend at least half of your fan base, not to mention your own band."

"It's been brewing for a while," Egg replied bluntly as he lay on his bed, head bent, staring down at his naked feet. He was alone. The excesses from the night before were giving him the shakes.

"I could tell," Jerome replied. "I had no idea you were so eloquent."

"Why not?" Egg snapped. "I write the lyrics, or did you believe what you read in the papers too?"

"Wow, touchy!" Jerome said. "It was supposed to be a compliment. Were you drunk, by any chance?"

Egg smiled reluctantly. "Yes, I had a few. I'd just been told Bex knows I tried to hit on Tyra."

"Tyra? Really? Wow. That's bad," Jerome said staring at Tyra, who was working away on her laptop on the other side of the office.

"All this has to mean something. I have to matter," Egg said with a sigh.

"It does matter, but bludgeoning people over the head with your intellect isn't the way to make your life count. It's your actions that will define you, Egg. And anyway, you write songs. You're an entertainer. That doesn't mean you have limitations, but it does mean that you live and die by the will of the public. We only have a few short years on this earth, mate. I chose a long time ago to work hard but not kill myself doing it. Be with family and friends often. Laugh more than you cry or shout, try not to take yourself too seriously."

"You think I take myself too seriously?"

"I think you're in danger of saying, 'Do you know who I think I am?' very soon if you don't get a handle on things. Look, it's a big deal becoming successful. The pressures are not to be sniffed at."

Egg put a hand across his face and groaned.

"Oh God! I'm turning into Burt!"

"No, no. You're nothing like Burt. In fact you're the opposite. Burt is very openly ambitious. He's refreshingly straightforward in a lot of ways. No, you're tortured, complex, and I think in many ways fighting against your ambition and growing self-worth."

Egg sat up in bed and stared at his reflection in his wardrobe mirror.

"I'm a pretentious prick?"

"No, but you can be. It's about learning to embrace all the aspects of your new life and then trying to enjoy it."

Egg frowned and stood up. "You can be pretty wise when you want to be, old man."

"I can?" Jerome smiled. "Why thank you, sir."

Egg started to get his shoes and socks on.

"I have to go over the park and meet Bex. We haven't seen each other in a while."

"Good luck, mate, I hope you work things out."

"Before I go, I wanted to ask why you let The Cloominator off the hook?"

Jerome leaned back in his chair. It was a question he'd asked himself a million times since the showdown.

"Honestly?"

"Of course honestly," Egg replied, shutting his front door and heading in the direction of Greenwich Park.

"I put it down to two things. One, I was taken by surprise and two, I really thought a draw was all I was going to get."

"But you had the tape recording," Egg replied. "Surely that would have buried him."

"I lost my nerve at the crucial moment, I admit that. At the time, I thought it was enough you were cleared of being fakes."

He paused and waited for a reply. Egg was silent.

"Did you see the paper? George Graves has been ordered to pay back all the money he received from the tabloids."

"Good, better go. I'm late for Bex."

Egg could see from a hundred metres away that she wasn't smiling. He watched as she made her way up the slope, wrapped up in an enormous puffa jacket. As she came closer, his sense of loss grew with every stride. Things had changed, that was plain from talking to Tyra, but Egg had pushed the inevitable away in the hope he could talk her round. She was only a few paces from him when she looked up and gave an abrupt wave.

"You look well," Egg said cheerfully.

"It's freezing," she replied.

She leant down and the pair shared an awkward kiss.

"So? How are you?" Egg asked.

"Good, I just signed a record deal."

Egg stared at her in disbelief.

"I don't understand?"

"Five album deal with Sir Wilson Cloom, worth half a million quid," she told him flatly.

"I don't even know how to respond to that," Egg said, shaking his head.

"I read your blog," she said, ignoring his tone.

"What's that got to do with anything?"

"Look, Egg, I love you. You were my first and before you lost your head up your arse, I thought we could last."

"So you think MY blog was an example of ME losing my head up MY arse?" he said indignantly. "That figures. You just signed a deal with the worst music offender on the planet!"

"Your second blog was even more egotistical. All you were really banging on about was yourself; all your neurotic worries and how jealous you are of Jack."

She paused, looked at him and shook her head.

"And that stuff about 'Satellites' being as good as 'Imagine'. Have you gone mad? What got into you?"

"*You* got into me. Tyra told me you knew I tried it on with her."

"Oh, so that's how you're coming at me?" Bex kissed her teeth. "YOU.TRIED.TO.GET.OFF.WITH.ANOTHER.GIRL.EGG!"

"I know and I'm sorry. But just to go back to the blog thing for a second. I'm not jealous of Jack, he's the last person I'm jealous of, and I wasn't saying 'Satellites' was as good as 'Imagine'. You didn't understand any of my blog!"

"Of course I understood your bloody blog, Egg, but just like everyone else who read it, I thought it was bitter, self-obsessed and far too long. You were busy trying to prove how clever you are but forgot to make any kind of real valid point."

Bex stared defiantly at him. His shoulders began to slump, his face dropped and she knew the fight had gone out of him.

"You're too late, Jerome already told me what a dickhead I was," he said morosely.

Bex sat back in surprise. "Have you ever asked yourself why you didn't know I could sing?" she said, more softly.

"Can you really sing?" Egg frowned.

"Do you think Sir Wilson Cloom would have signed me if I couldn't?"

"Yes I do. Most of the acts he signs can't sing."

Egg paused and fixed his ex-girlfriend with the most defiant look he could muster.

"If only you could hear yourself, Bex? How you sound? You sound like some airheaded, desperate wannabe."

Bex recoiled as if Egg had slapped her. It took her a few moments to compose herself.

"Look, I didn't come here to argue, I came here to ask you a favour and I think you owe it to me. You were the one that tried to cheat on me after all."

Her sudden change of tack took Egg by surprise. He stared at her in confusion.

"What?" he asked suspiciously.

"I want you to write three songs for my debut album."

Egg was unable to keep the contempt out of his voice.

"You don't ring me for weeks, you split up with me via text and then…"

To Egg's surprise, suddenly Bex reached over and took his gloved hand in hers.

"Wasn't some of that blog you wrote about being a better person, about creating artists that say something? So say something, Egg…" She squeezed his hand. "And let me sing it?"

Egg sat and stared at her.

"So you did like some of my blog?"

"Look, I don't want to spend all day talking about a self-important rant from a pop star having a nervous breakdown."

"A breakdown induced by a girl breaking his heart," Egg replied sulkily. "And I'm a rock star if you don't mind."

Bex smiled. He fought against it but her smile infected Egg and before he knew it he was smiling too.

"So you found your hidden ego then?" She laughed.

"I did!" he replied. "And there is plenty more where that came from."

Bex let go of his hand.

"I know it's a cliché, but I never meant to hurt you."

Egg's smile dropped and he struggled to fight back tears. He nodded and dropped his head.

"I will write the songs," he told her. "On one condition."

"And what might that be?"

He gazed at her through watery eyes.

"That you sing for me. Now." He paused and managed a sad smile. "You know, so I know what I'm working with."

SONG 14 DEADBEAT POETS

From Michael Twining <teabag22@gmail.com>

To Justin Clipper <justin.clipper @gmail. com>, Jack Skill <jackskilz@hotmail.com>, Egg <therockateers@gmail.com>

Date: 21 Jan 21:34

Subject: Deadbeat Poets

Lads, on Spotify they have this thing called related artists. On our page we are compared to all the usual suspects and then this band I have never heard of called Deadbeat Poets. Why are they robbing one of our songs for their band name? Anyway, I go and have a listen and guess what? They sound exactly like us but ultra-pop!! So then I checked them out online. They only have one single out but there is loads of heat around them. *Sound City* are sayin' they are the next "us". They wear all the same kinda gear we wear, there are four of them and the lead singer also has a stoopid name, Zander De Balland. It's a proper joke. I'm gonna ask Harry if we should sew them.

From Justin Clipper <justin.clipper@gmail.com>

To, Jack Skill <jackskilz@hotmail.com>,
Michael Twining <teabag22@gmail.com>, Egg
<therockateers@gmail.com>

Date: 21 Jan 22:14

Subject: Re: Deadbeat Poets

Wow, just been on Spotify. Me and Bex had a listen. They
sound sooo like us but more commercial. How awesome is
that? The lead singer is well hot too, Zander is such a cool
name. Bex said imitation is the highest form of flattery.
Nothing wrong with a bit of healthy competition. I think it
shows the highest level of respect they actually named the
band after one of our tunes.

From Jack Skill <jackskilz@hotmail.com>

To Justin Clipper <justin.clipper @gmail.com>,
Michael Twining <teabag22@gmail.com>, Egg
<therockateers@gmail.com>

Date: 22 Jan 01:27

Subject: Re: Re: Deadbeat Poets

Oh shit! That's the fella I blanked in the street. Clipper,
why you sayin' other lead singers are HOT? That's proper
selfish! I'm glad I was rude now I know he is ripping us
off. Isn't there something we can do if someone copies us?
THIS IS WAR! Maybe we should sew the bastards. HOW
CAN THEY STEAL OUR SONG NAME TOO?

Tea, I hope you're not implying my name is stupid?

From Egg <therockateers@gmail.com>

**To Justin Clipper <justin.clipper @gmail.com>, Jack
Skill <jackskilz@hotmail.com>, Michael Twining
<teabag22@gmail.com>,**

Date: 22 Jan 09:48

Subject: Re: Re: Re: Deadbeat Poets

See, this is exactly what I'm talking about! The music
industry doesn't have an inventive bone in their bodies, all
they do is copy, process and water down.

Tea and Burt, you need to learn to spell unless you intend
to ask Harry to get his needle and thread out. It's sue, not
sew. Clipper, I know it's late and you're obviously pissed
out of your head, but why have you got to mention Bex?
You know we just split up. I think that's pretty thoughtless.

Zander De Balland? Now that's a proper front man's name.
As for them calling it after my song, I guess it is quite
flattering.

They are proper pop. Sorry to say it but I think they are
gonna be massive.

Burt – 22nd January

I don't know what's happening to Egg. Saying
Deadbeat Pricks are going to be massive makes me
want to spider kick his stupid ginger face. And
his blog sucks ring too!! Bono on steroids!!!
I'm so glad I don't have to see him for a few
days. Also what the bollocks is he doing giving
away my real name AGAIN? We agreed to ignore the
utter shitness that is Deadbeat Poets and not

flatter those idiots by even talking about them.
#arsecharm #zanderdabellend

Me and Catalina have set up this system of
meeting in this hotel in Covent Garden. There's
a back entrance that the paps aren't allowed to
camp outside. I can honestly say she's the fittest
bird I've ever been with. Her naked body is
proper tonk, but she's still proper feminine. She
told me she works out two hours a day.

I met her daughter the other day, Kaye. She
thinks because she reads *The Guardian* newspaper
she's cleverer than me. We all had lunch, it
was well awkward. She made loads of sarcastic
comments about me being her mum's toy boy. #idiot

I can hear Lenny downstairs watching my DVD box
set of *Breaking Bad*. He wants me to sign a bunch
of papers about the management deal tomorrow.
He's sending Hazel round her nan's. If I don't
sign he says he's gonna cut my balls off.

"I love you, little fella. I promise I'll never treat you like my old
man treated me," Burt whispered, slurring slightly. He'd stayed
out the entire night hoping the binge would give him some clarity.
It hadn't. He reached down and took the sleeping baby's chubby
hand. Baby Burt stirred, but did not wake. He stared at the tiny
figure sleeping soundly in the cot, tears welling in the corners of
his bloodshot eyes. Watching his son sleeping stirred so many

emotions in him. How could a father treat his own child with anything but love?

He wiped the tears away. Today was D-day and he needed to focus. A decision must be made. Could he *really* allow Lenny to gain a stake in the band's management? He'd agreed to marry Hazel. Wasn't that enough? If he helped Lenny get a foothold, he would just want something more. The blackmail and bullying would never stop.

Burt made a decision. He would check himself into a hotel and ride it out until he left for America. He could see more of Cat before he left and totally avoid Lenny. But what about Millie? Was she really in danger, or was Lenny bluffing? He checked the time on his phone: 5 am. He would call her in a couple of hours and be honest; tell her to be on the lookout. It was Friday, she had half days on Friday. Yes, decision made.

He reached down and placed a palm on Double B's head.

"I'm off, little fella, I'll see you in a few weeks. Look after your mum, OK," he said softly.

"Is this OK?" Tea asked as he stood in front of Bex with only a pair of briefs between him and nakedness.

"Of course it is. You're beautiful, Tea," she replied smiling, her eyes twinkling. She lay on his bed in her underwear, her legs hitched up against her tummy, her head propped on an elbow.

"Beautiful? I think I prefer handsome or buff or some shit," he said, taking a step towards the bed.

All of a sudden Bex looked unhappy.

"I think about you all the time, Tea, but it doesn't feel right to go all the way with you just yet." A wistful gaze crossed her face. "It's getting harder and harder to keep my hands off you though."

"Same here," Tea said with a grin, before taking two quick steps and jumping on the bed. They wrestled playfully, Tea feeling increasingly aroused as they messed about.

"Why don't we take that off?" he said, as he straddled her belly, nodding down at her black lace bra.

"OK, but the knickers are staying on."

"Cool," Tea said, undoing the catch with one deft hand.

Burt sat at the roulette table and checked the time: 1 am. He looked down at his chips and smiled blearily. The pile had been three times the size an hour ago, ten times the size when he'd arrived twelve hours ago, but his luck was sure to change. He ordered another whiskey sour and pushed half his remaining chips into the rectangle marked red. His phone vibrated. It was Millie.

"Mills, what you doing phoning me at this time?" he garbled.

"Where are you, Burt? There's somebody in the house," she said, in a panicked whisper.

"What the hell you doing at home, Mills?!"

Burt stood abruptly, already clearing his chips off the table and stuffing them into his pockets.

"I wanted to surprise you, but you never came back."

"I came home this morning and went out again," he told her,

making for the exit. "Where are you right now!?"

"In my room," she whispered. "I heard someone come in the front door. I know Double B and Hazel are out for the night, I saw the message on the fridge."

"OK, OK, listen; hide in the wardrobe until I get there."

"Who's in the house? You're scaring me."

"It's Lenny, but he mustn't know you're there."

"What do you mean? Why mustn't he know I'm here?" Millie said, in a scared whisper.

"He was the one who sent the geezer up to Scotland to threaten you," Burt confessed.

"Burt, I don't understand you."

"Hide. I'll be there soon. I promise."

He hung up and bolted down the casino stairs.

Camped behind the high dividing hedge in the neighbour's garden, hidden from the pervasive photographers, Frank watched Burt's house patiently. He'd been there almost two hours already, his limbs stiff from the cold. He'd witnessed the sister moving around the property, turning lights on and off. He had watched her peer out of her bedroom window for over an hour before her light went out. At around midnight, Lenny entered the house. Why did he have a front door key?

Frank had obsessed about Lenny for weeks, but not because the butcher had hacked off his finger. He had threatened his nephew's dreams, caused someone he regarded as a son total misery and that was unacceptable. When Tea told him Lenny was blackmailing Harry, he made his mind up. Something needed to be done. Strong measures were required. Tea had mentioned Lenny regularly turned up at the singer's mansion. It was perfect. Lenny didn't have his cronies to protect him, he was as vulnerable as he was ever going to get.

Frank continued his vigil, the crouched position getting harder to maintain by the second. At a little after 1 am an upstairs light flickered on, after a minute it went off again. Then, the sister's light came on. Frank watched Lenny come to the window and draw the curtains.

Millie sat on the wardrobe floor, her legs drawn up close against her chest, her arms hugging her knees in a terrified clinch. She tried to breathe noiselessly, but the space seemed to resonate sound. She'd heard Lenny upstairs for the last few minutes. He seemed to be searching for something.

Suddenly, light streamed through the cracks in the wardrobe door. Millie filled her lungs with air and held her breath. Heavy boots thudded across the carpeted floor and she heard her curtains being drawn. She'd left them open, so she could watch for Burt arriving home. Why wasn't he here?

She heard the dull thump of Lenny moving around her room again. The mere presence of someone alien in their house, in her bedroom, was disturbing. Her lungs began to burn. She couldn't hold the air much longer. Her phone started to ring.

Burt arrived at his car and fumbled for the keys. Tea! He had to phone Tea. He was closer to where Millie was right now. He jumped into the car, switched his phone to hands free and dialled the number. Tea didn't answer. He rang again.

"Hello, Tea's phone," a girl answered breathlessly.

"Bex?" Burt said, as he started the car.

"Burt, why are you phoning this late?"

"Put Tea on," he demanded.

The phone went quiet.

"This better be good!" Tea said.

"Lenny is at my house. Millie's there too. She's in danger. You gotta get round there, mate. Get her out. I'm up West, I'm gonna be half-hour at least. Get in the back way, from the basement. The door's alarmed. The code is 3456. You got that? Lenny doesn't know she's there. She'll be in her room. She's hiding in the wardrobe," he told Tea, as the Lamborghini scraped over the speed bumps in the hotel car park. "Will you do it?"

Burt heard the alert of call waiting on his phone and checked the screen. It was Millie.

"Millie's calling. Gotta go. Will you do it, mate? I'm fucking begging you," he pleaded.

"Yes, I'll be there in five," Tea said decisively.

"Thanks, mate."

Burt hit the call waiting button.

"Millie, are you safe?" he shouted, as he raced down Shaftsbury Avenue.

The gruff voice filled his head.

"No, she ain't safe."

"Where is she?" Burt cried with a burst of rage.

"Here's what's gonna happen. You're gonna wake Harry up and the pair of you are going to sign all the relevant paperwork. I've already delivered it to his office. If it's not with me within the hour you're never gonna see your sister again."

"OK, OK." Burt whimpered, trying to keep the car steady as he hurtled down Charing Cross Road. "Don't hurt her. Please. I'll do anything."

The line went dead.

Tea and Bex ran across Blackheath.

"We have to go the back way," Tea said breathlessly.

They reached the wall on the side street, the one that Tea had climbed only weeks before and stopped. He knitted his fingers and crouched down to give her a leg-up. Bex put a hand on his shoulder and placed her foot in his hands. Tea pushed hard and Bex scrambled over the wall.

Once they were both safely over they jogged across the first lawn, repeated the process twice before arriving in Burt's vast garden.

They crept slowly towards the back of the house. As they reached the tiled porch, security lights flooded the whole of the back patio. Tea watched the house anxiously, his heart in his mouth. None of the lights inside came on. Finally he exhaled and nodded to Bex.

"I want you to stay here. It's not safe inside," he whispered.

"No way, I'm coming with you."

"I need you to call my uncle if anything happens."

"You called him five times already."

"The police then. You need to stay here and be my backup."

Bex nodded slowly. Tea leant over, took her head in his hands and kissed her firmly on the lips.

Bathed in the glare of the security lights, Tea reached the house and descended a short set of stairs leading down to the basement. At the foot of the stairs was a small window, just large enough for a slim man to fit through. The security lights timer clicked off. Tea jemmied the window, slid the sash upwards, and slipped inside the house. He crouched down in the darkness, reached inside his pocket, took out his iPhone and set it to torch. He scanned the disused basement. It looked like the Windsors used it as a storeroom. He settled the beam on a set of stairs leading up, walked hastily towards them and started to ascend. He froze as every step creaked. Once at the top he was confronted by a locked door and saw the alarm box, he dialled in the code, heard the door click and tried the handle. It opened smoothly and Tea found himself in the dimly lit hallway.

He scanned his surroundings. To his left was the regal staircase. He headed for it, faster now, adrenalin pumping. He took the carpeted stairs three at a time and turned left at the top. Millie's bedroom was at the front of the house, but which one was it?

Tea turned left, walked up the corridor and stopped outside the last door on the right. He gently eased the door open. It creaked loudly and Tea froze, his teeth gritted. All was silent. He pushed the door open and shone the torch into the room. Nothing. Then he heard a muffled shout, coming from the wardrobe.

Wham. Tea was suddenly sent sprawling across the room on to his front, the back of his head and neck searing with pain.

"Who the fuck are you?" Lenny barked.

Tea scrambled to his feet and stood facing the terrifying, thick-set man.

"I know you!" Lenny sneered. "You're the guitar player in the band!"

"I'm the bass player," Tea said, grabbing the lamp from the bedside table and whirling it at Lenny.

The lampshade hit true, hot glass from the jagged bulb slashing the gangster's cheek.

Lenny shook his head as if nothing had happened and made a backwards step, taking himself out of Tea's range. He put a hand to his wounded face, inspected the blood on his fingers and looked back at Tea. Lenny narrowed his turquoise eyes.

"You never should have done that, boy."

Lenny launched himself at Tea, catching him round the midriff. They careered into the chest of drawers, landing on the floor with a crash. Lenny pinned the younger man down, gripping him hard around the neck.

From downstairs they heard a loud crack. The sound distracted Lenny enough for Tea to arch his back and use his right hand to find a picture frame that had fallen from the chest of drawers in the struggle. He brought it down hard against Lenny's skull, inflicting just enough pain for Tea to wriggle free, scramble to his feet and dash to the wardrobe. He tried the door; it was locked. Suddenly, Tea was aware of another figure standing in the doorway.

"Unc!" he exclaimed.

Frank stood coolly, his eyes trained on Lenny, as the hulking man woozily got to his feet.

"Stay there, boy. I will deal with this."

Lenny stood, grinning. The injury to his cheek had covered his teeth in blood, making him appear even more monstrous. "What you gonna do to me with only nine fingers, Frank?" Lenny said, gesturing towards Frank's mutilated hand.

"I came to tell you to leave the kids alone," Frank said, gesturing to Tea.

Lenny took a step towards him.

"After I've killed you, I'm gonna cut your nephew's hands off so he can't play his guitar no more."

"It's a fuckin' bass," Frank said, before flying at him.

Burt crossed Tower Bridge at speed. The Lamborghini Veneno was eating up the deserted roads, but he was still miles from home. As he turned on to the Old Kent Road, he spotted the police car in his mirrors. He pulled sharply on the brakes and slowed to thirty. The police car trailed him for an excruciating thirty seconds before the siren sounded and Burt knew without a doubt they'd caught him speeding. He didn't have time for this. He floored the accelerator and the Lamborghini leapt forward. The empty, straight road rocketed past as he began to pull away. Despite his inebriation, Burt felt a surprising alertness brought on by the crisis.

He checked the rear view; the police were a hundred metres behind but chasing hard. He approached the turn on to New Cross Road. He needed to lose them now, before reaching the smaller streets. He applied the brakes and attempted the left-hander, but the car's back end swung away from him. The Veneno skidded sixty degrees and the engine stalled. By the time it came to a halt the police car had stopped at an angle in front of him. Burt pumped the accelerator desperately. Nothing. He slammed his hands on the wheel and watched as a uniformed officer got out of the police car and moved towards him cautiously. The stocky young officer arrived at Burt's driver's side window and peered in.

"Get out of your vehicle now, sir."

Burt let the window down a couple of centimetres.

"Do you know who I am, officer?"

"I know who you think you are, sir," the policeman replied. "You think you're Lewis Hamilton. Now GET out of the car!"

"No, no, I'm Jack Skill and my sister's been kidnapped and I'm trying to save her," he said.

"Have you been drinking, sir?"

"Yes. For about twenty-four hours straight. But that's irrelevant. Haven't you been listening? My sister's in big trouble!"

Burt heard a knock on the window on the passenger side and turned to see a second, older policeman gazing in. He let the other window down a fraction.

"Thank God you're here, officer. Are you this one's superior?" he asked, gesturing towards the first policeman.

"I'm afraid that's not going to work, sir. Now please will you kindly get out of the car?"

The sergeant narrowed his eyes and studied the singer.

"'Ere, are you Jack Skill?"

"Yes, yes, that's what I've been trying to tell you!"

"My twin daughters are in love with you, mate!" the sergeant beamed. "Posters of your band all over their rooms."

"I love your twins!" Burt screamed. "I'll do anything. My sister is in terrible trouble, please take me to my house."

Frank and Tea fought the gangster wildly, their relentless efforts pushing Lenny further and further down the hallway away from Millie's room.

Tea heard his name being called from below. What was Bex doing in the house? He didn't have time to think, as Lenny's huge ham-like fist clubbed his already swollen cheek and he was sent crashing against the far wall. His uncle stepped in, delivering two hard jabs to Lenny's torso. Lenny staggered backwards but managed to catch Frank by his bandaged hand. The smaller man screamed in agony as Lenny dragged him to the floor.

Tea scrambled to his feet and threw himself at Lenny, landing a solid blow to his temple. The gangster reeled, finally releasing Frank. Tea glanced down. Bex stood at the foot of the tall stairs, staring up at the bloodstained monster, her hand over her mouth and terror in her eyes. Lenny turned and swung at Tea, but it was a slow, laboured effort. Tea dodged, and with every ounce of his

265

remaining strength lashed out. Lenny let out a blood-curdling cry and teetered on the tip of the top step, before crashing down the stairs all the way to the hall floor.

"That's my house!" Burt shouted from the back seat of the police car as it turned on to his street.

The police sergeant had known the name Lenny Brown. He called it in and discovered they were the only car in the location.

"I need your keys, sir," the officer in the passenger seat said as they pulled into the drive. "You have to wait here."

"You're not getting them," Burt replied as he rocketed from the car and sprinted across the gravel.

The flash bulbs from the cluster of paparazzi popped as he ran up the stairs, unlocked the door and flew into the house.

Tea and his uncle stood at the foot of the stairs inspecting the body. Soon after the fight had ended, Tea had shepherded a shell-shocked Bex upstairs, freed an equally distraught Millie from the wardrobe and safely installed them in Burt's room. He left them huddled together as Bex hugged Millie tight and stroked her hair.

Frank crouched over Lenny and checked his vital signs. He looked up at Tea and shook his head gravely.

"Neck's broke. He's a goner."

Tea stared down, ashen-faced and exhausted at Lenny's lifeless form. He heard a car pull up outside.

"Old Bill," Frank hissed, climbing to his feet.

Tea glanced nervously at the door. Frank fixed his nephew a serious look.

"Tell your girlfriend it was me that pushed Lenny down the stairs. That's the story we're all sticking to. You got me?"

"No, Unc, I can't let you do that," Tea said, tears forming.

Frank took hold of Tea and hugged him. "I'm already implicated, boy. What's the point in both of us getting done?"

He pushed Tea up the stairs. "Now go!"

Burt - 23rd January

By the time I got there it was done. Millie was safe upstairs with Tea and Bex. Thank God Lenny locked her in the wardrobe and she didn't see any of it. I will never be able to thank Tea and his Uncle Frank enough.

Mills is made of strong stuff. She cried a lot but she was sort of calm. When I told her I was sorry, she said it wasn't my fault. And that's what made me cry. I just blubbed and hugged her for ages. She's well brave.

Frank said Lenny fell down the stairs when the two of them were fighting. Seeing that bastard's dead body didn't bother me. I'm glad he's gone. After a while they carted Uncle Frank off and my place was teeming with cops for hours. Then they took Lenny away in a body bag. The paps outside had a field day. All the papers ran the story front page this morning.

Crazel called me totally in bits, screaming and shouting at me. She was still round her nan's house. She asked when she could come home and I tried to tell her that it wasn't her home anymore. I've never heard anybody scream louder. I know I won't see Double B for a while and that does me in. I'm gonna be a proper dad to that little lad when I get back from America. I will make it right.

Tea – 25th January

I've been in a hole. I can't see no light and I can't breathe. All I want to do is tell the truth, but deep down I know it won't mean anything. My uncle will go down for murder. At best manslaughter. The Old Bill won't let me and Mum see him. He's still on remand. Thank God Bex is with me. She's pretty shocked too. When I told her what Frank wanted me to do she just nodded. She didn't say anything; she just nodded and hugged me. I couldn't believe it. She understood straight away. I won't ever forget her doing that. Never.

Egg had bought fingerless gloves specifically so he could write the letter on High Bench. Was it symbolic or sentimental? He wasn't sure. The day after he'd seen Bex he contacted a law firm that had nothing to do with his band or label and asked them to draw up a contract. He took out a pen and began to write.

Dear Bex,

Enclosed is a memory stick with three songs on it. They're yours now. I enclose contracts signed by me that hand over the copyright to you.

I've thought a lot about what you said up on High Bench. In fact, as I write this letter I'm here now. You were right about pretty much everything. I've been selfish and stupid. I wasn't listening when you tried to tell me to enjoy everything that was happening with the band, or when you tried to tell me about your singing, and that mortifies me. I know it's too late for us now, but I hope these songs will show you how sorry I am.

I reread the blogs I wrote. Some of it really embarrassed me. You always did know best.

I leave for the USA today. I'll be gone for six weeks. When I get back maybe we could meet up?

Sorry, Bex. I will always love you.

Egg

He pulled the legal document from his coat pocket added it to the letter, folded both and placed them in a pre-addressed jiffy bag. He took out his wallet, retrieved a stamp and stuck it on the top right-hand corner. Finally, he added the memory stick and sealed the parcel. He stood, shivering against the cold wind, and began to walk back down the hill. He passed through the black iron gates and made his way slowly down King William Walk. He came to a halt in front of a red pillar box at the end of the street, took out the letter, kissed it and pushed it through the slot.

Burt – 1st February
The US of fucking A. I'm literally gonna tear it a new arsehole. I can't wait to gig again. I'm gonna eat massive burgers and go to loads of bars called "Hooters". I will miss Double B so much and I suppose I will even miss Crazel a little bit. Millie has been with me and Mum and now she's gone back to school. She's so brave. Mum is still with Martin, which is well good. Dad hasn't contacted us and I don't give a flying arsehole.

Harry and Jerome reckon the word of mouth about us in The States is spreading like wild fire. They're calling it a British invasion.

I'm going to have sex with as many of them big-titted American women as I can.

BRING IT ON. #suckmeamerica

Egg ambled through Heathrow Airport, wheeling his suitcase behind him. He was three hours early for the flight; the rest of the lads wouldn't turn up for another hour at least. The crew had taken care of all his equipment. Ged had checked him on to the flight online. There was nothing for him to do but relax. It was a metaphor, he decided. The baggage had been lifted and he was free. He felt reborn. Why shouldn't he enjoy the ride? He had everything a teenage boy dreamed of: fame, money, girls and most importantly, talent. He'd browsed the shelves of the newsagent and picked up the latest *Sound City*. He even allowed himself a brief smile as he noticed the excruciating front cover of *OK!* magazine. George Graves and Sophia were on the cover, huddled together as if it was minus five degrees, on a magenta velvet sofa that Egg guessed must be in Sophia's plush Kensington flat "EXCLUSIVE: Our true love will get us through".

Egg spotted an open-fronted café and decided to indulge in a coffee and a brownie, something typically American to get him in the mood.

He approached the café and pulled up abruptly, his heart beginning to race.

She had her back to him, but he would recognise that jet-black hair and slender brown neck anywhere. For a split second, he was elated she was at the airport, thrilled at what it might mean. Then, a sharp shock coursed through him, as he watched her passionately embrace whoever was sitting opposite her at the tiny café table. He stared, unable to move or even breathe, until eventually, the lovers untangled. Bex looked round casually. Suddenly her eyes met his. Her lips mouthed words he was too far away to hear. The boy slowly rotated to reveal himself. It was Tea.

Egg fled towards the exit.

SONG 15 BONUS TRACK

Egg — 1st February
I received a letter from Bex this morning.

Dear Egg,

I really don't know where to start. I just
received your parcel and letter. I've listened
to the songs on repeat since I got them. I love
them more than words can say. They are truly
brilliant. "Sing For Your Supper" is a proper
wicked song, I can't help thinking it's directed
at me?

Egg, I am so sorry you discovered about me
and Tea like you did. I am so humiliated and
distraught about it. I could give you clichés.
It just happened, etc. etc. My betrayal was the
worst thing ever. I am so so sorry.

I wanted to tell you why I signed with Big Tone.
When I first went to see Sir Wilson and it was
obvious to me that he wanted to sign me, I told
him I wouldn't sign unless he put a clause in my
contract that promised that he would never ever
bother The RockAteers again. I couldn't stand you
thinking I signed with him to spite you. I signed
with him to ensure that he would leave you alone.

Me and Tea have finished BTW. I know that's not
much either but there it is.

Go back to the band, Egg. Please.

Love always, Bex

It was delivered by hand. She was only metres
away. I've been thinking about that more than the
letter. I've been reading the letter and lyrics
for "Sing For Your Supper" over and over.

Sing for winners when they bruise

Sing for losers when they lose

Sing for everyone you see

Sing for me

They'll make you dance, parade you, they'll spoil
and celebrate you

And when you're famous, they'll make you sing for
your supper

She says go back to the band? How can I? I never
in a million years thought Tea would be the one
to betray me like this. What he has done has
utterly destroyed me. I think they wanted me to
catch them, they must have.

I knew a long time ago, even before we got signed,

that this might not end well for me. I stayed in the band because I felt I owed a debt of gratitude to the people around us, the people who supported us. People like bloody Tea. People like Jerome. People like Bex. But it has worn me down and carved me up until I have nothing left to give.

The low I feel now is everywhere. I can't step out of it and I feel sure I won't be able to for a very long time. I see them together, holding each other. It is tattooed across my mind like a throbbing scar. How could I get on the plane after seeing that?

Did they honestly think I wouldn't see them, sitting there plain as day? The time I stood staring seemed like an eternity – watching as they caused me endless damage. She used to kiss *me* like that.

I'm a fool. I really thought after I met Bex on High Bench we were going to work stuff out. Every second I spent with her then, she had the knowledge that she was with Tea.

As I fled the airport I remember a Jonny Rotten quote burning into my head: "Have you ever felt like you've been cheated?"

I haven't answered the phone – Clipper, Ged, Harry and Jerome, not to any of them. I've had a million text messages from Clipper. He's the only one I don't want to let down, but he must understand that I can't do it anymore. I can't face anyone let alone take on America. Most of all, I cannot ever bear to be near Tea again.

I posted on our Twitter.
@The_RockAteers At Nine O'clock this morning I,
Edward (Egg) Poacher, left The RockAteers. Fun
while it lasted, thank you and goodnight.

Clipper - 2nd February
I can't ever forgive Tea or Bex if this is the
beginning of the end of the band.

Burt is all laid back about it. I had to remind
him that Egg is the songwriter and he can stop us
using the songs.

I've tried to call Egg a million times. He won't
answer. It's a proper catastrophe.

Tea - 2nd February
As soon as I got on the plane I got a text from
Bex saying it was over between us. I texted
back saying 'Don't do this.' She hasn't replied.
Clipper won't even look at me.

I'm in bits.

Jack Skill - 2nd February
America rocks me like a giant boner.

My balls are still inside my scrotum sack and
my dick is swinging free. I don't have to marry
Crazel. I'm the best looking man in New York. I'm
in the sickest hotel in Manhattan, I've scored a
giant bag of drugs and my shit-hot band are going
on tour in three days.

I don't want to be like all the other bands, so
I've asked Ged to order me one of those crooner

microphones. I'm going to decorate my mic stand with cool shit too. Zander BellWipe from DeadBeat Pricks wouldn't have the style to do that shizzle.

I've told Tea and Clip that if Egg doesn't come back, we'll be OK. Why worry? I'm the one everyone wants. I put five hundred dollars on him coming back within two weeks.

Perhaps now Egg gets how I felt when I found out Bex was seeing him. #tasteofyourownmedicine

Egg's guitar tech, Pete, is more than capable to take over anyway. He knows all the tracks, he's youngish and with a bit of styling he will scrub up twice as nice as Smeg.

By the time that ginger idiot turns up, America will be eating out of the palms of our hands. I'm fully cranked.

See you bitches on the front row!

✪

HELLO PERSON READING
THIS BOOK

I think I thanked everyone in Book 1. I hope I did. But if I did forget you or you feel that you've been supporting us for a while or even if you read the book and want to be in the next one, then please tweet me @JamieScallion and/or @thernrdiaries and we will try our hardest to put your Twitter handle in the back of Book 3.

Finally I wanted to thank my family. I love you BIG.

Jamie Scallion grew up in South East London. He spent twelve years writing, recording and touring in a band. Whilst on the road he wrote The Rock 'n' Roll Diaries.

About
the Author

Photo © Ami Barwell

THE ROCK'N'ROLL DIARIES

LOOK OUT FOR BOOK THREE:

LOSING IT

COMING SOON